STUNNING

Stunning

A PRETTY LITTLE LIARS NOVEL

SARA SHEPARD

HARPER TEEN

An Imprint of HarperCollinsPublishers

alloyentertainment
Produced by Alloy Entertainment
151 West 26th Street, New York, NY 10001

Library of Congress Cataloging-in-Publication Data is available.

ISBN 978-0-06-208189-6

Design by Liz Dresner

12 13 14 15 16 CG/BV 10 9 8 7 6 5 4 3 2 1
❖
First Edition

To Caron

It's not so important who starts the game but who finishes it.

—JOHN WOODEN

A BUNDLE OF SECRETS

Have you ever done something so shameful, so shocking, so unlike *you* that you wanted to disappear? Maybe you hid out in your room all summer, too mortified to show your face. Maybe you begged your parents to let you switch schools. Or maybe your parents didn't even *know* about your secret—you hid from them, too. You were afraid they'd take one look at you and know that you'd done something horrible.

A certain pretty girl in Rosewood carried a secret around for nine long months. She ran away from everything and everyone—except her three best friends. When it was all over, they swore they'd never tell a soul.

But this is Rosewood. And in Rosewood, the only way to keep your secrets safe is to have none at all . . .

That summer in Rosewood, Pennsylvania, a picturesque, wealthy suburb about twenty minutes from Philadelphia, had been one of the hottest ones on record. To escape the heat, people flocked to the country club pool, gathered around the local Rita's for extra-large strawberry ices, and skinny-dipped in the duck pond at Peck's organic cheese farm, despite the decades-old rumor that a dead body had been found there. But by the third week in August, the weather suddenly turned. "A Midsummer Night's Freeze," the local news called it, because the temperature got down to freezing a few nights in a row. Boys broke out their hoodies, and girls donned their brand-new, back-to-school Joe's jeans and puffer vests. A few leaves on the trees changed to reds and golds overnight. It was as though the Grim Reaper had come and ripped the season clean away.

On a chilly Thursday night, a beat-up Subaru cruised down a dark street in Wessex, a town not far from Rosewood. The glowing green clock on the dashboard read 1:26 AM, but the four girls inside the car were wide awake. Actually, there were five girls: best friends Emily Fields, Aria Montgomery, Spencer Hastings, Hanna Marin . . . and a tiny, nameless baby Emily had given birth to that day.

They drove past house after house, peering at the numbers on the mailboxes. When they approached number 204, Emily sat up straighter. "Stop," she said over the baby's cries. "That's it."

Aria, who was wearing a Fair Isle pullover she'd bought while on vacation in Iceland last month—a vacation she couldn't bear to think about—steered the car toward the curb. "Are you sure?" She eyed the modest white house. It had a basketball hoop in the driveway, a big weeping willow in the side yard, and cheerful flower beds under the front windows.

"I've seen this address on the adoption form a million times." Emily touched the window. "Two-oh-four Ship Lane. This is definitely where they live."

The car grew quiet. Even the baby stopped crying. Hanna glanced at the infant next to her in the backseat. Her tiny, perfect pink lips were pursed. Spencer looked at the baby, too, then shifted uncomfortably. It was obvious what everyone was thinking: How could this have happened to sweet, obedient little Emily Fields? They'd been Emily's best friends since sixth grade, when Alison DiLaurentis, the most popular girl at Rosewood Day, the private school they all attended, recruited them into her new clique. Emily had always been the girl who hated badmouthing people, who never instigated a quarrel, who preferred baggy T-shirts to tight-fitting skirts—*and* girls over guys. Girls like Emily didn't get pregnant.

They'd thought Emily was doing a program at Temple that summer, much like the one Spencer was attending at Penn. But then, one by one, Emily had told each of them the truth: She was hiding in her sister's dorm room in Philly because she was pregnant. Aria, Spencer, and Hanna had all reacted the same way when Emily broke the news: with jaw-dropping, speechless shock. *How long have you known?* they had asked. *I took a pregnancy test when*

I got back from Jamaica, Emily had answered. The father was Isaac, a boy she'd dated last winter.

"Are you sure you want to do this?" Spencer asked quietly. A reflection in the window caught her eye, and she cringed. But when she turned to stare at the house opposite them, a similarly modest brick ranch, no one was there.

"What other option do I have?" Emily twisted the pink rubber Jefferson Hospital bracelet around her wrist. The staff didn't even know she was gone—the doctors had wanted her to stay an extra day so they could monitor the incision from her C-section. But if she'd stayed in the hospital a minute longer, her plan wouldn't work. She couldn't possibly give the baby to Gayle, the wealthy woman who'd paid a huge sum of money for her, so she'd told Gayle she'd pushed back the date for her scheduled C-section to two days later. Then she'd solicited her friends' help to sneak out of the hospital shortly after the baby was born. Everyone had played a part in the escape. Hanna returned Gayle's money. Spencer distracted the nurses while Emily hobbled toward the exit. Aria provided her Subaru and even found an infant car seat at a garage sale. And they'd succeeded: They'd escaped without Gayle finding out and taking away the baby.

Suddenly, as if on cue, Emily's phone bleated, breaking the tense silence inside the car. She pulled it out of the plastic shopping bag the hospital had stashed her clothes in and looked at the screen. *Gayle.*

Emily winced and hit IGNORE. The phone quieted for a moment, then bleated once more. Gayle again.

Hanna eyed the phone warily. "Should you answer that?"

"And say what?" Emily hit IGNORE one more time. "'Sorry, Gayle, I don't want to give you my baby because I think you're psycho'?"

"But isn't this illegal?" Hanna looked up and down the street. There wasn't a car in sight, but she still felt on edge. "What if she turns you in?"

"For what?" Emily asked. "What Gayle did was illegal, too. She can't say anything without incriminating herself."

Hanna bit a thumbnail. "But if the cops do find out about this, what happens if they investigate other things? Like . . . Jamaica?"

A palpable tension rippled through the car. Although it was always on their minds, the girls had promised each other never to talk about Jamaica again. It was supposed to have been a getaway to forget about Real Ali, the diabolical girl who'd killed her twin sister, Courtney, the Ali they all knew and loved. Last year, Real Ali had returned to Rosewood and tried to pass herself off as the girls' old friend, but it was later revealed that she was the new A, the girls' text-messaging tormenter. She'd killed Ian Thomas, Rosewood Day heartthrob and suspect in the first murder, and Jenna Cavanaugh, who the girls and Their Ali had blinded in sixth grade. Real Ali's master plan was to murder the four girls. She'd brought them to her family's house in the Poconos, locked them in a bedroom, and lit a match. But things hadn't turned out as she'd hoped. The girls escaped, leaving Real Ali trapped in the house when it exploded. Even though her remains had never been found, everyone was positive she was dead.

But *was* she?

The trip to Jamaica had been a chance for the girls to move on with their lives and deepen their friendships. Once they got there, though, they met a girl named Tabitha who reminded them of Real Ali. She knew things only Ali would know. Her mannerisms were chillingly like Ali's. Slowly, they became convinced that she *was* Real Ali. Maybe she'd survived the fire. Maybe she'd come to Jamaica to finish off the girls as planned.

There was only one thing to do: stop her before she got revenge. Just as Real Ali was about to push Hanna off the rooftop deck, Aria had intervened, and Ali fell instead. Her broken body had vanished before the girls got down to the beach to see what they'd done, probably swept away by the tide. The girls vacillated between relief that Ali was gone for good . . . and horror that they'd killed someone.

"No one will ever know about Jamaica," Spencer growled now. "Ali's body is gone."

Emily's phone bleated again. *Gayle.* A beep followed. *Six new voicemail messages*, the screen announced.

"Maybe you should listen to those," Hanna whispered.

Emily shook her head, her hands trembling.

"Put the call on speaker," Aria suggested. "We'll listen with you."

Drawing her bottom lip into her mouth, Emily did as she was told and played the first message. "Heather, it's Gayle." A harsh voice blared through the car. "You haven't returned my calls in days, and I'm worried. You didn't have the baby a few days early, did you? Were there some complications? I'm calling Jefferson to make sure."

"Who's Heather?" Spencer whispered nervously.

"It's the fake name I gave everyone this summer," Emily said. "I even applied for my job using a fake ID I bought on South Street. I didn't want anyone making the connection that I was Alison DiLaurentis's best friend. Someone might have told the press I was pregnant, and then my parents would've found out." She stared at her phone. "God, she sounds really pissed."

Gayle's second message followed. "Heather, it's Gayle again. Okay, I called Jefferson—that *is* where you've scheduled your C-section, right? No one on the staff will tell me what's going on. Can you please pick up and tell me where the hell you are?"

The tones of the third and fourth messages increased in intensity and frustration. "Okay, I'm at Jefferson now," Gayle said in the fifth message. "I just talked to an orderly, and they don't have any record of anyone named Heather in the maternity ward, but then I described what you look like and she said you *are* here. Why didn't you call me? Where the hell is the baby?"

"What do you want to bet she *bribed* the orderly?" Emily murmured. "So much for checking in under my real name to throw Gayle off the scent." Checking in under Emily Fields had been a risk—even though Emily gave a PO box in Philly as her address and planned to use her babysitting savings to pay the hospital bill, what if, for some reason, her parents called Jefferson and found out she'd been there? But since Gayle knew her only as Heather, using her real name seemed like an easy way to lose her.

By the sixth message, Gayle had figured it out. "This was a setup, wasn't it?" she growled. "You had the baby and you left, didn't you? Was this your intention all along, bitch? Did you plan to scam me from the start? Do you think I give out fifty thousand dollars to just anyone? Do you think I'm an idiot? I'm going to *find you*. I'm going to hunt you and that baby down, and then you'll be sorry."

"Whoa," Aria whispered.

"Oh my God." Emily flipped her phone closed. "I should have never promised her anything. I know we gave it back, but I should have never taken her money in the first place. She's crazy. *Now* do you guys see why I'm doing this?"

"Of course we do," Aria said quietly.

The infant started to whimper. Emily stroked her tiny head, and then, steeling herself, pushed open the car door and stepped into the chilly air. "Let's do this."

"Em, don't." Aria opened her own door and grabbed

Emily's arm just as Emily fell against the side of the car, clearly in pain. "The doctor said you shouldn't strain, remember?"

"I need to get the baby to the Bakers." Emily pointed woozily to the house.

Aria paused. A truck horn honked far in the distance. Over the sound of the car's chugging engine, she thought she heard a brief, high-pitched laugh.

"Fine," Aria conceded. "But *I'll* carry her." She grabbed the baby seat from the back. A smell of baby powder wafted up to greet her, bringing a lump to her throat. Her father, Byron, and his girlfriend, Meredith, had just had a baby, and she loved Lola with all her heart. If she looked too long at this baby, she might love her just as much.

Emily's phone rang again, and Gayle's name flashed on the screen. She dropped it in her bag. "Come *on*, Aria."

Aria hefted the baby seat higher in her arms, and both girls staggered across the front lawn. Dew wet their feet. They narrowly missed a sprinkler head jutting out of the grass. When they climbed onto the porch, they noticed a cheerful wooden rocking chair and a ceramic dog dish that said GOLDEN RETRIEVERS WELCOME.

"Aw." Aria pointed to it. "Golden retrievers are awesome."

"They told me they have two golden retriever puppies." Emily's voice shook. "I've always wanted one of those."

Aria watched as a million emotions passed across

her friend's face in a split second. She reached over and squeezed Emily's hand. "Are you okay?" There was so much to say, but no words with which to say it.

Then Emily's expression hardened again. "Of course," she said through her teeth. Taking a deep breath, she grabbed the baby carrier from Aria and set it on the porch. The baby squeaked. Emily glanced over her shoulder at the street. Aria's Subaru idled at the curb. Something slipped into the shadows near the hedge. For a split second, she thought it was a person, but then her eyes blurred. It was probably the drugs that were still racing through her system.

Even though it made her incision hurt like hell, Emily bent down, pulled out a copy of the baby's birth certificate and the letter she had scribbled down shortly before going into the hospital, and tucked them into the top of the baby carrier. Hopefully, the letter explained everything. Hopefully, the Bakers would understand and love this baby with all their hearts. She kissed the baby's forehead, then let her fingers trail across her impossibly soft cheeks. *It's for the best*, a voice inside her said. *You know that.*

Emily pressed the doorbell. Within seconds, a light flipped on inside, and two sets of footsteps sounded behind the door. Aria grabbed Emily's hand, and they staggered for the car. The front door opened just as they were putting on their seat belts. A figure was silhouetted in the doorway, first looking out, and then looking down at the abandoned baby seat . . . and at the baby inside.

"Drive," Emily growled.

Aria zoomed into the night. As she rounded the first corner, she glanced at Emily in the rearview mirror. "It's okay."

Hanna placed her hand on Emily's arm. Spencer twisted around and squeezed her knee. Emily crumpled and started to sob, first quietly, then in huge, heaving gasps. Everyone's hearts broke for her, but no one knew what to say. This was yet another devastating secret in a long list of secrets they had to keep, along with Jamaica, Spencer's near-arrest for drug possession, what had happened to Aria in Iceland, and Hanna's car accident that summer. At least A was gone—they'd made sure of that. What they'd done might have been terrible, but at least no one would ever know.

They shouldn't be so sure about that, though. After all that had happened, they should know to trust their premonitions, to take those phantom laughs and shadows seriously. Someone *had* been there that night, after all. Watching. Studying. Plotting.

And that someone was just waiting for the opportunity to use all this against them.

1

REUNITED, AND IT FEELS SO GOOD

On a chilly Saturday evening in early March, Aria Montgomery sat down at the mahogany dining table at her boyfriend Noel Kahn's house. She smiled as Patrice, the family's private chef, served her a plate of ravioli with truffle oil. Noel sat next to her, and Mr. and Mrs. Kahn were across from them, fending off the Kahns' three prize-winning standard poodles, Reginald, Buster, and Oprah. Noel had given Oprah her name when he was little because he'd been obsessed with the talk show.

"It's so nice to see you, Aria." Mrs. Kahn, a stately woman with friendly crinkles around her blue eyes and hundreds of thousands of dollars' worth of diamonds on her fingers, gave Aria a genuine smile. Both Noel's parents had whisked into the house moments before dinner was served. "You've been such a stranger."

"Well, I'm glad to be back," Aria said.

Noel squeezed Aria's hand. "I'm glad you're back, too." He kissed her cheek.

Tingles rushed up Aria's spine. Though lacrosse-playing, Range Rover–driving, Typical Rosewood Boy Noel Kahn wasn't exactly Aria's type, he had slowly won her over. Aside from a brief breakup a few weeks ago, they'd been dating for almost a year.

Ever since they gotten back together, they'd been making up for the lost time. Monday night they'd gone to a Philadelphia Flyers game, and Aria had actually gotten into it, cheering as the team scored goal after goal. Tuesday, they'd attended an indie French movie that Noel said was thought-provoking, even though Aria was pretty sure he was just being nice. Wednesday, Thursday, and Friday they spent at Noel's house, lounging on the couch and watching *Lost* on DVD, and earlier that day they had gone snowshoeing after a freak snowstorm.

Patrice appeared again with salads, and the Kahns raised their glasses. "To my handsome husband," Mrs. Kahn said.

"To the most beautiful woman in the world," Mr. Kahn countered.

Noel pretended to vomit, but Aria gave an appreciative "*Awww.*" She'd gotten to know the Kahns in the year she'd dated Noel, and they seemed like a couple who communicated well and still planned romantic surprises on Valentine's Day. Aria's parents had never been like that, which was probably why they were divorced. Aria had told Noel just yesterday how lucky he was to have parents who still loved each other, and he said he thought so, too. Guys could be pretty dense sometimes, but Aria was happy her boyfriend recognized a good relationship when he saw one.

Mrs. Kahn sipped her wine. "So what's new, Aria? Are you excited about Hanna's dad's senate run?"

"Definitely." Aria speared a ravioli. "And it's fun to see Hanna on all those TV commercials." Truthfully, it was a relief to see any commercial that wasn't for *Pretty Little Killer*, the made-for-TV movie about Aria, Hanna, Emily, and Spencer, and their ordeal with Real Ali. It seemed like the movie was rebroadcast every other day.

"There's a big fund-raising party for Mr. Marin next weekend," Noel said between bites.

"Ah, yes, we're going to that, too," Mrs. Kahn said.

Mr. Kahn dabbed his mouth. "Actually, I can't. You'll have to go solo."

His wife looked surprised. "Why not?"

"I have a work dinner in the city." Mr. Kahn suddenly became very interested in his BlackBerry, which was sitting next to his plate. "I bet you kids are excited about the Eco Cruise coming up," he added, changing the subject. "Your mom told me all about it, Noel."

"I can't wait," Noel said enthusiastically. In a few weeks' time, most of the Rosewood Day senior class was going on a cruise to a bunch of tropical islands. It was part senior trip, part science excursion, and Aria was thrilled she and Noel were back together in time for it. Spending hours sunbathing next to him sounded like heaven.

The front door creaked open, and there were footsteps in the hall. "Hallo?" a familiar accented voice rang out.

"Klaudia!" Mrs. Kahn rose halfway from her seat. "We're in here!"

Klaudia, the Finnish exchange student who'd been with the Kahns for a little over a month, strutted into the dining room. As usual, she was wearing a skintight, ultrashort sweater dress that showed off her enormous boobs and minuscule waist. Over-the-knee boots accentuated her thin, long legs. Her white-blond hair spilled around her shoulders, and her sultry, raspberry-lined lips were pursed.

"Hallo, Noel!" She waggled her fingers. Then her gaze turned to Aria, and the smile turned sour. "Oh. *You*."

"Hello, Klaudia," Aria said in a clipped voice.

"Do you want some dinner, Klaudia?" Mrs. Kahn asked eagerly. "It's delicious!"

Klaudia stuck her nose in the air. "I fine," she said in her contrived pidgin English. Aria knew for a fact she spoke English perfectly, but she put on the innocent-little-foreign-girl act because it helped her get away with all kinds of things. "I already eat with Naomi and Riley." Then she spun on her heel and flounced upstairs.

As soon as the door slammed, Noel gave his parents an exasperated look. "Why is she still here? You said you were going to call the exchange program and send her home!"

Mrs. Kahn clucked her tongue. "Are you still upset about her borrowing your jacket?"

"She didn't *borrow* it." Noel's voice rose. "She *stole* it."

"*Shh.*" Mrs. Kahn glanced at the ceiling. "She'll hear you."

Aria fixed her eyes on her plate, feeling a secret rush of triumph. Not long ago, Aria had been certain Noel wanted to sleep with Klaudia—who wouldn't? She looked like a girl in a beer commercial, and she was diabolical and manipulative to boot. Even worse, Noel hadn't believed Aria when she said Klaudia was nuts—he just thought she was a sweet, hapless exchange student who needed coddling and protection from Big Bad America. It was so satisfying when Noel had come to Aria last week and said that Klaudia definitely wasn't for him. She was crazy, and he was doing everything in his power to get her sent back to Finland.

Mrs. Kahn's eyebrows knitted together. "Klaudia is a guest in our house, Noel. We can't just kick her out."

Noel's shoulders slumped. "You're taking her side instead of mine?"

"Just try to get along with her, honey. It's an amazing cultural experience to have Klaudia in the house."

"Whatever." Noel dropped his fork. "You know what? I'm not hungry."

"Noel," Mrs. Kahn protested, but Noel was already halfway out the door. Aria stood as well. "Thanks for dinner," she said awkwardly. She tried to carry her plate into the kitchen, but Patrice, who was waiting obediently in the corner, grabbed it from her and shooed her away.

Aria followed Noel up the stairs and into the second-floor family room, which had a huge flat-screen TV and five different video game consoles. Noel grabbed two Sprites from the mini fridge in the corner, flopped down on the couch, and started angrily flipping through the channels.

"Are you okay?" Aria asked.

"I just can't believe they aren't listening to me about her." Noel jutted a thumb in the direction of Klaudia's room down the hall.

Aria wanted to point out that not long ago, Noel hadn't listened to *her* about Klaudia, but now probably wasn't the right time. "You only have a few more months until she goes back to Finland, right? Maybe you can just ignore her. And anyway, now that she likes someone else, maybe she'll leave you alone."

"Mr. Fitz, you mean?" Noel raised an eyebrow. "Are you okay with that?"

Aria sank down into the couch and stared out the window at the Kahns' backyard guesthouse. Last week, while she and Noel were broken up, Ezra Fitz, Aria's teacher-slash-boyfriend, had returned to Rosewood in hopes of winning her back. Everything had played out like the fantasy that had been running constantly in Aria's head ever since Ezra had left town, until, unexpectedly, the dream turned sour. Ezra wasn't the guy she remembered, but instead someone who was needy and insecure. When Aria couldn't give Ezra the ego boost he needed, he'd turned to Klaudia instead. Last week, Aria had caught them making out in a coatroom at a cast party for the school's production of *Macbeth*. Since then, Klaudia had bragged loudly that she and Ezra had gone on sexy dates around Rosewood and that they were apartment-hunting in New York City, where Ezra lived.

"I don't care that Klaudia and Ezra are together," she said, meaning it. "I'm with *you*."

Noel put down the remote and pulled her close. Their lips met in a kiss. Noel pressed his hands along the sides of her face, then touched her neck and shoulders. His fingers grazed her bra strap, and she could tell he wanted more. She pulled away slightly. "We can't. Not with your parents downstairs."

Noel moaned. "So?"

"Perv." She hit him playfully, but felt a pang of longing, too. That was another thing that had changed: Since they'd reunited, they'd slept together for the first time. It had happened only a few days ago, in Noel's bedroom on a rainy afternoon, and it was all Aria could have hoped for—tender, slow, amazing. They'd whispered how much they cared about each other, and afterwards, Noel had told her it had been so special. Aria was glad they'd waited. They'd done it for the right reason—love.

Noel leaned back on his elbows and examined her. "Let's never let anyone get between us again. Not Klaudia, not Ezra, no one."

"Deal." Aria massaged Noel's forearm.

"I mean it." Noel sat up straighter and looked into her eyes. "I want us to be completely honest with each other. No more secrets. That's why my parents are still together—they don't hide anything. I don't want us to, either."

Aria blinked hard. What would he say if she told him about what she'd done in Iceland this past summer? What would he say if she told him that she and her old friends had shoved the person they thought was Real Ali off the roof in Jamaica, only to find out later that it was actually an innocent girl named Tabitha Clark? What would he say about New A, the anonymous text messenger who'd begun to torment Aria and her friends with their darkest secrets?

And who *was* new A? Spencer's ex-friend, Kelsey Pierce, had made so much sense—she'd been in Jamaica over spring break, and Spencer had framed her for drug possession last summer. But when they'd confronted Kelsey at the Preserve at Addison-Stevens mental hospital, she genuinely hadn't seemed to know about Tabitha or A.

And then there was the inscription on the bench they'd seen outside the hospital. TABITHA CLARK, RIP, it said, listing the dates Tabitha had been a patient at the Preserve. They matched the dates Real Ali had been there, too—clearly Tabitha and Real Ali had known each other.

"Hello? Aria?"

Noel was staring at her curiously. "You disappeared on me. Everything okay?"

"Of course," Aria lied. "I . . . I was just thinking about

how amazing you are. How I completely agree with being honest all the time."

Noel's face relaxed into a smile. He held up his Sprite. "Great. So no more secrets?"

"No more secrets." Aria lifted her Sprite, too, and they touched the cans just like the Kahns had toasted at dinner. "Starting now."

Okay, so "starting now" was a little bit of a cheat. But the horrible crimes Aria had committed were in the past, and they needed to stay that way—forever.

2

SPENCER'S NEW CHALLENGE

That night, a slim woman in skinny black pants proffered Spencer Hastings and her family four slices of cake on a silver tray. "Okay, we have chocolate with coffee frosting, vanilla sponge with lemon buttercream, chocolate cake with Frangelico liqueur, and carrot." She placed them on the table.

"Looks delicious." Spencer's mother grabbed her fork.

"You're trying to make my wife-to-be fat, aren't you?" Mr. Pennythistle, Mrs. Hastings's new fiancé, joked.

Polite laughter ensued. Spencer clutched her own silver fork hard, trying to keep a smile pasted on her face even though she thought the joke was pretty lame. She was with her mother, her sister, Melissa, Melissa's boyfriend, Darren Wilden, Mr. Pennythistle, and Mr. Pennythistle's daughter, Amelia, at Chanticleer House. Mrs. Hastings and Mr. Pennythistle had chosen the stone mansion with its enormous private garden for their upcoming summer nuptials.

Amelia, who was two years younger than Spencer and

went to St. Agnes, the snootiest school on the Main Line, tentatively poked her fork into the slice of carrot cake. "The cakes from Sassafras Bakery are prettier," she said, wrinkling her nose.

Melissa took a bite and swooned. "They might be prettier, but this buttercream frosting is heaven. As maid of honor, I vote we go with this one."

"You're not the only maid of honor," Mrs. Hastings pointed her fork in Spencer's direction. "Spencer and Amelia get a vote, too."

All eyes turned to Spencer. She wasn't really sure why her mother was going through all the bridal bells and whistles, including purchasing a Vera Wang gown with a ten-foot-long train, putting together a guest list of more than three hundred people, and charging Spencer, Amelia, and Melissa with maid of honor duties, which so far had included interviewing wedding planners, drafting the *New York Times* and *Philadelphia Sentinel* announcements, and choosing the perfect gift bags for the reception. There were still days when Spencer thought her mom was going to wake up and realize that divorcing Spencer's father had been a mistake. Okay, so her dad had had an affair with Jessica DiLaurentis and secretly fathered twin girls, Courtney and Alison. But still—all this for a second wedding?

Spencer cut a perfect rectangle of chocolate Frangelico cake, careful not to get any crumbs on her new Joie dress. "This one's pretty good," she said.

"Great minds think alike. That's my favorite, too." Mr.

Pennythistle wiped his mouth. "I've been meaning to tell you, Spencer. I got in touch with my friend Mark, who's an off-Broadway producer. He was very impressed with your Lady Macbeth performance and might want you to audition for one of his upcoming plays."

"Oh," Spencer breathed, surprised. "Thanks." She shot him a smile. In a family of standouts, it was nice to be noticed.

Amelia wrinkled her nose. "Is this the same Mark that produces dinner theater? Aren't his plays usually about medieval jousts?" She snickered nastily.

Spencer narrowed her eyes. *Jealous much?* Even though Amelia had lived in the Hastings house for a few weeks now, their interactions consisted mostly of bitchy snipes, one-word grunts, or seething looks across the dinner table. Spencer had once had a sisterly relationship like that with Melissa. She and Melissa had finally made peace; she didn't need another sibling adversary to take her place.

Amelia was still staring at Spencer. "By the way, have you heard from Kelsey lately? She, like, dropped off the face of the earth. My orchestra group is minus a violinist."

Spencer shoved another bite of cake in her mouth to delay responding. Spencer's old friend from the UPenn summer program was now at the Preserve at Addison-Stevens mental hospital and rehab center to get over her drug abuse—and it was partly Spencer's fault. Spencer had framed Kelsey last summer for drug possession and gotten her sent to juvie. When she'd resurfaced in Spencer's life recently, Spencer had thought Kelsey was the new A, exacting her revenge.

She knew now that Kelsey wasn't A—she and her friends had received a text from A while Kelsey was in the Preserve, which didn't allow phones. But who *else* could know so much about all of them?

"I haven't heard from Kelsey at all," Spencer said, which was the truth. She snuck a look at Darren Wilden, who was diving into a slice of chocolate cake. Though he'd been the head investigator for the Alison DiLaurentis murder case, he wasn't a cop anymore. But Spencer felt slightly uneasy in his presence all the same. Especially now that she was keeping dangerous new secrets.

The waitress reappeared and smiled hopefully. "Are the cakes okay?"

Mrs. Hastings nodded. Melissa waved her fork in the air, her mouth full of food. As the waitress pranced away, Spencer looked around the huge dining room. The walls were lined in stone and the floors were marble. Huge floral bouquets sat in small alcoves next to the floor-to-ceiling windows. Outside, an enormous hedge labyrinth stretched as far as the eye could see. There were a few other people eating in the dining room, most of them stuffy old men, probably conducting business deals. Then, she locked eyes with a tall, forty-something woman with ash-blond hair, steely gray eyes, and a Botoxed forehead. When she noticed Spencer looking, she quickly turned her attention to the menu in her hands.

Spencer looked away, too, feeling jittery. Ever since A

had resurfaced, she couldn't shake the feeling that she was being watched wherever she went.

Suddenly, Spencer's iPhone let out a *bloop*. She pulled it out and inspected the screen. *Princeton Dinner Reminder!* the subject line read. Spencer pressed OPEN. *Don't forget! You are cordially invited to a dinner honoring all of the Princeton early-admits in Pennsylvania and New Jersey!* The dinner was Monday night.

Spencer smiled. She loved correspondence from Princeton, especially since her future there had seemed so precarious last week—A had sent a letter saying that Spencer hadn't been admitted after all, and Spencer had jumped through hoops trying to prove herself worthy until she realized the letter was a fake. She couldn't wait until September, when she could start over somewhere fresh. Now that there was a new A, Rosewood felt more like a prison than ever.

Mrs. Hastings glanced at Spencer with curiosity, and Spencer flashed her phone screen. Mr. Pennythistle looked at it, too, and then took a sip of the coffee the waitress had just poured. "You're going to really enjoy Princeton—you'll make such great connections. Do you plan on joining an Eating Club?"

"Of course she does!" Melissa said matter-of-factly. "I bet you've already got your top three picked out, right, Spence? Let me guess. Cottage Club? Ivy? What else?"

Spencer fiddled with the wooden napkin ring next to her plate, not immediately answering. She'd heard of Eating Clubs, but hadn't looked into them carefully—she'd been too busy studying vocabulary words, volunteering for a zillion community service activities, and chairing various school organizations just to get *into* Princeton. Maybe they were like the Rosewood Day Foodie Club, a group of kids who went out to fancy restaurants, had *Top Chef* viewing parties, and used the home ec ovens to cook *boeuf bourguignon* and *coq au vin*.

Wilden laced his fingers over his stomach. "Anyone care to enlighten me about what an Eating Club is?"

Melissa looked a little embarrassed for her boyfriend—preppy, Ivy-League Melissa and blue-collar Wilden came from very different worlds. "The Eating Clubs are like secret societies," she explained in a slightly patronizing voice (which Spencer wouldn't have stood for if *she* were Melissa's boyfriend). "You have to compete to get in through this process called bicker. But once you're in, it's like instant popularity, instant friends, and tons of perks."

"Sort of like a frat?" Darren asked.

"Oh, *no*." Melissa looked appalled. "For one thing, Eating Clubs are coed. For another, they're way classier than that."

"You can go a long way if you're part of an Eating Club," Mr. Pennythistle interjected. "I had a friend who was in Cottage Club, and a Cottage Club alumni who worked in the senate snapped him up for a job, sight unseen."

Melissa nodded excitedly. "The same thing happened to my friend Kerri Randolph. She belonged to Cap and Gown, and she got an internship with Diane von Furstenberg's design team through an Eating Club connection." She looked at Spencer. "You have to let them know you're interested early, though. I knew people who started buttering up Eating Clubs when they were sophomores in *high school.*"

"Oh." Spencer suddenly felt nervous. Maybe it was a huge gaffe that she hadn't gotten on the Eating Club bandwagon earlier. What if every early admission student had already brown-nosed their way into the Eating Club of their choice, and, like in an elaborate game of musical chairs, she would be left without a seat when the music stopped? She was supposed to feel grateful that she was going to Princeton, *period*, but that wasn't how she functioned. She couldn't just be a regular old student there. She had to be the best.

"An Eating Club would be stupid not to invite me," she said, pushing a lock of long blond hair over her shoulder.

"Absolutely." Mrs. Hastings patted Spencer's arm. Mr. Pennythistle gave an "*Mm-hmm*" of support.

When Spencer sat back again, a high-pitched, keening giggle echoed off the walls. She tensed and looked around, the hair on her arms standing on end. "Did you guys hear that?"

Wilden paused from his coffee and peered about the room. Mr. Pennythistle's brow furrowed, then he tutted. "Bad windows. It's just a draft."

Then everyone went back to eating like nothing was amiss. But Spencer knew that noise wasn't from a draft. It was the same laugh she'd been hearing for months. It was A.

3

THE BOY WHO GOT AWAY

Hanna Marin and her stepsister, Kate Randall, sat at a long table in the central corridor of the King James Mall. They tossed huge, irresistible, we're-cute-and-we-know-it smiles at all the passersby.

"Are you registered to vote?" Hanna asked a middle-aged woman toting a bag from the artisanal cheese shop Quel Fromage!

"Want to come to Tom Marin's town hall meeting Tuesday night?" Kate handed a flyer to a guy wearing a Banana Republic name tag.

"Vote for Tom Marin in the next election!" Hanna bellowed at a bunch of fashionable grandmothers checking out the Tiffany window display.

There was a lull in the crowd, and Kate turned to Hanna. "You should have been a cheerleader."

"Nah, cheerleading isn't my style," Hanna said breezily.

It was seven o'clock on Saturday night, and they were

trying to drum up interest for Mr. Marin's senate run. He was gaining in the polls, and the hope was that the town hall meeting and fund-raiser he was holding the next week would give him an advantage over his competitor, Tucker Wilkinson. Hanna and Kate were the youth voices in the campaign, launching Twitter feeds and organizing flash mobs.

Kate fiddled with the large VOTE FOR TOM MARIN button she wore on the lapel of her fitted jacket. "By the way, I saw another picture of Liam in the paper this morning with some skank on South Street," she whispered. "It looks like he gained weight."

Ordinarily, Hanna would have thought that her step-sister's mention of Liam, a boy Hanna had gotten burned by a week before, was just to make her squirm—especially since Liam was Tucker Wilkinson's son. But amazingly, Kate had been really cool. She laid off the snarky, I'm-better-than-you comments at the dinner table. She let Hanna have the bathroom first three mornings in a row. And the night before, she dropped off the new LMFAO album, saying she thought Hanna would like it. Hanna had to admit the New Kate was kind of awesome, though she'd never actually *tell* Kate that.

"Maybe he's stress-eating because I'm not picking up his calls," Hanna said, snickering. "He's left me a bunch of voicemails."

Kate inched closer. "What do you think Tom's going to do about what you told him?"

Hanna stared absently at a bunch of seventh-grade girls clumped in front of Sweet Life, a gourmet candy shop. After she found out Liam was a big fat cheater, she'd told her father a juicy, damaging bit of gossip about Liam's dad.

"I don't know," she answered. "I'm not sure dirty politics is really his style."

"Too bad." Kate pressed her lips together and folded her hands over the stack of flyers in front of her. "That jerk deserves to go down."

"So where are Naomi and Riley tonight?" Hanna stretched out her long, thin legs under the table, eager to change the subject. "I thought you always spent Saturdays with them." Naomi Zeigler and Riley Wolfe were Kate's BFFs. They had been Hanna's biggest enemies when she was best friends with Mona Vanderwaal, the girl who had turned out to be the first A.

Kate shrugged. "Actually, I'm taking some time off from Naomi and Riley."

"Really?" Hanna sat up with interest. "Why?"

Kate passed a flyer to a college-age girl in a leather jacket. "We had a fight."

"About what?"

Kate coughed awkwardly. "Um, about the upcoming Eco Cruise. And about you, actually."

Hanna wrinkled her nose. "What about me?"

"Forget it." Kate looked away. "It doesn't matter."

Hanna was about to press Kate for more details when her father appeared from the food court with a cardboard container of Starbucks lattes and a bag of assorted muffins. "You girls are doing an amazing job," he said, clapping a hand on Kate's shoulder. "I've seen tons of people with flyers. I bet we'll get a great turnout at the town hall meeting on Tuesday. And Hanna, I'm still getting a lot of positive feedback on the commercial. I may ask you to film another one." He winked.

"Of course!" Hanna said brightly. In the six years since her father had divorced her mom, moved out of the house, and forgotten Hanna existed, she'd yearned for his acceptance, trying so hard to get him to notice her. Ever since she'd tested well in the focus groups, she was a star in his eyes. Her dad asked her opinion about campaign strategy, and he actually *wanted* to be around her.

Then Mr. Marin turned and took the arm of a woman behind him. Hanna expected to see Isabel, her dad's new wife and Kate's mother, but instead it was a tall, stately woman in her early forties. She wore a gorgeous camel hair coat and high, pointed Jimmy Choo boots.

"Ladies, this is Ms. Riggs," he said. "She just moved to Rosewood, and she's promised a huge donation to the campaign."

"You deserve it, Tom." Ms. Riggs's voice was very refined, like Katharine Hepburn's. "We need more people like you in Washington."

She turned to the girls, shaking Kate's hand, then Hanna's. "You look very familiar," she said, looking Hanna up and down. "Where have I seen you?"

Hanna's lips twitched. "*People* magazine, probably."

Ms. Riggs smiled. "Goodness, why?"

Hanna's eyebrows shot up. Did this woman seriously not know?

"*People* did a profile on Hanna," Mr. Marin said. "Her best friend was Alison DiLaurentis. The girl murdered by her twin sister."

Hanna squirmed in her seat, not wanting to correct her dad on the details. Technically, her best friend had been *Courtney* DiLaurentis, the girl who'd impersonated Alison while Alison had been forced to take Courtney's place at the mental hospital. But it was way too complicated to get into.

"I *did* hear something about that." Ms. Riggs gazed at Hanna sympathetically. "You poor thing. Are you all right?"

Hanna shrugged. She was sort of all right . . . and sort of not. Could you ever really get over something like that? And then there was a new A on the scene. A knew about Tabitha, about Hanna's naughty pictures with Patrick, the photographer who'd promised he'd make her a model but just wanted to get in her pants, and about her tryst with Liam. Any of those things could ruin her life—*and* her dad's campaign. Thank God A didn't know about the accident she'd been in last summer.

Ms. Riggs checked her watch. "Tom, we're late for the strategy talk."

"You go on ahead. I'll be there in a second," Mr.

Marin said. Ms. Riggs waved good-bye to the girls, and then headed in the direction of The Year of the Rabbit, an upscale Chinese restaurant. Mr. Marin lingered behind, eyeing Hanna and Kate when Ms. Riggs was a safe distance away. "Be nice to Ms. Riggs, okay?" he murmured.

Hanna made a face. "I *was* nice!"

"I'm always nice, Tom," Kate added, looking offended.

"I know, I know, girls, just keep it up." Mr. Marin's eyes were wide. "She's a huge philanthropist and very influential. We need her funds to air our commercials throughout the state. It could mean the difference between winning and losing."

Her father scampered after Ms. Riggs, and Kate headed to the bathroom. Hanna gazed at the passersby again, annoyed that her father had lectured her like she was a naughty six-year-old. Since when did Hanna need a lesson on being nice to donors?

A figure emerged from Armani Exchange, and Hanna perked up. Hanna took in the boy's wavy hair, square jaw, and slim-cut, beat-up leather jacket. Something inside her stirred. It was her ex, Mike Montgomery. She'd avoided him ever since the *Macbeth* cast party a few weeks ago, where he'd asked for her to take him back and she'd rejected him. But he looked positively delicious tonight.

Hanna called his name, and Mike looked up and smiled. As he walked toward her, Hanna adjusted her polka-dotted silk blouse so that a teensy bit of her bra strap was showing and quickly checked her reflection in the back of her iPod. Her auburn hair was shiny and full, and her eyeliner was smudged to perfection.

"Hey." Mike leaned his elbows on the table. "Campaigning, huh?"

"Yup." Hanna crossed her legs coquettishly, a nervous buzz in her stomach. "And you're . . . shopping?" She wanted to smack herself for sounding so lame.

Mike held up the A/X bag. "I got that black sweater you and I looked at a while back."

"The slimming one?" Hanna wound a piece of hair around her finger. "That looked really good on you."

Two dimples appeared on either side of Mike's face when he smiled. "Thanks," he said bashfully.

"Mike?"

Mike jumped, as if caught. A petite girl with long, brown hair, an oval face, and large, doll-like eyes stood behind him. "*There* you are!" she chirped.

"Oh, hey!" Mike's voice rose in pitch. "Uh, Hanna, do you know Colleen? My . . . girlfriend?"

Hanna felt as though Mike had kicked her in the boobs. Of course she knew Colleen Bebris—they'd only been going to the same school for ages. But she was his . . . *girlfriend*? Colleen was one of those ass-kissy types who tried to be everyone's best friend. Back in the day, Colleen had made it her personal goal to be BFFs with Hanna and Mona, even though she was two years younger and ridiculously dorky. They made Colleen take notes for them in Latin I while they skipped school to go shopping, schlep their clothes to the dry cleaner's, and camp out in front of the Apple store all weekend so they wouldn't have to wait in line for the latest iPod. Eventually, Colleen had gotten the hint and started hanging out with the Shakespeare Festival kids instead. But she always had a big smile for Hanna and Mona in the halls, saying "Kiss kiss!" whenever she passed. Mona used to nudge Hanna and mutter, "No *no*!"

"Nice to see you," Hanna said tightly. Suddenly feeling awkward, she shoved a flyer in Colleen's face. "Vote for Tom Marin."

"Oh, Hanna, I'm not old enough to vote." Colleen sounded crushed, as if Hanna wasn't just trying to make conversation. "But your dad's awesome. That Wilkinson guy seems like a jerk, don't you think? And his son is such a player."

Hanna's eyes widened. How did Colleen know Liam was a player?

Colleen touched Mike's arm. "We should get going. Our dinner reservations are at seven-fifteen." She beamed at Hanna. "We have Rive Gauche reservations tonight. It's a Saturday tradition. I absolutely love the *moules frites*."

"I read that *moules frites* are loaded with the worst kind of fat. But you don't really look like you care about that kind of thing," Hanna said sweetly to Colleen. Then she glared pointedly at Mike. He'd always wanted to go to Rive Gauche when they were dating, but Hanna had refused because Lucas Beattie, her ex, worked there. Rive

Gauche was *the* Rosewood Day hangout, though, and Hanna hated the idea of the school's elite seeing Mike Montgomery and Colleen together. Dating Mike would automatically make Colleen *in*, and she so didn't deserve it.

"See ya later, then," Mike said, not catching Hanna's snarkiness—or her frustration. As he walked away, his hand entwined in Colleen's, Hanna felt a strange sense of loss and longing. She hadn't realized how cute Mike's butt was. Or how attentive he was to his girlfriends. All of a sudden, she missed everything about him. She missed the shopping trips where he had patiently sat outside the dressing room and critiqued Hanna's outfits, the lustful comments he made about the Kardashian girls when they watched their shows on E!, and how he let Hanna put makeup on him once—he'd looked surprisingly good in eyeliner. Hanna even missed the stupid Hooters keychain that hung from his backpack zipper. Her time with Liam might have been electric and intoxicating, but with Mike, she'd been silly and immature and utterly herself.

All of a sudden, it hit her like a shocking note from A: She wanted Mike back. She could even imagine the type of note A might write for the occasion:

The grass is always greener, isn't it, Hannakins? Looks like you're as out as last season's wide-leg jeans!

4

A DRIVE DOWN MEMORY LANE

The following evening, Emily Fields's mother gripped the steering wheel of the family Volvo and turned out of Lyndhurst College, where Emily had just competed in her final long-course swim meet of the year. The windows in the car were steamed up, and the mingling aromas of chlorine, UltraSwim shampoo, and Mrs. Fields's vanilla latte wafted through the air.

"Your butterfly is looking so good," Mrs. Fields gushed, patting Emily's hand. "The UNC team is going to be thrilled to have you."

"Mm-hmm." Emily ran her fingers over the furry insides of her swimming jacket. She knew she should be excited about her swim scholarship to the University of North Carolina next year, but she was just relieved that this swim season was over. She was exhausted.

She pulled out her cell phone and checked the screen for the eleventh time that day. *No new messages.* She turned her phone off and then on again, but the inbox was still blank. She clicked over to her Daily Horoscopes app and read Taurus, her sign. *You will shine at work today*, it said. *Prepare for surprises ahead.*

Surprises . . . as in bad surprises or good surprises? A whole week had passed without a single note from New A. There had been no threats, no taunts about what Emily and the others had done in Jamaica, no "tsk tsk" for believing that Kelsey Pierce, a girl Emily had fallen for, was the person after them. But A's absence was even spookier than a barrage of texts about her darkest secrets. Emily couldn't help but picture A lying in wait and plotting a new assault, something dangerous and devastating. She dreaded what it might be.

Emily's mother paused at a stop sign in a small housing development. Modest homes were framed by old oaks, and there was a basketball hoop at the end of a cul-de-sac. "This isn't the usual route we use to go home," she murmured. She checked the GPS. "I wonder why this thing is sending me on these back roads." She shrugged and kept driving. "Anyway, have you been in touch with any of the girls on the UNC team? It might be nice to start getting to know them."

Emily ran her hands over her damp reddish-blondish hair. "Uh, yeah. I should do that."

"A few of them live in 'clean' dorms—you know, the kind where smoking, alcohol use, and sexual activity are frowned upon? You should request one of those rooms.

You wouldn't want to lose your swim scholarship from too much partying."

Emily stifled a groan. Of course her über-conservative mom would want her to live like a nun at college. Earlier in the week, when her mom had found out that Kelsey, the girl she'd been hanging around with, had a drug problem, she'd grilled Emily, figuring Emily was using drugs, too. Emily was surprised her mom hadn't asked her to pee in a cup for an at-home drug test.

While Mrs. Fields blathered on about the clean dorms, Emily picked up her cell phone again and scrolled through the previous texts she'd received from A, ending with the last one:

Dig all you want, bitches. But you'll NEVER find me.

She sucked in her stomach. In some ways, she almost wished A would just expose all of them and get it over with—the guilt and lying were too horrible to bear. She also wished that A would reveal herself as the person Emily knew she was—Real Ali. Her friends might not believe it, but Emily knew deep down in her bones that Ali had survived the fire at the Poconos house. After all, Emily had left a way for Ali to escape, opening the door for her before the house exploded.

The pieces were starting to fit together. Ali and Tabitha were at the Preserve at the same time, and maybe that was why Tabitha had acted so much like Ali in Jamaica.

Perhaps the two of them had been working together somehow—maybe Ali had gotten in touch with Tabitha after she'd escaped the fire in the Poconos. Maybe Ali even sent Tabitha to Jamaica to screw with the girls' minds and drive them crazy.

The whole thing broke Emily's heart. She knew, logically, that their tormenter wasn't *Her* Ali, the girl she'd adored for years, spent lots of time with, and kissed in the DiLaurentis's tree house at the end of seventh grade. But she couldn't help but dwell on that moment last year when Real Ali had returned, impersonated Their Ali, and kissed Emily with such passion. She'd seemed so . . . *genuine*, not like a cold-hearted psycho.

"You know, you should probably sign up for a spot in the clean dorms now," Mrs. Fields was saying as they drove up a hill past a large school playground. Several teenagers were sitting on the swings, smoking cigarettes. "I'd love to have this settled before your father and I go out of town on Wednesday." Mr. and Mrs. Fields were taking a trip to Texas for Emily's grandma and grandpa's sixty-fifth wedding anniversary, leaving Emily alone in the house for the first time ever. "Want me to call the student living office tomorrow and ask?"

Emily groaned. "Mom, I don't know if I want to—"

She trailed off, suddenly noticing where they were. SHIP LANE, said a green street sign. Up ahead was a very familiar little white ranch house with green shutters and a big front porch. It was on that very porch that she and her friends had left a certain baby carrier months earlier.

"Stop," she blurted.

Mrs. Fields hit the brakes. "What's wrong?"

Emily's heart was pounding so fast she was sure her mother could hear each valve flapping open and closed. This house had appeared in Emily's dreams almost every night, but she'd vowed never to drive by it again. It seemed extra-creepy that the GPS had guided them here, almost like the computer knew this house held painful memories. Or maybe, she thought with a shiver, it was someone else who knew, someone else who'd somehow programmed the GPS.

A.

Either way, now that she was here, she couldn't tear her gaze away. The dog bowl that said GOLDEN RETRIEVERS WELCOME was missing from the front porch, but the rocking chair was still there. The bushes in the front yard looked a little overgrown, like they hadn't been pruned in a while. The windows were dark, and there were a bunch of wrapped newspapers on the lawn, a sure sign that the family was on vacation.

All kinds of memories flooded back to Emily, unbidden. She saw herself staggering off the plane from Jamaica, nauseated and dizzy and exhausted. She'd figured it was just because of something she'd eaten at the resort, but as time went on, the symptoms got worse. She could barely stay awake through class. She couldn't keep food down. Certain things, like coffee, cheese, and flowers, smelled horrible.

Then, a week later, she'd been flipping through channels and caught the end of a *True Life* episode on MTV about kids who'd been pregnant in high school. A girl had felt sick for months but thought it was mono; by the time she'd taken a pregnancy test, she was already four months along. Watching it, a light had gone on in Emily's brain. The next day, she'd driven to a drugstore a few towns away from Rosewood and bought an EPT test. Terrified her mom would find the evidence, she took the test in a dank, dark bathroom in the local park next door.

It was positive.

She'd spent the next few days in a horrified daze, feeling confused and lost. The father had to be Isaac, her one and only boyfriend of that year. But they'd only had sex *once*. She wasn't even sure she *liked* guys. And what the hell were her parents going to say about this? They would never, ever forgive her.

When her head cleared, she'd begun to make plans: She would escape to Philly that summer and stay with her sister Carolyn, who was doing a summer program at Temple University. She'd wear baggy blazers and blouses to hide the weight gain until school was over. She'd see a doctor in the city and pay cash so her appointments wouldn't show up on her parents' insurance bill. She'd contact an adoption agency and make arrangements. And she had done all those things, which was how she'd met the Bakers, who lived in this very house.

After Emily called Rebecca, the adoption coordinator,

and told her she'd made her choice, she took SEPTA to New Jersey to visit Derrick, her friend from Poseidon's, the fish restaurant in Philly where she worked as a waitress. Derrick was the only friend she'd confided in all summer, his soft eyes and easy manner calming her down. He'd been her sounding board, her rock, and she'd told him almost everything about herself, from her ordeals with A to her crush on Maya St. Germain. Sometimes, Emily lamented that she was the one always dumping on him—she didn't know much about him at all—but Derrick just shrugged and said his life was boring in comparison to hers.

Derrick was working as a gardener at a big house in Cherry Hill on the weekends and told Emily to meet him there. It was the kind of mansion with iron gates, a guest house in the back, and a long, winding driveway made of pretty blue paver stones instead of blacktop. Derrick said the owners wouldn't mind if they talked in the gazebo, and that was where Emily told him her news. He'd listened patiently and hugged her tightly when she was done, which had brought tears to her eyes. Derrick was a godsend—he'd swooped in just when she needed him, listening to all of her problems.

As they were talking, the back door to the mansion, which looked out onto a lavish patio with a long, rectangular swimming pool, swung open, and a tall woman with short blond hair and a long, sloping nose stepped out. She noticed Emily immediately and looked her up and down, from her frizzy hair to her huge boobs to her enormous stomach. A small, tormented squeak escaped from her mouth. She crossed the patio and approached Emily, staring at her with such a sad expression it made Emily's heart break.

"How far along are you?" she asked softly.

Emily flinched. Since she was a teenager, most people averted their eyes from her pregnancy like it was a huge tumor. It was strange to hear someone sound so genuinely interested. "Um, about seven-and-a-half months."

The woman had tears in her eyes. "That's so precious. Are you feeling well?"

"I guess." Emily glanced cautiously at Derrick, but he just bit his lower lip.

The woman thrust out her hand. "I'm Gayle. This is my home."

"I'm, uh, Heather," Emily answered. It was the fake name she'd given everyone that summer, except for Derrick. *Heather* was even on her name tag at the restaurant. The skinny, pre-pregnant Emily was all over the Internet, connected to the Alison DiLaurentis story, and Emily could just picture an item about her illicit pregnancy on a local gossip blog, followed by a horrified call from her parents.

"You're so lucky," Gayle murmured, staring lovingly at Emily's belly. She almost looked like she wanted to reach out and touch it. Then, Gayle's smile suddenly wobbled into a frown, and tears rolled down her cheeks. "Oh,

God," she blurted, then turned around and ran crookedly into the house, slamming the door hard.

Emily and Derrick were silent for a while, listening to the sounds of a Weedwacker next door. "Did I do something to upset her?" Emily asked worriedly. The woman seemed so fragile.

Derrick rolled his eyes. "Whatever. Don't worry about it."

And so Emily hadn't worried about it. Little did she know she would be promising her baby to Gayle only a few short weeks later . . . and then going back on her word.

The furious messages Gayle left the day Emily placed the baby on the Bakers' doorstep flashed through her mind. *I'll hunt you down. I'll find you.* Luckily, Gayle never had.

"Emily, honey, are you okay?" Mrs. Fields asked, shattering Emily's thoughts.

Emily clamped down hard on the inside of her cheek. "Uh, I know the girl who lives here," she floundered, feeling her cheeks turn hot. "I thought I saw her at the window, but I guess not. We can go now."

Mrs. Fields peered at the yard. "Goodness, their lawn looks terrible," she murmured. "They'll never sell this house with all those weeds."

Emily squinted. "What do you mean, sell the house?"

"It's for sale. See?"

She pointed at a sign in the front yard. FOR SALE, it said, with a picture of the realtor and a phone number. Starbursts at the top right-hand corner said QUICK

TURNAROUND! and OWNERS RELOCATED! and BUY THIS NOW! There was also an announcement that an open house would be held the following Saturday from noon till four o'clock.

A sick feeling rushed through Emily's body. Just knowing that this house was here, that her baby was nearby, had made her feel comforted and relieved—she could close her eyes and picture where her baby was at all times. But the Bakers weren't on vacation—they'd moved.

Her baby was gone.

5

THE THINGS YOU DISCOVER IN
THE PRODUCE SECTION . . .

The following day, the bell rang in Art History class, and all twenty-two students stood en masse. "Read chapter eight for tomorrow!" Mrs. Kittinger called after them.

Aria shoved her books into her backpack and followed the herd out the door. As soon as she was in the hallway, she glanced at her cell phone, which had been blinking for the last hour. *New Google alert for Tabitha Clark*, said the screen.

Her stomach twisted. She'd been tracking Tabitha-related news, reading accounts of bereft friends, grieving relatives, and angry parents protesting drunken spring break trips. Today, there was a story in a newspaper. The headline read FATHER OF DECEASED SPRING BREAK TEEN TO SUE JAMAICAN RESORT THAT SERVED HIS DAUGHTER ALCOHOL.

She clicked on the link. There was a picture of Tabitha's father, Kenneth Clark, a tall, bespectacled man who was a captain of industry. He wanted to crack down on teenage drinking and punish bars that served underage drinkers. "I'd be curious to know what her blood-alcohol level was when she died," he said. There was also a quote from Graham Pratt, who'd been Tabitha's boyfriend when she died. "I think it's very possible The Cliffs resort served her, even though she was visibly drunk."

Whoa. What if Tabitha's family and friends somehow found out Tabitha *hadn't* died from an alcohol overdose? Aria's throat felt dry, and her heart started to pound. It was hard enough getting through the day without thinking about the innocent girl falling to her death—she hardly slept some nights, and she wasn't eating much. But if Tabitha's father found out, if the police linked it to them, if Aria's friends' lives were ruined because of something *she* technically did . . . well, she wouldn't know how to go on.

"Aria?"

Aria whirled around and saw Emily behind her. She was wearing a Rosewood swim-team parka, skinny black jeans, and had a curious look on her round, pleasant, freckled face.

"Um, hi." Aria slipped the phone into her pocket. There was no use showing this to Emily and getting her worried over what was probably nothing. "What's up?"

"I was wondering if you were going to Hanna's dad's town hall meeting on Tuesday." Emily moved out of the way as some guys on the crew team shouldered past. "She asked if I'd be there."

"Yep." Aria had already told Hanna she'd attend her dad's political events. "Want to sit together?"

"That would be nice." Emily gave Aria a small, watery smile that Aria recognized instantly. Back when they were part of Ali's clique, Aria had dubbed it Emily's Eeyore smile. She'd seen it on Emily's face a lot after Their Ali disappeared.

"What's the matter, Em?" Aria said softly.

Emily stared at her gray New Balance sneakers. Behind her, a bunch of sophomore boys shoved each other playfully. Kirsten Cullen gazed into the trophy case glass, fixing her lipstick. "I drove by that house on Ship Lane yesterday," Emily finally said.

Aria blinked, remembering Ship Lane's significance. "How did it go?"

Emily swallowed hard. "There was a FOR SALE sign on the lawn, and the house looked empty. They *moved*." Her jaw trembled like she was going to cry.

"Oh, Em." Aria wrapped her arms around her friend. Words couldn't describe how shocked she'd felt last summer when Emily told her she was pregnant. She'd called Aria out of the blue and begged her not to tell the others. *I've got it under control*, she'd said. *I've picked out a family for the baby once it's born. I just had to tell someone.*

"I wish I knew why they left," Emily murmured.

"It makes sense, don't you think?" Aria asked. "I mean, they suddenly had a baby. It probably looked strange to the neighbors. Maybe they moved to avoid questions."

Emily considered this. "Where do you think they went?"

"Why don't we try to find out?" Aria suggested. "Maybe the realtor knows."

Emily's eyes lit up. "The FOR SALE sign did say there's an open house this weekend."

"If you want company, I'll go with you," Aria offered.

"Really?" Emily looked relieved.

"Of course."

"*Thank* you." Emily threw her arms around Aria again and squeezed her tight. Aria squeezed back, grateful that they were close again. They'd spent so much time avoiding each other, shying away from the secrets they shared, but it hadn't done them much good. It was better to fight A together. Plus, Aria missed having good friends.

Aria's cell phone rang, and Emily broke away, saying she had to get to class. As she drifted down the hall, Aria looked at the screen and frowned. *Call from Meredith.* It was unusual for her father's fiancée to be calling her.

"Aria?" Meredith said when Aria answered. "Oh my God, I'm so glad I caught you." In the background, Meredith and Byron's toddler, Lola, was wailing. There were also sounds of banging pots and shattering dishes. "I really need your help," she went on. "I want to re-create this amazing pasta dish we had at an Italian restaurant in Philly for your dad tonight, but I just went to Fresh Fields, and they're out of tatsoi. The Fresh Fields in Bryn Mawr has it, but I can't go right now—Lola's super-fussy and I don't want to make it worse by lugging her out in public. Can you go for me after school?"

Aria slumped against the wall and stared absently at a poster reminding seniors to sign up for shore excursions on the upcoming Eco Cruise. "Can't you make it tomorrow?" Bryn Mawr wasn't exactly close.

"I really need it tonight."

"Why?" Aria asked. "Does Byron have visiting professors in town or something?"

Meredith made an uncomfortable noise at the back of her throat. "Never mind. It doesn't matter."

Now Aria was curious. "Seriously. What's the occasion?"

Another long pause. Meredith sighed. "Okay, it's the anniversary of our first kiss."

Nausea rippled through Aria's gut. "Oh," she said nastily. Her parents had still been married when Byron and Meredith had their first kiss.

"You asked!" Meredith protested. "I didn't want to tell you!"

Aria shoved her free hand into her blazer pocket. If Meredith really wanted to keep it from her, then why had she called up Aria in the first place?

"Aria?" Meredith's voice rang through the phone. "Are you there? Look, I'm sorry I told you. But I really *do* need your help. Can you do this for me just this once?"

Lola started to wail even louder in the background, and Aria shut her eyes. Even though she didn't support this anniversary, the more stressed out Meredith was, the more Lola would suffer. Saying no would probably get back to Byron, too, and she'd never hear the end of it.

"Fine," she said as the second bell rang. "Except you have to tell me what tatsoi *is*."

A few hours later, Aria pulled into Fresh Fields in Bryn Mawr. The town was about ten miles away, had a small liberal-arts college, an art house theater that produced avant-garde plays, and an old inn that with a sign that said GEORGE WASHINGTON SLEPT HERE. The cars in the grocery store's parking lot were covered with bumper stickers beseeching people to SAVE THE WHALES, GO GREEN, LIVE IN PEACE, and KILL YOUR TELEVISION.

After passing through the grocery store's automatic doors and between at least thirty barrels of olives, she headed to the greens section of the produce department. Apparently, tatsoi was like spinach. Why Meredith couldn't have just *used* spinach for the stupid let's-celebrate-our-affair dinner was beyond her.

The whole thing still made Aria squeamish. She'd been the one who caught Byron and Meredith kissing in a back alley in seventh grade. Byron had begged her not to say anything to Ella, and even though Aria wanted to tell, she'd thought that by keeping her dad's secret, her parents would stay together.

For a long time, Their Ali was the only one who knew about her dad's dalliances, and Aria had wished she didn't. Ali used to tease her about it all the time, asking if Byron had had affairs with other girls, too. When Ali disappeared, Aria had been partly relieved—at least she couldn't taunt her about the secret anymore. But it was lonely keeping the secret to herself, too. She'd tried to bury it deep, telling herself she was making a sacrifice for her family. In the end, though, her sacrifice didn't matter. A had revealed the affair to Ella, and her parents had separated.

Aria passed a hanging scale and touched it lightly with her fingertips. Maybe this wasn't worth dwelling on. It wasn't like Ella and Byron were the perfect couple, anyway, even long before Meredith. They were nothing like, say, Noel's parents. Nothing like what Aria wanted her and Noel to be.

She passed a bunch of bulbous, dark-purple eggplants and huge, fragrant bins of Thai basil and apple mint, and sampled a bite of sautéed Swiss chard from a woman in a Fresh Fields apron. At the end of the aisle, there was a small bin full of greens marked TATSOI. Aria grabbed a plastic bag from the dispenser and started to fill it up. Out of the corner of her eye, she noticed a woman by the heirloom tomatoes. She wore a swirled-print, Pucci-style dress, and had tanned skin, bushy eyebrows, and lots of makeup. There was something about her that reminded Aria of Noel's father. This woman could be his sister.

As Aria moved closer, considering asking the woman where she got her dress—Ella would love it—the woman pivoted, revealing more of her face. Something suddenly soured inside Aria, and she ducked around the corner. After a moment, she snuck another peek at the woman's face and gasped.

The woman wasn't Mr. Kahn's sister. She was *Mr. Kahn*.

SPENCER'S IN

That night, shortly after six, Spencer walked into Striped Bass, a restaurant on Walnut Street in Philadelphia. The place had echoing high ceilings, Brazilian cherry floors polished to a glossy shine, and Corinthian columns around the perimeter. Huge, barrel-shaped lights swung overhead, waiters swirled around white tablecloth–draped tables, and the air smelled like melted butter, grilled swordfish, and red wine.

PRINCETON EARLY ADMISSIONS WELCOME DINNER read a small sign just past the maître d' stand, pointing to a small room off to the right. Inside, thirty eager kids her age were standing around tables. The guys were all dressed in khakis, button-downs, and ties, and had that slightly nerdy, over-confident look of every class valedictorian Spencer had ever met. The girls wore sweater sets, knee-length skirts, and demure, I'm-going-to-join-a-law-firm-someday high heels. Some of them were whip-thin and looked like models, others were chubbier or wore dark-framed glasses, but they all looked like they had 4.0 GPAs and perfect SAT scores.

A flashing TV screen above the main bar caught Spencer's eye. THIS FRIDAY, AN ENCORE PERFORMANCE OF *PRETTY LITTLE KILLER*, a banner announced in bold yellow letters. The girl playing Alison DiLaurentis appeared, telling the Spencer, Aria, Hanna, and Emily actresses that she wanted to be their BFF again. "I've missed all of you," she simpered. "I want you back."

Spencer turned away, heat rising to her face. Wasn't it time they stopped showing that stupid docudrama? Anyway, the movie didn't tell the whole story. It left out the part about all of the girls thinking Real Ali had surfaced in Jamaica.

Don't think about Ali—or Jamaica, Spencer scolded herself silently, squaring her shoulders and marching into the dining room. The last thing she needed was to freak out, Lady Macbeth–style, at her first Princeton fete.

As soon as she swept through the double doors, a girl with blond hair and wide, violet eyes gave her an enormous smile. "Hi! Are you here for the dinner?"

"Yes," Spencer said, straightening up. "Spencer Hastings. From Rosewood." She prayed no one would recognize her name—or notice that a slightly heavier, twenty-something version of her was on TV in the room behind them.

"Welcome! I'm Harper, one of the student ambassadors." The girl shuffled through a bunch of name tags and found one with Spencer's name written in all caps. "Hey, did you get that at the D.C. Leadership Conference two years ago?" she asked, eyeing the silver Washington Monument–shaped keychain that hung from Spencer's oversize leather tote.

"I did!" Spencer said, glad she'd stuck the keychain on the zipper pull at the last minute. She'd hoped someone would recognize it.

Harper smiled. "I have one of those somewhere. I thought they only asked college students to that."

"Normally they do," Spencer said with mock-bashfulness. "You were there, too?"

Harper nodded eagerly. "It was pretty great, don't you think? Meeting all those senators, doing those mock-UN meetings, although that opening dinner was kind of . . ." Harper trailed off, making an awkward face.

"Weird?" Spencer ventured, giggling. "You're talking about that mime, right?" The event coordinators had hired a mime as entertainment. He'd spent the entire dinner pretending he was trapped in an invisible box or walking his imaginary dog.

"Yes!" Harper snickered. "He was so creepy!"

"Remember how that senator from Idaho *loved* him?" Spencer tittered.

"*Totally.*" Harper's smile was warm and genuine. Her gaze moved to Spencer's name tag. "You go to Rosewood Day? One of my best friends went there. Did you know Tansy Gates?"

"She was on my field hockey team!" Spencer cried,

thrilled for another connection. Tansy was one of the girls who'd petitioned Rosewood Day to let seventh graders on the JV field hockey team, hoping that Spencer would be chosen. Ali had been picked instead, and Spencer had been relegated to the lame sixth-grade squad, which let anyone play.

Then Spencer looked at Harper's name tag. It listed the activities she was involved in at Princeton. Field Hockey. The *Daily Princetonian*. At the very end, in small letters, were the words *Bicker Chair, Ivy Eating Club*.

She almost gasped. She'd done a ton of research about Eating Clubs since she'd been caught unaware at the cake-tasting. The coed Ivy, which boasted heads of state, CEOs of major companies, and literary giants as alums, was at the top of her must-join list. If Harper ran Bicker, that meant she was in charge of picking new members. She was definitely *the* person to know.

Suddenly, someone started clapping at the front of the room. "Welcome, incoming freshmen!" a gangly guy with curly reddish-blondish hair yelled. "I'm Steven, one of the ambassadors. We're going to start dinner, so could everyone take their seats?"

Spencer looked at Harper. "Want to sit together?"

Harper's face fell. "I'd love to, but our seats are assigned." She pointed to Spencer's name tag. "That number on your name tag is the table you're sitting at. I'm sure you'll meet some awesome early admits, though!"

"Yeah," Spencer said, trying to hide her disappointment.

And then, before she could say anything else, Harper flounced away.

Spencer found her way to table four and sat down across from an Asian boy with spiky hair and angular glasses who was glued to his iPhone screen. Two guys in matching Pritchard Prep jackets were talking about a golf tournament they'd competed in the summer before. A petite girl in a Hillary Clinton–esque pantsuit was scream-ing into a cell phone about selling stock. Spencer raised an eyebrow, wondering if the girl already had a job. These Princeton kids didn't mess around.

"*Hola.*"

A guy with a billy-goat chin-beard, shaggy brown hair, and sleepy bedroom eyes gazed at Spencer from the adja-cent seat. His gray dress pants had a ragged hem, his shoes were thick-soled and surely made of hemp, and he smelled like the enormous bong Mason Byers had brought back from Amsterdam.

The stoner kid stuck out his hand. "I'm Raif Fredricks, but most people call me Reefer. I'm from Princeton, so I feel like I'm going to the local community college. My folks are begging me not to board, but I'm like, 'Hell no! I need my freedom! I want to hold drum circles in my room at four in the morning! I want to have killer protest meetings during dinner!'"

Spencer blinked at him. He'd said everything so fast she wasn't sure she caught it all. "Wait, *you* got into *Princeton?*"

Reefer—God, that was a stupid nickname—grinned. "Isn't that why we're all here?" His hand was still hanging in front of Spencer. "Uh, normally, this is the part where people shake. And you say, 'Hi, Reefer, my name is . . . '"

"Spencer," Spencer said dazedly, clasping Reefer's enormous palm for a split second. Her mind reeled. This dude belonged on a grassy knoll at Hollis with the other kids who'd graduated from their high schools in the middle of the pack. He didn't look like the type who agonized over AP exams and made sure he'd fulfilled enough community service hours.

"So, Spencer." Reefer sat back and eyed Spencer up and down. "I think it's fate that we got seated together. You look like you get it, you know? You look like you aren't a prisoner to the system." He nudged her side. "Plus, you're totally cute."

Ew, Spencer thought, purposely turning the opposite direction and pretending to be enamored with the endive salads the waiters were serving. It was just her luck to be seated next to this loser.

Reefer didn't get the hint, though. He leaned closer, tapping her shoulder. "It's okay if you're shy. So get this: I was thinking of heading over to Independence Hall and checking out the Occupy Philly rally after this. Are you in? It's supposed to be really inspiring."

"Uh, that's okay," Spencer said, annoyed at how loud this guy was talking. What if everyone thought they were friends?

Reefer shoved a piece of endive into his mouth. "Your loss. Here, in case you change your mind." He ripped a piece of paper from a ragged spiral-bound notebook in his bag, scribbled something down, and passed it to Spencer. She squinted at the words. *What a long, strange trip it's been.* Huh?

"Jerry's my guru," Reefer said. Then he pointed to a bunch of digits below the quote. "Call anytime—day or night. I'm always up."

"Uh, thanks." Spencer slipped the paper into her bag. She noticed Harper watching her from across the room, met her eyes, and gave her an *Oh-my-God-I-think-he's-gross* eye roll.

Thankfully, Steven, the other ambassador, started speaking, and his long, ego-stroking speech about how everyone in the room was wonderful and amazing and would surely change the world someday because they went to Princeton took up the rest of the hour. As soon as the waiters cleared the desserts, Spencer shot out of her seat as fast as her toned-from-field-hockey legs could carry her. She found Harper by the coffee urn and gave her a huge smile.

"I see you met Reefer." Harper winked.

Spencer scrunched up her face. "Yeah, lucky me."

Harper gave Spencer an inscrutable look, then moved in closer. "Listen, I know this is last minute, but do you have plans for this weekend?"

"I don't think so." Aside from helping her mom

taste-test yet more confections for the wedding. Did a second wedding really need a cake *and* a cupcake tower?

Harper's eyes glittered. "Great. Because there's a party I'd love to bring you to. I think you'd really get along with my friends. You could stay with me in this big house I live in on campus. Get a sense of things."

"That sounds wonderful," Spencer said quickly, as though if she paused even a millisecond, Harper would rescind her offer. The *big house on campus* was the Ivy House—as Bicker Chair, Harper got to live there.

"Awesome." Harper tapped something on her phone. "Give me your e-mail. I'll send you my number and directions of where to find me. Be there by six."

Spencer gave Harper her e-mail address and phone number, and soon enough, Harper's e-mail appeared in her inbox. When she read it, she almost whooped aloud. Sure enough, Harper had given her directions to the Ivy House on Prospect Avenue.

She filed out of the room, walking on air. As she pushed through the revolving door to the street, her cell phone, which was tucked in her purse, let out a muffled chime. When she pulled it out and saw the screen, her heart plummeted like a stone. *New text message from Anonymous.*

Hi Spence! Think your college friends would let you into their Eating Club if they knew about your appetite for murder? Kisses! —A

7

HANNA GETS STEAMED

The following night, Hanna stood outside the boys' locker room, tugging down the curve-hugging dress she'd changed into after the final bell. All around her, students bustled to catch their after-school buses, rushed to activities, or climbed in their cars to head to the King James Mall.

Hanna's cell phone beeped, and she quickly turned down the volume. It was yet another message from Isabel, reminding Hanna to be at her father's town hall meeting that night a little early to meet and greet some of the donors. *Duh*—as if she didn't already know that. She'd helped *organize* the whole thing. And she'd get there when she got there. The task at hand was the only thing on her mind right now.

The aromas of dirty socks and Axe body spray wafted into the hall. Muffled voices and hissing shower sounds echoed. It just so happened that the boys' indoor track team had come in from a grueling workout of wind sprints around the iced-over parking lot. It also just so happened that Mike was on the indoor track team to keep in shape for lacrosse. Operation Get Mike Back was about to begin.

The blue door swished open, and two sophomores in track jackets emerged, giving Hanna strange looks as they passed. She glared at them in return, then edged toward the door again.

"It was genius of the gym to introduce a pole-dancing class," Mason Byers's telltale gravelly baritone rang out. "Have you seen the girls that take it?"

"Dude, don't even get me started," James Freed answered. "I didn't even work out the last time I was there—I just watched them the whole time."

"That girl Mike's dating takes it," Mason said.

Hanna frowned. Colleen was pole dancing now? For an eighth grade talent show, Colleen had dressed in a Latvian costume and danced her ancestors' native steps. Hanna and Mona had made fun of her for months afterward.

"I *know*." James made a weird boy grunt. "No wonder he's doing her." He snickered. "Did you know Bebris means *beaver* in Latvian?"

Wait. The guys didn't just say Mike was *doing* her, did they? Hanna felt a hurt twinge. She and Mike hadn't done it, and they'd dated for over a year.

Two more guys emerged from the locker room, and Hanna peeked inside. James and Mason were nowhere to be seen, but Mike was at his locker. He was standing in his boxers, his black hair wet and matted against his head, little water droplets on his broad shoulders. Had he *always* been that muscled?

Hanna rolled back her shoulders. *Go time.* She sauntered into the steamy room. She'd never been inside the boys' locker room before and was disappointed to find that it didn't look all that different from the girls', aside from the jockstrap lying on the floor in one of the aisles. The room smelled like talc and sweaty socks, and the trash can was overflowing with empty Gatorade bottles.

She tiptoed across the gray tiled floor until she was only a few feet away from Mike. On his back was the crescent moon–shaped scar he'd gotten from falling off his bike when he was little. They'd shown each other all their scars one afternoon at Hanna's house, stripping down to their underwear but not going any further. In some ways, Hanna had been too afraid to have sex with Mike—she'd never slept with anyone before, and it seemed like such a big deal with him. And despite how Mike was always talking about how sex-crazed he was, Hanna had wondered if he had been a little afraid, too.

Hanna reached out and clapped her hands over Mike's eyes. "Boo."

Mike jumped, but then relaxed. "Heeeyy," he said, drawing out the word. "What are *you* doing in here?"

Instead of saying anything, Hanna began to pepper the back of Mike's neck with little kisses. Mike leaned into her, his bare skin warm against her tight dress. He reached back and raked his fingers through Hanna's long ringlets. Suddenly, he whipped around, opened his eyes, and stared.

"Hanna!" Mike grabbed the towel from the bench and covered his bare torso. "What the hell?"

Hanna grabbed for the rope necklace Mike had worn ever since his family returned from Iceland and yanked him closer. "Don't be shy. Just go with this. Isn't this one of your sex fantasies?"

Mike stepped away from her, his eyes bulging. "Have you lost your mind?" He wasn't checking out Hanna's skintight dress or the super-high-heeled shoes that made her ankles ache. Instead, he was glaring at her like she was being wildly inappropriate. "You need to go."

Hanna stiffened. "You seemed into it just a few seconds ago."

"That's because I thought you were someone else." Mike pulled a T-shirt over his head and stepped into his pants.

Hanna leaned against the lockers, not budging. "Look, Mike, I want you back, okay? Things are over with me and my boyfriend. I know you want me back, too. So stop acting like an idiot and kiss me already!"

She punctuated this with a little laugh so that she didn't sound complete pushy, but Mike just stared at her blankly. "You heard me at the mall the other night—I have a girlfriend now."

Hanna rolled her eyes. "Colleen? *Please*. Don't you remember how she had her head flushed in the Old Faithful toilet four times in sixth grade? And Mike, she's a drama geek. You're totally bringing down your popularity quotient by dating her."

Mike crossed his arms over his chest. "Actually, Colleen has an agent for her drama stuff. She's been on auditions for some big stuff on TV. And I don't care about popularity."

Yeah, right. "Is she easy or something?" Hanna was surprised by how bitter she sounded.

Mike's face hardened. "I *like* her, Hanna."

He stared at her unflinchingly, and the clouds in Hanna's head began to lift. Mike wasn't going out—and sleeping–with Colleen because she was willing, but because he cared about her.

Someone snickered from near the sinks, and Hanna spied James and Mason hiding behind the wall, hanging on every word. She wrapped her arms around her body, suddenly feeling exposed. They were laughing at her. Dorky Hanna, throwing herself at her ex. Dorky Hanna, making an idiot out of herself. She might as well have been fat again, with poop-brown hair and braces on her teeth. The ultimate chubby, ugly loser who nobody loved.

Without another word, she whipped around and marched out of the locker room, not even stopping when her ankle twisted beneath her. *This isn't happening, this isn't happening*, she silently repeated over and over. There was no way she had been beaten by someone as milquetoast as Colleen.

She slammed the locker room door hard and emerged into the silent hall. Suddenly, a new laugh rang through the corridor, high-pitched and even more sinister than the boys'. Hanna froze and listened. Was she crazy, or did that sound like Ali's laugh? She cocked her head to the side, waiting. But just like that, the sound disappeared.

HELLO, MY NAME IS HEATHER

That night, Emily walked into the Rosewood Arms, a hotel near Hollis that was half quaint B&B, half fancy resort. The old mansion was once owned by a railroad baron, and each room was decorated with priceless antique cabinetry and a smattering of deer, bison, and lion heads. One of the wings had been converted into a spa. The baron's old garage, which used to house dozens of top-of-the-line carriages and early race cars, was now the banquet hall.

On this particular night, the space had been rented out for Mr. Marin's town hall talk. There were long rows of chairs facing a stage. A lone microphone stood in the center, and there were banners proclaiming messages like TOM MARIN FOR CHANGE and PENNSYLVANIA NEEDS MARIN. It was weird to see Hanna's dad's face on campaign posters. Emily still thought of him as the guy who'd once reprimanded Ali for throwing her Bubble Yum out his car window. Later, Ali had made them all go around in a circle, calling Hanna's dad Mr. *Moron*—even Hanna, who had done it with tears in her eyes.

Emily scanned the crowd. There were people here she hadn't seen in years—Mrs. Lowe, her old piano teacher, whose angular face always reminded Emily of a grey-hound's, was sipping from a Starbucks thermal mug in the corner. Mr. Polley, who used to emcee Emily's swim team banquets, was looking at his BlackBerry near one of the windows. Mr. and Mrs. Roland, who had moved into the Cavanaughs' old house, sat on folding chairs that had been set up near the stage, their daughter, Chloe, perched next to them. Emily ducked. Mr. Roland had gotten her the scholarship to UNC, but his lascivious behavior had cost Emily her friendship with Chloe.

The only people Emily didn't see were her friends. As she turned mid-stride to look for them in a different room, she smacked into a caterer who was carrying a silver tray loaded with appetizers. The caterer shot forward, but he miraculously caught the tray before it fell to the floor. "I'm so sorry!" Emily cried.

"No worries," he answered breezily. "Luckily, I have lightning-quick reflexes." Then he turned around and did a double take. "*Emily?*"

Emily blinked. Staring back at her, dressed in a cater-er's tuxedo, was Isaac Colbert, her ex-boyfriend—*and* the father of her child. She hadn't seen him since they'd broken up over a year ago.

"H-hey." Emily's heart pounded. Isaac looked taller than she remembered—broader, too. His brown hair was down to his chin, and a tattoo peeked out from under his collar. She stared at the black spiral pattern on his skin. What did his overprotective mother have to say about that? Given that Mrs. Colbert had cut Emily's head out of all the photos of her and Isaac together and called her a whore, Emily couldn't imagine she was thrilled her son had gotten inked.

"What are you doing here?" she blurted.

Isaac gestured to the logo on his breast pocket. COLBERT CATERING. "My dad's company is providing refreshments. He's a Tom Marin fan." Then he stood back and looked Emily up and down. "You look . . . different. Have you lost weight?"

"I doubt that. I still feel like I'm hanging onto some weight from being—" She caught herself before she could say *being pregnant* and almost swallowed her tongue. What was *wrong* with her?

She'd almost called Isaac to confess a few times while she was pregnant—Isaac had been wonderful to her before that stuff happened with his mom. They used to talk for hours, and he'd been so accepting when she told him that she'd dated girls in the past. Then one wintery afternoon, they'd undressed slowly in his bedroom. He had been so sweet about wanting to make their first time meaningful.

But every time she picked up the phone to call him, she couldn't figure out how to break the news. "Hey! I've got a story for you!" Or, "Hey, remember that one and only time we slept together?" And what would Isaac have said? Would he have wanted to give the baby up for adoption, too, or would he have demanded that they raise it together? Emily couldn't imagine doing something like that—she loved kids, but she wasn't ready for her own. Then again, Isaac might not even have believed her. Or he might have gotten really, really angry that she hadn't told him earlier. It was something, she'd decided, she had to handle on her own. And so she'd flipped through the online profiles of hopeful adoptive couples by herself. When she came to an account for two happy, smiling people that read *Loving couple married for eight years so excited to be a mommy and daddy*, she stopped. Charles and Lizzie Baker said they were soul mates, went on kayaking trips on the weekends, read the same book at the same time so they could discuss it over dessert, and were fixing up their old house in Wessex. *We will always let your child know that he or she was placed for adoption out of love*, their profile had said. Something about it had touched Emily at her core.

Now, Isaac set the tray down on a nearby table and laid his hand on her arm. "I wanted to call so many times. I heard about the horrible thing you went through."

"*What?*" Emily felt the color drain from her face.

"Alison DiLaurentis coming back," Isaac said. "I remember you talking about Ali, how much she meant to you. Are you okay?"

Emily's heart slowly returned to its normal rhythm. Of course—Alison. "I guess," she answered shakily. "And,

um, how are you? Is the band still together? And what's
that?" She pointed to his tattoo. Anything to get him off
the topic of her.

Isaac opened his mouth to speak, but a tall, older guy
in a caterer's uniform tapped his shoulder and told him
he was needed on prep duty. "I should go," he said to
Emily, starting toward the door. Then he stopped and
faced her again. "You wouldn't want to get together after
the meeting tonight and catch up, would you?"

For a moment, Emily considered taking him up on it.
But then she thought about how tense she'd be the whole
time, the secret bulging inside her like an overfilled water
balloon. "Um, I already have plans," she lied. "Sorry."

Isaac's face fell. "Oh. Well, maybe another time, then."

He followed the other caterer into the crowd. Emily
spun around and darted in the opposite direction, feeling
like she'd just narrowly escaped something awful, but also
sad and regretful that she'd blown Isaac off.

"Emily?"

Emily turned to her left. Hanna stood next to her,
dressed in a fitted pinstriped sheath and chunky heels.
Mr. Marin was at her side, looking senatorial in his red
power-tie. "Hey," she said, hugging both of them.

"Thanks for coming." Hanna sounded grateful.

"We're happy to have you, Emily," Mr. Marin said.

"I'm happy to be here," Emily answered, though after
her run-in with Isaac, all she wanted to do was go home.

Then Mr. Marin turned to a woman who'd just joined

the group. She had ash-blond hair, perfect posture, and wore an impeccable suit that looked like it cost a small fortune. Emily started, her body suddenly on fire. *No.* It couldn't be. Emily had to be seeing things.

The woman noticed her, too, and stopped talking mid-sentence. "Oh!" she blurted, her face going white.

Bile rose in Emily's throat. It was Gayle.

Mr. Marin noticed the strange look pass between both of them and cleared his throat. "Uh, Emily, this is Ms. Riggs, one of my biggest donors. She and her husband recently moved to the area from New Jersey. Ms. Riggs, this is my daughter's friend Emily."

Gayle pushed a strand of blond hair from her eyes. "I thought your name was Heather," she said in a measured, ice-cold voice.

All eyes were on her. Hanna shot around and stared at Emily. It felt like ten years passed before Emily spoke again. "Uh, you must have me confused with someone else," she blurted. And then, unable to stand there a moment longer, she whipped around and ran as fast as she could for the nearest door, which led to a back storage room. She shut herself inside and leaned against the wall, her heart thudding in her ears.

As if on cue, her phone chimed. Emily grabbed for it, her stomach jumping all over the place. *One new text,* the screen said.

Hey, baby mama. Guess the jig is up! —A

9

HELL HATH NO FURY LIKE
A RICH LADY SCORNED

As Mr. Marin took the stage at the town hall meeting, beaming at his adoring crowd, Spencer banged through the back doors of the banquet room into a small parking lot. Only a few spaces were occupied, taken by beat-up pickup trucks and compact cars. At the back of the lot, next to a green Dumpster stuffed with empty cardboard boxes, Emily hopped from foot to foot as if her sweater dress was on fire.

The door opened again, and Aria and Hanna stepped outside. They were both holding their phones and looking confused. Just moments ago, Emily had sent all of them a cryptic text saying they needed to talk and to meet her here. Spencer had texted back asking if they could talk inside—it was cold out—but Emily had written back *NO!*

"Em?" Aria called out, walking down the rickety metal steps. "Are you okay?"

"My dad's going to wonder where I am." Hanna held

the railing tight, cautious in her high heels. "What's going on?"

Emily thrust her phone toward them when they were close. "I just got this."

The girls read the note on the screen. Spencer's stomach flipped as she took in the words. "Wait. A knows about the baby?"

Emily nodded, looking terrified.

"But how is that possible? And why didn't A mention it before?" Spencer asked. She still couldn't believe Emily had had a baby. Before school was dismissed last year, Emily had looked—and seemed—so normal, like nothing was bothering her at all. But halfway through July, shortly after Spencer's run-in with the police for possession of Easy A, Emily had called Spencer in a panic, saying she was pregnant. At first, Spencer had thought it was a joke. Not a very funny one, either.

"I don't know," Emily answered, tears in her eyes. "Maybe because A knows everything. Has anyone else gotten a note?"

Spencer shakily raised her hand. "Actually, I did. Last night. I was going to tell you tonight."

She pulled up the text on her phone, and the others gathered around.

Think your college friends would let you into their Eating Club if they knew about your appetite for murder?

Just reading it again made Spencer's heart gallop. She'd barely slept a wink last night, running over the possibilities of who A might be.

"How could A know about Tabitha *and* the baby?" Emily whispered.

Hanna exhaled sharply, her breath visible in the frigid air. "The same way A knows everything."

"Plenty of people saw you." Spencer shivered in the thin blazer she'd chosen to wear. "You were in Philly all summer. A could have been, too. Maybe that's how A knew about me and Kelsey."

Emily paced up and down a faded yellow line demarcating a parking space. "You know how big I got. I didn't look like the girl on that *People* cover. But I suppose someone could have figured it out." She arched her back and stared at the spindly tree branches above their heads.

"This isn't just any random someone," Aria pointed out. "It's a person who's out to get us. Someone we wronged. Someone who wants revenge."

"But *who*?" Hanna cried.

Emily stopped pacing. "You all know who *I* think A is."

Spencer groaned. "*Don't* say Ali, Em."

"Why not?" Emily's voice cracked. "She and Tabitha were at the Preserve together. Ali could've found out we killed Tabitha. Maybe she wants revenge for that, on top of everything else we did to her."

Spencer sighed. She couldn't believe Emily was still on

this Ali-is-alive mission. "So Ali and Tabitha were at the Preserve at the same time. That doesn't prove anything. And for the last time, Ali's bones weren't found in the rubble, but we all saw her in the house just before it blew up."

A shadow passed over Emily's face. "It's just, who other than Ali would know to follow us around everywhere, track our every move?" she said, staring at her feet. "And you guys aren't going to believe who's here—*Gayle*. What if A is planning to tell her what I did with the baby? And what if Gayle tells everyone about me?"

"Wait a minute." Hanna furrowed her brow. "Gayle, the woman who wanted the baby, is *inside*?"

Emily nodded. "It was the woman your dad introduced me to. Ms. Riggs."

"So that's why she called you Heather." Hanna shut her eyes. "Gayle is promising my dad a lot of money for his campaign."

"Well, isn't that a lovely coincidence," Spencer said sarcastically.

Aria cleared her throat. "Maybe it's not a coincidence at all."

Everyone looked at her. Aria turned to Emily. "Let me get this straight, Em. You just saw the woman you promised a baby to, the woman you screwed over in the end. Right?"

"I had to screw her over," Emily interrupted, a tormented look on her face. "I had to do what was right for the baby!"

"I know, I know." Aria waved her hands impatiently. "Just go with me, okay? You were worried sick about Gayle tracking you down, though. And you said Gayle was crazy. Isn't that why you didn't want to give the baby to her?"

Emily wrinkled her nose. "I don't see what you're getting at."

"Isn't it obvious?" Aria exclaimed. "You saw Gayle inside. And then, seconds later, you got a note from A *about* the baby. Gayle is A! Maybe she figured out what you did—what we all did! And now she wants to get revenge on all of us for helping you take her baby away!"

Emily squinted. "That makes no sense. How could Gayle know about Spencer's drug problem? How could she know about what happened in Jamaica?"

"Maybe she has a connection to Penn and Jamaica," Aria said. "She's really rich. Maybe she hired a PI. You never know."

"But what does she want from us?" Hanna asked.

Everyone thought for a moment. "Maybe she wants to know where the baby is," Aria suggested.

"Or maybe Gayle just wants to hurt you like you hurt her," Spencer said with a shiver. "Remember those messages she left on your voicemail, Em? She sounded crazy." She shut her eyes and recalled the woman's grating voice coming through the tiny cell phone speaker. *I'm going to find you,* the last voicemail had said. *I'm going to hunt you and that baby down, and then you'll be sorry.*

Inside, Tom Marin's voice boomed through the micro-phone. Hanna cast a glance at the door. "What did you mean when you said Gayle being my dad's biggest donor might not be a coincidence, Aria?"

"Think about it." Aria fiddled with one of her feather earrings. "If Gayle is A, maybe she got involved with your dad's campaign to get closer to you. Maybe it's part of her master plan."

Hanna squeezed her eyes shut. "My dad said that her funds are crucial to the campaign, though. If she withheld them for any reason, he might not have the money to air his commercials throughout the state."

"Maybe that's part of A's master plan, too," Spencer said somberly.

"Guys, do you hear yourselves?" Emily looked annoyed. "There's *no way* Gayle is A. Yeah, it's awful that I ran into her. And yeah, I don't know what I'm going to do now that she's seen me. But we have to think about A *getting* to Gayle, not A *being* Gayle."

"I think we need more facts," Spencer said. "Maybe there's a way we could prove if Gayle is or isn't A. If she's your dad's biggest donor, Hanna, maybe you could snoop around a little?"

"Me?" Hanna pressed her hand to her chest. "Why do *I* have to do it?"

They were suddenly interrupted by a loud creak. The back door opened, and Kate stuck her head out. "*There* you are," she said, sounding more relieved than annoyed.

"I've been looking everywhere for you. Dad wants us on the stage with him."

"Got it." Hanna moved toward the door. She glanced over her shoulder at the others, indicating that they should follow. Aria and Spencer fell in line, but Emily stayed where she was. *I'm not going back inside*, her stubborn expression said. *Not with Gayle there.*

Spencer gave Emily an apologetic wave before ducking back into the banquet hall. The room was even more crowded than before—every seat was filled. Mr. Marin stood on the stage, answering questions and flashing his politician's smile. Spencer caught Hanna's arm before she joined her father. "Which one is Gayle, anyway?"

Hanna pointed to a woman in a red skirt suit in the front row. "Her."

Spencer gazed at the woman, assessing her blond hair, thin face, and the enormous diamonds on her fingers. All of a sudden, something clicked. The cake tasting. Gayle had been a few tables over, wearing a Chanel suit. Spencer had felt the woman's gaze on her back, but had shaken off Gayle's weird, smug expression, telling herself she was just being paranoid.

But maybe she wasn't. Maybe Gayle *had* been watching her. Because maybe, just maybe, Gayle was A.

10

FOOD FOR THOUGHT

Wednesday afternoon, Aria and Noel stood at a counter in the basement of the Rosewood Culinary College, where they were taking Introduction to Cooking. Shiny pots and pans surrounded them. Ground-up spices waited in small, clear prep bowls, and a half-chopped leek lay limply on their cutting board. The room smelled of boiling chicken broth, gas from the burners, and the pungent cinnamon Trident that Marge, the lady behind them, chewed nonstop.

All eyes were on Madame Richeau, their instructor. Even though she'd only been a cook on a Carnival cruise ship for all of six months in the eighties, she acted as though she were a celebrity chef on the Food Network, wearing a tall toque and speaking with a dubious French accent.

"The key to good risotto is constant stirring," Madame Richeau said, inserting a wooden spoon into a pot and

rotating it slowly around. She pronounced *the* like *zee.*
"Never stop stirring until the rice is creamy. It's a hard
technique to master! Now, stir, stir, stir!"

Noel nudged Aria. "You aren't stirring fast enough."

Aria snapped to attention and looked down at her
pot, which was full of Arborio rice and bubbling broth.
"Oops," she said distractedly, giving the concoction a few
good mixes.

"Would you rather chop?" Noel held up the Japanese
knife he'd brought from his parents' kitchen. He was at
work cutting a red onion for a side salad. "I don't want
our risotto to be ruined. Madame might give us the
guillotine," he said with a sly smile.

"I'm cool," Aria said, glancing at his workstation. "Besides,
I could never slice that onion as well as you." Surprisingly,
Noel had turned out to be pretty good at the class—especially
the chopping part. Aria always got bored halfway through
and left her vegetables in big, unwieldy chunks.

She could feel Noel studying her, but she pretended
not to notice, instead vigorously stirring the risotto.
Thankfully, Noel had missed the town hall meeting last
night because he and his lacrosse buddies had a team dinner. And their schedules didn't intersect in school for the
past two days, which meant she hadn't seen him in the
halls. She'd considered not coming to cooking class, too,
but then Noel would ask why. And what was she supposed
to say—that she'd seen his father squeezing tomatoes in a
dress at Fresh Fields?

She shuddered, the image swimming into her mind again. The moment she'd realized Mr. Kahn's long-lost sister might just be Mr. Kahn himself, she'd shot out of the produce section as fast as she could and hidden behind a rack of French bread. She'd watched the man from afar, praying that she was wrong. Maybe it was another dude in drag. Maybe it was a really ugly woman. But then the person's cell phone rang. "Hello?" a man's voice said into the receiver—a man's voice that sounded exactly like Mr. Kahn's. Game over.

Aria wasn't sure who she felt more embarrassed for— Mr. Kahn or herself. She couldn't shake the feeling that the whole thing was *her* fault, which was how she'd felt when she discovered Byron kissing Meredith in seventh grade. If she hadn't walked down that alley, if she hadn't turned her head *at that moment*, she wouldn't have been burdened with her dad's secret—or the agonizing struggle of whether to tell Ella. Likewise, if she'd only gone to Fresh Fields a few moments later, or lingered at the cheese counter, she wouldn't know something so damaging about Noel's dad.

But now that she did know, she was dying to dig deeper. Was this something Mr. Kahn did often? He *was* a little odd—he'd dressed up as a cavemannish Viking for Klaudia's welcome-to-the-U.S. party a month ago, and he was always drunkenly belting out opera songs and show tunes at Rosewood Day school board fund-raiser parties. But dressing up as a woman—in *public*? Didn't he realize how that would look if someone caught him? And surely Mr. and Mrs. Kahn's marriage wasn't as solid as Aria had thought. Were they one of those couples who put up appearances but secretly didn't love each other at all? That just made her heart break for Noel even more. He idolized his parents' strong bond.

Aria had promised no more secrets, but this was definitely something Noel didn't need to know—or *want* to know. And she could only hope A would never find out.

From the moment she'd woken up yesterday, Aria kept waiting for a taunting A message to arrive about Mr. Kahn. But miraculously, no note had been slipped under her windshield wiper, left in her locker, or beamed to her cell phone. Which meant one of two things: A was waiting for the perfect moment . . . or A didn't know.

If Gayle was A, maybe Gayle had been too busy stalking Spencer and Emily to make time for Aria, too. It wasn't like Gayle could be everywhere at once. And if A didn't know, the best thing Aria could do was pretend she'd never seen Mr. Kahn. She wouldn't even *think* about it.

"Everyone, get out your *beurre* and measure one half cup!" Madame Richeau crowed from the front.

"What's *beurre* again?" Noel grumbled. "I hate when she says stuff in French."

"Butter." Aria reached into the mini fridge under the counter and pulled out a stick of Land O'Lakes. As she unwrapped it, her mind wandered again. Why was Gayle, a wealthy, successful woman, wasting her time and money stalking four high schoolers? Then again, she *was* nuts. Aria had only met Gayle once before, and she could tell immediately that there was something wrong with her.

It had been shortly after Emily admitted to Aria that she was pregnant. Aria was meeting Emily in the city. They'd planned to peruse the Italian Market, but then Emily asked if they could stop off to have coffee with Gayle, a strange, wealthy woman she'd met a week before.

"She got in touch with me through Derrick," Emily explained, referring to her friend from the restaurant. "He works for her on the weekends. He's asked her for more hours and listed me as a character reference." She smiled apologetically. "It'll only take a couple of minutes, I promise. And oh, I should warn you. She's a little . . . weepy. But she seems nice enough."

Aria had agreed, and Emily asked her to wear a wig and sunglasses so that Gayle wouldn't recognize her and make the connection that both of them were the famous Pretty Little Liars. The only wig Aria had was a pink one from a few Halloweens earlier, but she'd worn it anyway.

The café was next to a yoga studio and a store that did tongue piercings. It was the kind of place that had reclaimed-wood farmhouse tables, weathervanes nailed to the walls, and a hand-printed menu on a chalkboard that said breakfast was served all day. Gayle was waiting for them in a booth, a big stack of blueberry pancakes already on the table. As soon as she spied Emily waddling up the aisle, she pushed the plate across the table. "Eat up. Blueberries are good for the baby's developing brain."

"Oh." Emily looked startled. "That's nice of you."

"I'm just doing what's best for the baby," Gayle said, her gaze squarely on Emily, a sweet smile on her face.

"I appreciate it." Emily took a bite of the pancakes and smiled. "They're really good."

Gayle cleared her throat awkwardly. "Pardon me if you think this is a little forward, but I assume you are putting your baby up for adoption. Can I ask if you've found a family yet?"

A muscle in Emily's cheek twitched. Aria reached under the table and took Emily's hand as if to say, *If you want to run out of here right now, I'm right behind you.* But instead, Emily had taken a breath. "Uh, yes. I found a nice couple who lives in the suburbs, not that far from me."

Gayle looked crestfallen. "I figured as much. I recently lost a child, and it was devastating. My husband and I want a baby, and I've gone through countless fertility treatments, spent tens of thousands of dollars, but we haven't had any luck."

"That must be so rough for you," Emily said, her features softening.

Gayle's eyes welled with tears. "I want a baby of my own so badly. You seem like a beautiful, smart, well-rounded girl. I would be honored to raise your child, but I guess that's not meant to be." She hung her head.

"Gosh, if I'd have known," Emily murmured, fiddling with her fork. "I'm really sorry."

"Are you sure you couldn't change your mind?" Gayle's voice rose. "I could make it worth your while. My husband and I do very well for ourselves, and we would reward you handsomely."

A zillion alarms blared in Aria's head. Did this woman seriously mean she was going to *pay* Emily for her kid?

But Emily didn't appear fazed. She reached for her water glass and took a long sip, nodding for Gayle to go on.

"The baby would have every privilege in the world," Gayle said. "Private schools. Lessons of all kinds. Amazing trips around the world. You name it."

Aria glanced around at the other patrons in the café, amazed no one had overheard what had just transpired. Wasn't this illegal? Then Gayle dropped a twenty-dollar bill on the table and stood. "Think about it, Heather. I'll call you in a few days, or you call me." She passed Emily a business card. A second later, she was gliding out of the café, waving good-bye to the balding owner in suspenders behind the counter as though she hadn't just offered to buy a stranger's baby.

As soon as Gayle disappeared down the sidewalk, Aria let out a breath. "Do you want to call the police, or shall I?"

Emily looked surprised. "What?"

Aria stared at her. "Are you high? She just offered you money for your baby."

Emily picked at the pancakes. "I feel terrible for her. It's obvious she really wants a baby. She seems so sad."

"You bought that sob story?" Aria shook her head. Emily always was the most sensitive of the group, the one who saved baby birds when the mother pushed them out of the nest too early, or who tried to stop Ali when she teased someone too nastily. "Em, normal people don't walk into cafés and offer to buy teenagers' unborn children. Even people who are desperate to have kids. There's something seriously wrong with her."

But Emily was staring wistfully at her belly, appearing not to hear a word of what Aria said. "Wouldn't it be nice to have everything you wanted in the world? Exotic trips? Fantastic summer camps? The baby's life would be incredible."

"Money isn't everything, you know," Aria pointed out. "Look at Spencer. She had every privilege in the world, and her family's a mess. Can you honestly tell me that woman would be a caring, nurturing mother?"

"It's possible," Emily said, an empathetic look on her face. "We don't even know her."

"*Exactly!*" Aria pounded her fork on the table for emphasis. "I loved the sound of the first family you chose, Em. You got to know them. You picked them for a reason."

"But they're both teachers," Emily protested. "Neither of them make that much money."

"Since when do you care about that?"

"Since I got pregnant!" Emily's cheeks flushed. She said it so loudly a couple of patrons looked up, startled, then sheepishly went back to their meals.

Aria talked on and on, listing reason after reason why Emily shouldn't pay any attention to Gayle, but Emily still had that torn, faraway look on her face. It wasn't surprising when Emily told her a few days later that she'd accepted Gayle's offer. It also wasn't that surprising that, only a few weeks later, Emily called Aria back in a panic, saying she'd changed her mind and that Aria had to help her get out of the Gayle mess.

"Your risotto has gone gelatinous!"

Madame Richeau was standing over Aria, peering into her pot with a look of abhorrence on her face. Sure enough, the rice had congealed into a thick paste. She tried to rake the wooden spoon through it, but the slop wouldn't budge.

Madame Richeau shook her head and strode away, muttering. The whole class looked at Aria with tiny smirks on their faces. Noel stared at Aria curiously. "Are you sure everything is okay?" he asked.

Heavy pressure settled behind Aria's eyes. She considered telling Noel about what was going on with Emily's pregnancy . . . maybe even with A. Couples told each other everything, after all. They were supposed to trust each other, right?

But then the image of Mr. Kahn in that dress rushed to the forefront of her mind again. She straightened up and gave Noel a self-deprecating smile. "Sorry. I was thinking about what I was going to wear to Hanna's dad's benefit on Sunday. Do you think I should go vintage or buy something new?"

Noel studied her for a moment, looking puzzled, then shrugged and wrapped his arm around her shoulder. "You'll look fantastic in anything."

Aria snuggled into him, her insides feeling as sludgy and unappetizing as the risotto she'd just botched. So much for the honesty pact. Out of the corner of her eye, she saw a flicker of white at the window. Was that . . . a flash of blond hair? But when she broke away from Noel and looked closer, the flicker had already vanished.

11

WORK IT

Later that night, Hanna walked through the steamed-up double doors of The Pump, a musclehead gym at the King James Mall. The gym smelled like sweat, spilled Gatorade, and that unidentifiable but utterly boy smell of burgeoning testosterone that always made Hanna gag. A slick-haired guy straight out of *Jersey Shore* central casting sat behind the check-in desk, drinking a protein shake and reading a bodybuilding magazine. Across from him was a giant mural of a gorilla lifting weights, his ab muscles well defined, his biceps bulging. She supposed it was meant to inspire people to work out more, but who wanted to look like a gorilla?

Hanna paid for a day pass and walked into the main exercise room, which consisted of racks of free weights, lines of bench-press machines, and a long bank of mirrors. There was the ear-splitting *clang* of metal weights hitting steel bars. When Hanna looked in the corner by the windows, her heart began to pound. James Freed and Mason Byers were doing pull-ups on side-by-side machines. Standing next to them, dressed in an old Phillies T-shirt with the sleeves cut off, staring dreamily at something across the room, was Mike.

Hanna swiveled around and followed Mike's gaze to a large exercise classroom. On the front of the door was a sign that said POLE DANCING, 6:30. A bunch of metal poles had been spaced evenly in front of the mirrors. A few middle-aged women dressed in tight-fitting leotards, flirty miniskirts, and wobbly high heels stood around the room. Positioned in the very center, balanced perfectly in pointy stripper heels, was Colleen.

Mike's new girlfriend raked her fingers through her hair. It didn't seem quite so mousy brown today, and her body looked both curvy and lithe at the same time in tight spandex shorts and a yellow bra top. When Colleen noticed Mike's reflection, she turned around, waved, and blew him a kiss. Mike blew one back.

Hanna balled up her fists, thinking of the two of them in bed together.

She stormed to the dressing room, dropped her duffel on the floor, and stepped into a tiger-printed, stripper-style crop top she'd found at the mall earlier that afternoon. After pouring herself into it—she'd bought a size smaller than normal for maximum cleavage—she checked herself out in the mirror. Her hair was full and wild, thanks to tons of hairspray. She had on triple the amount of makeup she normally wore, though she'd stopped before applying false eyelashes. And then there was the pièce de résistance: a pair of incredibly high, incredibly spiky, silver Jimmy Choo sandals. She'd only worn them once before, to last year's prom; Mike had thought they were so sexy he even made her wear them to the after-party with her jeans. Hanna slipped them on her feet and pivoted back and forth. They looked perfect. She just hoped she could pole dance in them.

Her cell phone buzzed, and she eyed it nervously. *One new text message.* Luckily, it was only from Kate, asking if she'd be willing to help her hand out fliers at a 10k race around Rosewood Saturday morning. *Sure,* Hanna wrote back, trying to ignore her shaking hands as she typed. Now that Spencer and Emily had received new notes from A, she'd been waiting all day for hers.

Could Gayle be A? Hanna hadn't met the woman over the summer—she only heard about her when Emily reached out shortly before her C-section—but the phone messages Gayle had left the night they sneaked Emily and the baby out of the hospital had stayed with her. They weren't the desperate, sobbing voicemails most people would leave if they thought they might not get the child they'd hoped and prayed for—they were steely and enraged. Gayle was not the kind of person you crossed, and now she was knee-deep in Mr. Marin's campaign.

That morning at breakfast, Hanna had sat down next to her dad at the table. "How do you know Gayle? Are you old friends?"

Mr. Marin continued to butter his toast. "I actually didn't know her until about a week ago. She called me up to say she'd recently moved to Pennsylvania and really liked my platform. The amount of money she's promised is astounding."

"You didn't do a background check on her? What if she's, I don't know, a Satan worshipper?" Hanna's face had felt hot. *Or a crazy person who's stalking your daughter?*

Her father gave her a curious look. "Gayle's husband just gave a substantial donation to Princeton to build a new cancer research lab. I don't know too many Satan worshippers who would do *that*."

Discouraged, Hanna had gone upstairs and Googled Gayle's name, but nothing damning came up. She was influential in countless charities in New Jersey, and she'd participated in a dressage competition at the Devon Horse Show ten years ago. Then again, what *would* come up? It wasn't as if Gayle would keep a blog about how she was systematically torturing four high-school girls and calling herself A.

The door to the locker room squeaked open and a buff, sweaty woman strutted in. Hanna stuffed her duffel in a locker, spun the combination lock, and tottered toward the fitness classroom. Mason and James stopped their pull-ups as she passed. They nudged Mike. Hanna pretended not to notice as he turned and looked, rocking her hips back and forth and praying that her butt looked amazing.

"Welcome!" A woman in a skimpy black leotard and tights and tall eighties bangs waved as Hanna walked through the door. "You're new, right? I'm Trixie." The instructor gestured to a spare pole in the center of the room, right next to Colleen. "That pole has got your name on it."

Hanna sauntered up to it and shot Colleen a smile. "Oh, hey!" she chirped in a mock-surprised voice, as though their meeting was completely by accident and Hanna hadn't strategically planned this out from the moment she'd heard the boys talking about it in the locker room at school.

"Hanna?" Colleen looked Hanna up and down. "Omigod! How fun! I didn't know you pole danced."

"It's not like it's hard," Hanna sniffed, summoning her inner Ali. She checked out her reflection in the mirror. Her hips were thinner than Colleen's, but Colleen had bigger boobs.

"Well, you're going to love this class," Colleen said. "Of course, if you pole dance all the time, you'll probably find it really easy. I bet you're *really* good." She leaned in closer. "And we're cool about Mike, right?"

Hanna wasn't sure if Colleen was genuinely being sweet or diplomatic, so she stuck her nose in the air. "Whatev," she said coolly. "Mike was just too much work for me. There was so much pressure to look like a Hooters hostess. And he's always checking out other girls at parties—it used to drive me crazy." She shot Colleen an apologetic smile. "I'm sure he doesn't do that to *you*, though."

Colleen opened her mouth to speak, looking so worried that Hanna wondered if she'd gone just a teensy bit overboard. Just then, the song "Hot Stuff" blared through the speakers. Trixie sauntered to the front of the class, hooked her leg around her pole, lifted her butt in the air, and did a half-raunchy, half–Cirque de Soleil spin. "Okay, everyone!" she squawked into a headset. "Let's start off with some low squats!"

She bent her knees out to the side and lowered herself toward the ground. The class followed, pumping in time with the beat. Hanna peeked at Colleen; her squats were low, balanced, and perfect. Colleen glanced back at her and gave her a broad smile. *You're doing great!* she mouthed. Hanna fought the urge to roll her eyes. Could she *be* any more nauseatingly positive?

Trixie led them through a series of neck rolls, shoulder raises, and provocative hip bumps. Next, they tried out a series of dance moves that involved whipping around the pole like Gene Kelly in *Singin' in the Rain*. Hanna kept up just fine, her heart pounding hard and just the teensiest bit of sweat beading on her forehead. *Sexy* sweat, of course.

The next time Hanna glanced over her shoulder, the boys were sitting on the mats outside the classroom, staring at the girls like ravenous dogs. Fueled by their presence, she scooped up her hair and dropped it behind her back, wiggling her butt at them. James Freed visibly shuddered. Mason whistled. Colleen noticed the boys and did a sexy shimmy. The boys nudged each other appreciatively.

Colleen gave Hanna a conspiratorial wink. "They can't get enough of us, huh?"

Hanna wanted to smack her. Didn't she realize they were competing?

"Advanced students only for this next move," Trixie announced as the soundtrack shifted to a sultry Adele song. She marched up to the pole, wrapped her arms and legs around it, and climbed it like a monkey. "Use your thighs to grip the pole, girls!"

Colleen proceeded to wriggle up the pole. She took one hand off, arched her back, and hung upside down for a moment. The boys applauded.

Hanna gritted her teeth. How hard could the move be? She grabbed the pole and began to climb. She was able to stay up for a moment, but then her thighs gave out, and she began to slip toward the ground. She sank farther and farther until her butt kissed the floor. Her reflection in the mirror looked ridiculous.

"Good try, Hanna," Colleen chirped. "That move is *really* hard."

Hanna dusted off her butt, then gazed around at the other girls in the room all making love to their poles. Suddenly, they didn't look like strippers, just chubby middle-aged women making fools out of themselves. This was the most idiotic fitness class she'd ever taken. There was a much easier way to get the boys' attention.

She turned to the window again and eyed the boys. When she was sure they were looking at her, she casually tugged down her leopard-print, too-small shirt, exposing the top of her red, scalloped-lace bra.

By the looks on the boys' faces, she knew they saw it. Their jaws dropped. James grinned. Mason pretended he was going to faint. Mike didn't crack a smile, but he couldn't keep his eyes off her. It was good enough for Hanna. She sauntered out of the class, swishing her hips to the strip-club beat.

"You're not staying?" James called out, his voice full of disappointment.

"Gotta leave something for your imagination, don't I?" Hanna said coyly. She could tell without turning around that Mike was still staring. She also knew that Colleen was watching her in the mirror, probably feeling a little confused. But whatever. She knew what Their Ali would say if she were still alive: All's fair in love and pole dancing.

12

WORDS OF WISDOM

That night, Emily stood in the hallway at Holy Trinity, the church her family attended. A bunch of construction-paper balloons bearing psalms and Bible verses were tacked up on the walls. A long gold runner stretched from one end of the hall to the other. The air smelled like a mixture of incense, stale coffee, and rubber cement, and the wind whistled noisily under the door. Years ago, Ali had told her that the whistling wind was the wails of the people buried in the cemetery out back. Sometimes Emily still believed that was true.

A door at the far end of the hall opened, and a graying man peered out. It was Father Fleming, the oldest and sweetest priest at the church. He smiled. "Emily! Come in, come in!"

For a second, Emily considered turning and bolting back to her car. Maybe this was a huge mistake. Yesterday, when she'd come home from swim practice, her mom had sat her down at the kitchen table and said she and her dad were considering postponing their trip to Texas. "Why?" Emily had asked. "You've planned this trip for months!"

"You just don't seem like yourself," Mrs. Fields said, folding and unfolding a cloth napkin again and again. "I'm worried about you. I thought, with the scholarship to UNC, you'd turn a corner and put everything behind you. But it's still weighing on your mind, isn't it?"

Tears inadvertently filled Emily's eyes. Of course everything was still weighing on her—nothing had changed. Even worse, the woman who'd wanted her baby had found her. If A didn't tell everyone about her pregnancy, Gayle probably would. And then what would happen? Would Emily still have a home to live in? Would her parents ever speak to her again?

She put her face in her hands and murmured that everything was so hard. Mrs. Fields patted her shoulder. "It's okay, honey." Which made Emily feel even worse— Emily didn't deserve her mom's sympathy.

"I have an idea." Mrs. Fields picked up the cordless phone from its cradle. "Why don't you talk to Father Fleming at the church?"

Emily made a face, thinking about Father Fleming. She'd known him forever. He'd listened to her first confession when she was seven years old, telling her not to sweat calling Seth Cardiff a walrus in the schoolyard. But admitting to a priest she'd had premarital sex? It seemed so wrong.

The thing was, Mrs. Fields wouldn't take no for an answer—in fact, she'd already set up a meeting with Father Fleming the following day without asking Emily first. Emily relented, if only to reassure her parents that it was okay for them to go to Texas as planned. They'd left for the airport that morning, although Mrs. Fields had left a miles-long list of emergency contacts on the kitchen table and arranged for several neighbors to check in on Emily during the time they would be gone.

But now here she was, shuffling toward Father Fleming's office. Before she knew it, she was hanging her coat on a hook shaped like a hand making a thumbs-up sign on the back of the door and looking around the room. The décor took her aback. A ceramic head of Curly from The Three Stooges leered from the windowsill. The sanctimonious preacher from *The Simpsons* gave her a puckered-lipped pout from next to a gooseneck lamp. There were a lot of religious texts on the bookshelves, but Agatha Christie mysteries and Tom Clancy thrillers as well. On the desk were two tiny handmade Guatemalan worry dolls.

Father Fleming noticed her looking at them. "You're supposed to put them under your pillow to help you sleep."

"I know. I have some, too." Emily couldn't hide the surprise in her voice. She didn't think priests were superstitious. "Do they work for you?"

"Not really. What about you?"

Emily shook her head. She'd bought six worry dolls

at a head shop in Hollis shortly after what happened in Jamaica, hoping that placing them under her pillow would calm her down at night. But the same thoughts still zoomed through her mind.

Father Fleming sat down in the leather chair behind his desk and folded his hands. "So. What can I do for you, Emily?"

Emily stared at her chipped green nail polish. "I'm okay, really. My mom was just worried about my stress levels. It's not a big deal."

Father Fleming nodded sympathetically. "Well, if you want to talk, I'm here to listen. And whatever you say goes no further than this room."

One of Emily's eyebrows shot up. "You won't tell my mom about . . . anything?"

"Of course not."

Emily ran her tongue over her teeth, her secret suddenly feeling like a festering sore inside of her. "I had a baby," she blurted. "This summer. No one in my family knew about it except for my sister." Just saying it out loud in such a holy place made her feel like the devil.

When she snuck a peek at Father Fleming, though, he still had the same unflappable expression on his face. "Your parents had no idea?"

Emily nodded. "I hid in the city for the summer so they wouldn't find out."

Father Fleming fingered his collar. "What happened to the baby?"

"I gave her up for adoption."

"Did you meet the family?"

"Yes. They were very nice. It all went very smoothly."

Emily stared at the cross on the wall behind Father Fleming's desk, nervously hoping it wouldn't shoot off of its hook and impale her for lying. Her baby was with the Bakers, but things had gone the *opposite* of smoothly.

After Gayle had met with Emily and Aria in the café, Emily couldn't get Gayle's offer out of her mind. The Bakers seemed special, but what Gayle brought to the table was special, too. Aria had scolded Emily for being so preoccupied with Gayle's money, but she didn't want this baby to grow up the way she had, listening to her mom agonize about money every Christmas, missing out on a Washington, D.C., field trip because her dad was out of a job, being forced into keeping with a sport she wasn't interested in anymore because it was her only ticket to college. Emily wanted to say that money didn't matter to her, but since she'd always had to *think* about money, it definitely did.

Two days later, after her shift at the restaurant, Emily called Gayle and said she wanted to talk more. They arranged to meet at a coffee shop near Temple that very night. A little before 8 PM, Emily cut through a small Philadelphia park, and a hand had shot out from the darkness and cupped her belly. "Heather," a voice said, and Emily screamed. A figure stepped into the light, and Emily couldn't be more surprised to see Gayle's smiling face. "W-what are you doing here?" she gasped. Gayle shrugged. "It was such a nice night I thought we could talk outside. But *someone's* jumpy," she said with a laugh.

Emily should have turned around and left, but instead she told herself that maybe she *was* being jumpy. Maybe Gayle was just playful. So she accepted Gayle's carryout cup of decaf coffee and stayed. "Why do you want *my* baby?" she asked. "Why can't you go through an adoption agency?"

Gayle patted the seat next to her, and Emily plopped down on the bench. "The wait with an adoption agency is too long," she said. "And we suspect that potential mothers wouldn't choose me and my husband because of what happened to our daughter."

Emily raised an eyebrow. "What *did* happen to her?"

A faraway, uncomfortable look came over Gayle's face. Her left hand kneaded her thigh. "She had problems," she said quietly. "She was in an accident when she was younger and never quite recovered."

"An . . . accident?"

Suddenly, Gayle put her head in her hands. "My husband and I are dying to be parents again," she said with urgency. "Please let us have the baby. We can give you fifty thousand dollars cash for your trouble."

Emily felt a palpable jolt of surprise. "Fifty thousand dollars?" she repeated. That could pay for all four years of college. She wouldn't have to swim on scholarship every year. She could take a gap year and travel the world. Or she could donate it all to charity, to other babies who wouldn't have an opportunity like this one.

"Maybe we can work something out," Emily said quietly.

Gayle's face twitched. She let out a whoop of joy and wrapped her arms around Emily tight. "You won't regret this," she said.

Then she jumped up, rattled off information on how they would meet again in a few days, and was gone. The darkness swallowed Gayle up entirely. Only her laugh lingered, a haunting cackle that echoed through the woods. Emily sat on the bench for a few more minutes, watching the long, bright line of traffic on the 76 expressway in the distance. She wasn't left with a feeling of comfort, as she'd hoped. Instead, she just felt . . . *weird*. What had she just done?

A single pipe-organ note echoed through the church hall. Father Fleming lifted a jade paperweight on his desk and put it back down. "I can only imagine how much of a burden this has been for you. But it sounds like you did the right thing, giving the child up to a family who really wanted her."

"Uh huh." Emily's throat itched, a sure sign she was about to cry.

"It must have been hard to give her up," Father Fleming went on. "But you'll always be in her heart, and she'll always be in yours. Now, what about the father?"

Emily jolted up. "What about him?"

"Does he know about this?"

"Oh my God, no." Emily's face felt hot. "He and I broke up long before I knew I was . . . you know. Pregnant." She wondered what Father would think if he knew that the dad was Isaac, one of his parish members. Isaac's band had played at quite a few church functions.

Father Fleming folded his hands. "Don't you think he deserves to know?"

"No. Absolutely no way." Emily shook her head vehemently. "He would hate me forever."

"You can't know that." He picked up a ballpoint pen and clicked it on and off. "And even if he's angry with you, you might feel better if you tell the truth."

They talked for a while longer about how Emily had weathered having a baby on her own, what her recovery had been like, and what her college plans were. Just as the pipe organist launched into a long, droning variation of *Canon in D*, Father Fleming's iPhone chimed. He smiled at her kindly. "I'm afraid I'll have to leave you now, Emily. I've got a meeting with the church board of trustees in about ten minutes. Do you think you'll be all right?"

Emily shrugged. "I guess."

He stood, patted Emily's shoulder, and guided her toward the door. Halfway down the hall, he turned and looked at her. "It goes without saying, but everything you've told me is just between us," he said softly. "Still, I know you'll do the right thing."

Emily nodded dumbly, wondering what the right thing

was. She considered Isaac again. He'd been so nice at Hanna's dad's town hall meeting. Maybe Father Fleming was right. Maybe she owed it to him. It was his baby, too.

Heart thumping, Emily pulled out her cell phone and composed a new text to Isaac.

I have something to talk to you about. Can we meet tomorrow?

Before she could change her mind, she pressed SEND.

13

RING, RING, IT'S REAL ALI

A few hours later, Aria sat in the kitchen at Byron and Meredith's house, her laptop on the table in front of her. An IM from Emily appeared on the screen. *Any news?*

Emily obviously wanted to know if Aria had gotten a message from A. *Nope*, Aria replied. *I haven't gotten anything yet.* She hoped to keep it that way. As far as she was concerned, she didn't know anything interesting about Mr. Kahn. A had no new reasons to torment her. The secret would stay locked away forever.

Are we still on for Saturday? Emily wrote next.

It took Aria a moment to remember that Emily had wanted her to go to the open house at the property on Ship Lane. *Definitely.*

The front door slammed, and then came the sounds of keys dropping into a bowl and Meredith cooing soothingly to Lola. Meredith strode into the kitchen and grabbed a water bottle from the fridge. She was dressed in stretch pants and a baggy white sweatshirt, a yoga mat tucked under her arm. Her dark hair was in a ponytail, her cheeks were flushed, and she looked very relaxed. Lola was strapped to her torso in a baby carrier, sound asleep.

"Ugh, I'm so out of shape," Meredith moaned, rolling her eyes. "Maybe I went back to teaching a little too soon. I couldn't even do a handstand today."

"I was *never* able to do a handstand," Aria said, shrugging.

"I could teach you how if you want," Meredith offered.

"Sorry, I'm not really into yoga," Aria said. The last thing she wanted was for Meredith to teach her something.

Meredith placed the water bottle on the island and cleared her throat. "I really appreciate you going to Fresh Fields for me the other day."

Aria grunted, staring at an abstract painting of the Wicked Witch of the West from *The Wizard of Oz* that Meredith had brought from her old apartment. If it weren't for Meredith's stupid dinner, Aria wouldn't have happened upon Mr. Kahn's awful secret. She couldn't help but blame her a little.

"And I am sorry . . . about the reason behind the dinner." Meredith's voice cracked.

At first Aria bristled, but then realized she actually had something she wanted to ask Meredith. "When you and my dad were dating, did you tell anyone about it?"

Meredith stiffened. After a moment, she adjusted the

baby carrier so that Lola was more comfortable. "No," she said quietly. "I couldn't. I mean, when we were first together, your dad was my teacher—I didn't want to get him fired. It wasn't until you guys left for Iceland and I thought things were over that I told my mom. She was furious at me. She thought it was awful that I was fooling around with a married man."

Aria stared at the floor, surprised. She had assumed that Meredith bragged about her older professor boyfriend to her friends, laughed about the family she was destroying, and snickered at how much of an idiot Ella was for not suspecting something was going on.

"When you guys came back from Iceland and your dad and I started dating again, I didn't dare tell my mom what was going on," Meredith went on. "I worried about telling anyone else, too, in case they told her—or judged me harshly. I knew what I was doing was wrong."

Aria traced her finger over a jute placemat, surprised again. Meredith had seemed so confident when she and Byron were secretly dating, insisting that she wasn't a home wrecker because she and Byron were in love. She hadn't expected Meredith to care about what other people thought.

"So you didn't say anything to anyone? That whole time?" Aria asked incredulously.

Lola stirred, and Meredith grabbed a pink pacifier from the table and popped it into the baby's mouth. "I was afraid the secret would get out. I was terrified your mom would catch us."

"But she was going to find out eventually," Aria pointed out.

"I know, but I didn't want to be the one to break the news." Meredith pressed her fingers to her temple. "I really didn't set out to destroy anyone's life, I swear. It might not have seemed like it, but I had a very hard time with what we were doing."

Aria shut her eyes. She wanted to believe Meredith, but she wasn't sure if she could.

"You know, I saw you when you discovered me and Byron kissing in his car," Meredith said softly. "I saw the look on your face, how devastated you were."

Aria turned away, that horrible memory flooding back to her.

"I felt terrible about it. I wanted to explain myself. But I knew you wouldn't want to talk to me."

"You're right," Aria admitted. "I wouldn't have."

"And then you started showing up everywhere," Meredith went on. "You came to the yoga studio—I recognized you right away. Then you showed up at my art class. You threw paint at me, remember?"

"Uh huh," Aria mumbled, staring at the floor. She'd drawn a red scarlet *A* for "adultress" on Meredith's dress. It seemed so immature now.

Neither of them said anything for a while. Meredith retied her ponytail. Aria stared at the ragged edges of her fingernails. Lola let out a loud burp in her sleep, the pacifier tumbling from her mouth. Aria giggled. Meredith laughed, too, then let out a long sigh. "It's not fun to keep secrets," she said. "But sometimes you have to do it to protect yourself. And to protect people around you."

For the first time ever, Aria agreed with Meredith. Protecting someone was exactly what she was doing by not telling Noel about his dad's cross-dressing. Just hearing it put that way made her feel better about her decision.

Meredith opened the fridge and pulled out a bottle for Lola. "I have to tell you, though. I felt like crap when your friend called me and chewed me out."

Aria frowned. "What friend?"

"You know. The friend you were with that day you saw us. Alison."

A chilly jolt whizzed through Aria's veins. "Wait. She *called* you?"

Meredith cocked her head. "She called me a while after you guys caught us in the car—sometime in June. She asked me all these questions about me and your dad—if we were in love, when we started dating, if we'd done it yet. She made me feel awful." She searched Aria's face. "You didn't put her up to it?"

"No . . ." Ali had tormented Aria about Meredith constantly, but she'd never told Aria that she'd called Meredith behind her back. What had Ali expected to accomplish? And why had she waited until June to call her? Aria and Ali had caught Meredith and Byron in April.

Suddenly, a horrible thought popped into her mind. "*When* in June did Alison call you?"

Meredith drummed her fingers on the table. "The morning of the fifteenth. I remember it because it was my brother's birthday. I thought it was him calling, but it was her."

The room began to spin. *June fifteenth.* That was the day of their end-of-seventh-grade sleepover with Their Ali. According to the events pieced together by letters, testimonies, public documents, and the police investigation, the secret DiLaurentis sister had been picked up from the Preserve the day before. An unhappy family reunion had occurred. Two twins who hated each other were together again.

The day of the sleepover, Aria, Spencer, Hanna, and Emily had gone into Ali's room and discovered her sitting there, reading what looked like her diary with a big smile on her face. To this day, Aria wondered if it had been Their Ali in her bedroom . . . or her twin.

"Aria? Are you okay?"

Aria jumped. Meredith was staring at her with round blue eyes. Aria nodded faintly, feeling woozy. Ali had called Meredith all those years ago, all right—but it might not have been to make Meredith feel bad. It could have been to dig for dirt. And it wasn't *Her* Ali, either.

It was Real Ali.

14

CATCHING UP

Thursday night, Emily walked into Belissima, the Italian bistro at the Devon Crest Mall across town, where she was meeting Isaac for dinner. The restaurant floor was made of bronze-colored terra-cotta tile, and the walls were painted to look as if they were part of an old, crumbling farmhouse. A shiny brass espresso machine sat behind the counter, bottles of wine were lined up on shelves around the big room, and the air smelled pungently of olive oil and mozzarella. Emily hadn't been to this mall since two Christmases ago, when she'd agreed to be the mall's Santa. She'd come to this restaurant with Cassie, one of Santa's elves, and they'd bonded over their friendships with Ali.

Her phone beeped, and when she checked the screen, there was a Google Alert for Tabitha Clark. A lot of Tabitha-related news she didn't read—it was just too painful—but because she was nervous and wanted something to do with her hands, she stared at the screen.

The alert linked to a message board from the Tabitha Clark Memorial website. The site mostly consisted of pictures of Tabitha and her friends. A prom video showed Tabitha in a purple satin dress, her gold necklace glinting in the strobe light as she danced with her boyfriend, a cute boy with longish brown hair and clear green eyes, to a Christina Aguilera song. There were some mournful posts from friends and rants about how The Cliffs resort should be shut down. But the most recent post was what caught Emily's eye: *Tabitha's dad should conduct an autopsy. I don't think she died from too much drinking.*

A chill gripped Emily. With all of the drama about her baby and Gayle, she'd lost focus on the other horrible thing A knew. She shut her eyes and saw the picture A had sent to Spencer's phone of Tabitha's body, twisted and broken on the sand after they'd shoved her off the roof.

"Emily! Over here!"

Isaac was sitting in a banquette in the corner, a plate of fried calamari in front of him. His hair was pushed back off his face, and he wore a blue T-shirt that brought out his sapphire eyes. "Hey!" he called, gesturing for her to come over.

Emily's stomach swooped, and she shoved the phone back into her bag. Then she stared down at the green wool skirt she'd picked out from the back of her closet. Was she honestly going to tell Isaac the truth? All afternoon, instead of paying attention in English, Calculus, and Bio II, she'd rehearsed how she'd broach the subject. *So, you know how we had sex that one time last year? Well, it had a, um, lasting effect.*

Even worse, Isaac looked so *happy* right now, like he was overjoyed she'd shown up. This was going to kill him. But she had to say something. She owed it to him. She certainly didn't want A telling him first.

Her hands shook as she wound around the busy tables and dodged a waitress with a tray of tiramisu. Isaac half-stood as Emily approached. "I ordered calamari. I hope that's okay. You used to like it back when we . . . you know." His words rushed out in a nervous jumble.

"I still love calamari." Emily slid into the cushy leather seat.

Isaac touched her arm, then pulled away, perhaps worried it was too forward. "Are you still swimming?"

Emily nodded. "I got a scholarship to UNC for next year."

"UNC?" Isaac beamed. "That's awesome. Congratulations."

"Thanks," Emily said. "Have you figured out where you're going to go yet?" She reached over and speared a piece of calamari from the plate. The batter was perfect, and the dipping sauce was thick and tangy.

Isaac shrugged. "I'd love to go to Juilliard, but I'll probably end up at Hollis."

"You never know. You're talented enough for Juilliard."
Emily thought of Isaac's band performances. His voice
was rich and full, and he sounded a lot like the lead singer
of Coldplay. Plenty of girls had swooned over him at his
show; Emily had been astounded when he'd singled
her out.

Isaac took a long sip of sparkling water. "Nah. I didn't
even apply. I was terrified to audition. I'd probably freak
out on stage."

"Since when do you freak out on stage?" Emily asked,
surprised. "Have you changed that much since I've last
seen you?"

"Tons." Isaac cupped his chin in his hands and smiled
at her.

"Well, maybe you *have* changed." Emily pointed at the
tattoo on his neck. "I don't remember you being a tattoo
kind of guy."

Isaac glanced at it. "I got it when I turned eighteen.
Everyone in the band was getting one, but they all chick-
ened out at the last minute. I was the only one who went
through with it."

"Did it hurt?"

"Yeah. But I powered through."

"Can I see it?"

"Sure." Isaac pulled down the collar of his shirt even
further, revealing a black pattern that looked like a giant
abstract moth.

"Whoa!" Emily cried. "It's huge!"

"Yeah." Isaac pulled the collar back to cover it. "I wanted something significant."

Emily wanted to touch the part that was still visible, but she stopped herself. Maybe that would give Isaac the wrong idea. "Does it mean something special?"

"Well, I've always been really into moths." Isaac reached for another calamari. "Did you know they can see ultraviolet light? And they can smell their mates from up to seven miles away?"

"Seriously?" Emily made a face.

Isaac nodded. "I've always thought moths were really beautiful, but no one pays attention to them the way they do with butterflies. They're sort of . . . forgotten."

It was such an Isaac thing to say, sensitive and moony and a little goofy all at the same time. Emily had forgotten that about him. She'd forgotten how cute he was, too. An unexpected wave of longing came over her. Then a voice boomed inside her, ripping her back to reality. *You had his baby. Tell him.* She pressed the tines of her fork lightly into her palm.

The waitress appeared. "Have you guys had a chance to look at the menu?"

Emily looked down, feeling a little relieved that they'd been interrupted. She ordered the pasta special, and Isaac asked for veal Parmesan. By the time the waitress closed her notepad and strolled away, the brave feeling had passed. So Emily asked Isaac a few more questions about himself—what was happening at school, how many shows his band had played, what his plans for summer vacation were. Then she told him more about UNC, the Eco Cruise she was going on in a few weeks, and how she was thinking about getting a summer job. For the most part, the conversation was smooth and effortless, and before Emily knew it, there were only a few pieces of calamari left on the plate. She'd forgotten how easy it was to talk to Isaac, how he laughed at all the appropriate parts of a story. Her fists unclenched. Maybe this would be okay.

"So how's your family?" Isaac asked as the waitress served them their food.

"Oh, you know." Emily shrugged nonchalantly. "The same. My mom's still really active in the church. She's BFFs with Father Fleming. She made me go see him the other day."

"Oh really? Why?"

Emily pushed a bite of pasta into her mouth so she wouldn't have to speak. *Tell him. You owe it to him.* Yet again, her mouth couldn't form the words.

She must have taken too long to answer, because Isaac cleared his throat. "How's your older sister? What was her name . . . Carolyn?"

A sharp odor of milky Alfredo sauce wafted into Emily's nostrils, turning her stomach. "She's . . . fine."

"Where'd she go to school?"

"Stanford."

"Does she like it?"

"I think so."

Not that Emily really knew. After sharing a bedroom for almost eighteen years, Carolyn had barely said a word to Emily since last summer. Emily hadn't known who to turn to when she found out she was pregnant, but since Carolyn was spending the summer in Philly, she seemed like the best option. Emily thought Carolyn would step up and be her big sister, and while Carolyn did let Emily stay, Carolyn never let her forget how disappointed and disgusted she was. She never asked how Emily was feeling. She never wanted to know how her latest anatomy scan had been. She didn't even ask who the father was. When Emily had found out she had to have a scheduled C-section because the baby was breech, she called Carolyn and told her right away. All Carolyn had said was, "I heard recovery from a C-section is awful."

Emily didn't dare tell Carolyn about the struggle to choose adoptive parents. Nor did she tell her that Gayle had offered her fifty thousand dollars, or about the day she'd gone to Gayle's enormous house in New Jersey to collect the check. Gayle had looked at her like she was a specimen in a jar. And when Emily pocketed the check Gayle gave her, she felt dirty and awful.

Carolyn wasn't there for her, but maybe Isaac would have been, if only she'd given him the chance.

She took a breath. "Isaac, there's something I need to talk to you about."

He nodded. "Yeah, you said that in your text. What's up?"

Emily pushed her fork around her plate, her heart

hammering. *Here goes.* "Well . . ."

"What are you doing here?"

Emily's head snapped up. Standing over them, dressed in a powder-blue suit from sometime in the eighties—and not the *cool* eighties, either—was Isaac's mom. As Mrs. Colbert's gaze bounced from Isaac to Emily and back to Isaac again, her expression shifted from annoyance to rage.

"You told me you were going out to dinner with your bandmates," Mrs. Colbert hissed, her eyebrows drawn together. "Not . . . *her.*"

"Mom, stop," Isaac warned. "I knew you'd get crazy and irrational if I told you I was meeting Emily. She's a good person—I don't know why you can't see that. We're having a really nice dinner, catching up."

Emily's cheeks flushed as she felt a mix of pleasure and guilt. She couldn't remember the last time someone had stood up for her like that.

Mrs. Colbert let out an unflattering snort. "I hardly think she's a good person, Isaac."

"What would make you say that?" Isaac asked.

Mrs. Colbert didn't answer. Instead she stared at Emily with a pointed look on her face. It was almost like she knew what Emily had done. Emily drew in a breath. Had A contacted her?

Finally, Mrs. Colbert wrenched her gaze away and turned to Isaac. "Your father is looking for you. One of the caterers for the event tonight dropped out, and he needs you to fill in."

"Now?" Isaac asked. He gestured to his plate. "I'm in the middle of dinner."

"Have them wrap it up." Mrs. Colbert turned on her heel and stormed toward the bar, clearly expecting Isaac to follow.

Isaac looked at Emily, his eyes big and sad. "I'm so sorry. Can we take a rain check? Do something later in the week?"

"Uh, sure," Emily said dazedly, staring at Mrs. Colbert as she typed something on her cell phone.

They flagged down the waitress, who brought them the check and a Styrofoam carryout container. Then Isaac pushed cash into the bill envelope and handed it back to the waitress.

"You were saying something before we got interrupted." He touched Emily's hand lightly. "Is it important?"

Emily's mouth went dry. "It doesn't matter," she said quietly.

"Are you *sure*?" Isaac looked worried.

Emily nodded. "Absolutely. I promise."

Isaac gave Emily a hug. As he squeezed her tight, so many emotions flooded her. She'd forgotten how soft his hair was, the feel of his slightly scratchy face against her neck, and how he smelled like freshly squeezed oranges. Long-repressed feelings awoke inside her, those tingles growing stronger.

He pulled away too soon. "Let me make it up to you. I'm off Saturday—we could go to the ice cream shop in

Hollis." His soft blue eyes beseeched her.

After a moment, Emily nodded, and Isaac left her to join his mother at the counter. Mrs. Colbert shot Emily one last nasty look, then flounced out of the restaurant.

Emily sank back into the booth, relief settling over her. All at once she was glad Mrs. Colbert had interrupted them—and that she hadn't told Isaac her secret. If Mrs. Colbert ever found out, she'd call Emily's parents immediately, and probably tell the entire church that Emily was a slut.

And Isaac might not want to go to ice cream with you if he knew what you did, a tiny, selfish voice whispered in her ear. But Emily couldn't change the past. What was done was done, and what Isaac didn't know would hurt him.

Right?

15

IVY OR BUST

Late Friday afternoon, Spencer got out of a cab at the Princeton University gates, zipped up her leather jacket, and looked around. Students in stadium-cloth coats and Burberry-plaid scarves bustled to and fro. Professors wearing wire-rimmed glasses and blazers with corduroy patches on the elbows strolled together, no doubt having Nobel prize–quality conversations. The bells in the clock tower struck six, the sound bouncing off the cobblestones.

A thrill went through Spencer. She'd been to Princeton plenty of times for debate competitions, field trips, summer camps, and college tours, but the campus felt very, very different today. She was going to be a *student* here next year. It was going to be such a dream to get the hell out of Rosewood and have a whole new start. Even this *weekend* felt like a fresh start. As soon as the train had pulled out of Rosewood, her shoulders had fallen from her ears. A wasn't here. Spencer was safe . . . at least for a little while.

She looked at the directions Harper had sent her to the Ivy Eating Club. It was on Prospect Avenue, which everyone at Princeton simply called "The Street." As she turned left and walked up the tree-lined boulevard, her phone chimed. *Have you done any research on you-know-who?* Hanna wrote.

That was code for Gayle. *Nothing that's led anywhere*, Spencer wrote back. She'd scoured the Internet for details on Gayle, seeing if there was any possible way she could be A. The first order of business was to figure out if Gayle could have been in Jamaica last year at the same time the girls were—maybe, like they'd hypothesized about Kelsey, Gayle had seen what they'd done and then, later, after Emily screwed her over, she connected the dots and used it against them.

The Cliffs wasn't the kind of place a classy, middle-aged woman would have stayed, but Spencer phoned a few resorts near The Cliffs, identifying herself as Gayle's personal assistant and asking when Gayle had vacationed there. None of the reservations associates had any record of Gayle staying with them—*ever*. She'd fanned out her search, calling resorts ten, fifteen, even fifty miles away, but as far as Spencer could tell, Gayle had never even *been* to Jamaica.

So how could Gayle know about what they'd done to Tabitha? How would she have gotten that photo of Emily and Tabitha or of Tabitha lying twisted and broken on the sand? Had Gayle gone to Jamaica under a fake name? Was she working with someone else? *Had* she hired a PI, like Aria had suggested?

Furthermore, even if Gayle *was* A, the issue of Tabitha was still puzzling. Why had she acted so Ali-like at The Cliffs? Had she and Ali been friends when they were at The Preserve, and had she been trying to get revenge for Ali's death? Or was it all an awful coincidence?

Before she knew it, she'd arrived at the address Harper had given her. It was a large, Gothic-style brick house with gorgeous leaded-glass windows, manicured bushes, and an American flag protruding from the front porch. Spencer walked up the stone path and rang the front doorbell, which let out a few impressive *bongs* to the opening notes of Beethoven's Fifth Symphony. There were footsteps, and then the door flung open. Harper appeared, looking fresh-faced in a purple top with dolman sleeves, skinny jeans, and leather ankle boots. A navy cashmere blanket was draped around her shoulders.

"Welcome!" she cried. "You made it!"

She ushered Spencer inside. The foyer was drafty and smelled like a mixture of leather and jasmine perfume. Blond-wood beams crisscrossed the ceiling, and stained-glass windows decorated the walls. Spencer could just picture past Pulitzer Prize winners standing by the roaring fire or sitting in the wing chairs, having important discussions.

"This is amazing," she gushed.

"Yeah, it's okay," Harper said nonchalantly. "I have to apologize in advance, though. My bedroom upstairs is really drafty and kind of small."

"I don't mind," Spencer said quickly. She'd sleep in the Ivy broom closet if she had to.

Harper took Spencer's hand. "Let me introduce you to the others."

She led Spencer through a long hallway lit by chrome and glass lamps to a larger, more modern room in the back of the house. A wall of windows faced the woods behind the property. Another boasted a flat-screen TV, bookshelves, and a large papier-mâché statue of the Princeton tiger mascot. Blanket-swaddled girls lounged on suede couches, tapping their iPads and laptops, reading books, or, in one blond girl's case, playing an acoustic guitar. Spencer was almost positive the Asian girl fiddling with her phone had won the Golden Orchid a few years ago. The girl in bottle-green jeans by the window was a dead ringer for Jessie Pratt, the girl who'd gotten her memoir about living in Africa with her grandparents published at sixteen.

"Guys, this is Spencer Hastings," Harper said, and everyone looked up. She pointed at the girls around the room. "Spencer, this is Joanna, Marilyn, Jade, Callie, Willow, Quinn, and Jessie." So it *was* Jessie Pratt. Everyone waved happily. "Spencer is an early admit," Harper went on. "I met her at the dinner I hosted, and I think she's a natural for us."

"Nice to meet you." Quinn set aside her acoustic guitar and shook Spencer's hand. Her fingernails were painted a preppy pink. "Any friend of Harper's is a friend of ours."

"I like your guitar," Spencer said, nodding at it. "It's a Martin, right?"

Quinn raised her perfectly plucked blond eyebrows. "You know guitars?"

Spencer shrugged. Her dad was into guitars, and she used to go to some of the vintage expos with him, searching for new ones to add to his collection.

"How do you like that?" Jessie Pratt said, pointing to the book Spencer was carrying. It was a copy of *V.* by Thomas Pynchon.

"Oh, it's great," Spencer said, even though she didn't really get the gist of the story. The writer barely used any punctuation.

"We'd better get going." Harper grabbed a sweater from the back of one of the couches.

"Going where?" Spencer asked.

Harper gave her a cryptic smile. "A party at this guy Daniel's house. You'll love him."

"Awesome." Spencer dropped her duffel by the front door, waited as Harper, Jessie, and Quinn put on their coats and gathered their purses, and followed them into the cold night. They trudged down the snowy sidewalks, careful not to slip on patches of ice. The moon was out, and aside from a few cars swishing down the main avenue, the world was very quiet and still. Spencer eyed a hulking SUV parked at the curb, its motor running, but couldn't see its driver through the tinted glass.

They turned up the walkway of a big, Dutch-style mansion on the corner. Bass thundered from inside, and shadows passed in front of the brightly lit windows. There were a bunch of cars parked in the driveway, and more kids were making their way up the front lawn. The front door was open, and a handsome guy with thick eyebrows and longish chestnut-colored hair stood in the foyer, the official welcoming committee.

"Greetings, ladies," he said in a smarmy voice, sipping from a plastic cup.

"Hey, Daniel," Harper gave him an air kiss. "This is Spencer. She's going to be a freshman next fall."

"Ah, new blood." Daniel looked Spencer up and down. "I approve."

Spencer followed Harper into the house. The living room was packed, and a 50 Cent track blared loudly. The guys were drinking Scotch; the girls were in dresses and heels and wore diamond studs in their ears. In the corner, people were sitting around a hookah, bluish smoke wafting around their heads.

When someone grabbed her arm and pulled her toward him, Spencer figured it was a hot guy—there were so many of them to choose from. But then she looked at the guy's droopy eyes, dirty dreadlocks, crooked smile, and tie-dyed Grateful Dead 1986 Tour T-shirt.

"Spencer, right?" The guy's smile stretched wide. "You missed an amazing time the other night. The Occupy Philly rally rocked."

Spencer squinted at him. "Excuse me?"

"It's Reefer." The guy raised his arms in a *ta-da!* gesture. "From the Princeton dinner last week. Remember?"

Spencer blinked. "What are you doing here?" she barked.

Reefer looked around the room. "Well, a professor invited me to lunch. And then I met Daniel in the dining hall, and he told me about tonight's shindig."

It was the most preposterous thing Spencer had ever heard. "A *professor* invited you here?"

"Yeah, Professor Dinkins," Reefer said, shrugging. "He's in the quantum physics department. That's what I'm majoring in next year."

Quantum physics? Spencer stared again at Reefer's dirty jeans and beat-up hemp shoes. He didn't even look capable of using a washing machine. And was it normal for professors to invite incoming freshmen to tour the campus? No one from the faculty had invited Spencer to visit. Did it mean she wasn't special?

"*There* you are." Harper grabbed Spencer's arm. "I've been looking all over for you! Wanna keep me company outside?"

"*Please*," Spencer said, relieved.

"You can ask Reefer if he wants to come, too," Harper stage-whispered.

Spencer glanced over her shoulder at Reefer. Luckily, he was now talking to Daniel and paying no attention to either of them. Maybe Daniel would realize how much of a dork Reefer was and ask him to leave.

"Uh, I think he's busy," Spencer said, turning back to Harper. "Let's go."

Harper kicked open the back door and led Spencer across a brick patio to a small gazebo. Several kids were sitting around a fire pit, drinking wine. A couple was making out near the hedges. Harper settled down on a bench, pulled a cigarette from her jacket pocket, and lit it. Smelly smoke swirled around her head. "Want some?"

It took Spencer a few seconds for her to realize it was a joint. "Um, that's okay. Pot makes me sleepy."

"Come *on.*" Harper inhaled hard. "This stuff is amazing. It gives you the best high."

Snap. A twig broke in the woods. A whooshing sound filled the air, and then soft, feathery whispers. Spencer looked around nervously. After what had happened last summer with Kelsey, the last thing she wanted was to get caught with drugs.

"Do you really think you should do that?" Spencer said, eyeing the joint. "I mean, couldn't you get in trouble?"

Harper flicked a bit of ash off the tip. "Who's going to tell on me?"

There was another *snap.* Spencer gazed into the dark woods, feeling more and more nervous. "Um, my drink's running low," she mumbled, holding up her empty cup.

She ran into the house, feeling relieved as soon as she returned to the overheated room. Refilling her cup with lemon-infused vodka, she strutted onto the dance floor. Quinn and Jessie invited her into their dancing circle, and she let three songs go by without thinking, trying to lose herself in the music. A junior boy named Sam cut in, dipping Spencer dramatically. The vodka zoomed through her veins, fiery and potent.

When she saw the flashing lights reflecting across the window, she thought someone had been pulled over on the street outside the house. But then, two uniformed cops opened the front door and poked their heads inside. Most of the guests hid their drinks behind their backs. The music stopped dead.

"What's going on in here?" One of the officers shone a flashlight into the room.

Everyone scattered. Doors slammed. The other cop raised his megaphone to him mouth. "We're looking for Harper Essex-Pembroke," his muffled voice boomed. "Miss Essex-Pembroke? Are you here?"

Murmurs rippled through the crowd. At that very moment, Harper appeared at the back door, her hair mussed, and a startled look on her pale face. "I-I'm Harper. What's the problem?"

The cop stepped toward her and grabbed her arm. "We got an anonymous tip that you're in possession of marijuana, with the intent to sell."

Harper's mouth dropped. "W-what?"

STUNNING ✦ 133

"That's a serious offense." The corner of the cop's mouth turned down.

Everyone watched as Harper was escorted through the room. Quinn shook her head in horror. "How the hell did the cops find out Harper had weed?"

As if she'd heard Quinn's question, Harper turned around and glared at Spencer. "Nice job," she hissed. "You ruined this party for everyone—*and* yourself."

Spencer's eyes bulged. "*I* didn't say anything!"

Harper just gave her an incredulous look as the cops escorted her out the door. Jessie and Quinn gaped at Spencer. "You *told*?" Quinn exclaimed.

"Of course not!" Spencer said.

Jessie's brown eyes were wide. "But you were outside with her, weren't you? None of *us* would tell."

"It wasn't me!" Spencer exclaimed. "I swear!"

But her words fell on deaf ears. Within seconds, everyone else at the party was looking at her suspiciously. Spencer slipped out of the room, her face burning. What the hell had just happened? How was she suddenly to blame?

Bzz.

She pulled out her phone. *One new text from Anonymous.* She looked around at the towering trees and the silent stars. It was so quiet out, yet she felt distinctly like someone was lurking close, trying hard to keep from laughing. Taking a deep breath, she looked at her phone's screen.

Just be happy I didn't call the cops about YOUR secrets. —A

16

RUNNING FOR HER LIFE

"Looking good, everyone!" Hanna called to the crowds thundering down Rosewood's main drag in the annual Rosewood Hospital 10k race. It was Saturday morning, and a steady rain was falling. Hanna's hair looked like crap and her makeup was smudged, but she'd promised her dad she'd hand out Tom Marin buttons and treats.

"Have a banana!" she said to a skinny older man who was puffing along in a see-through rain slicker, passing him a banana with a VOTE FOR TOM MARIN sticker on the peel. "Vote for Tom Marin!" She handed water cups printed with TOM MARIN to two chubby middle-aged women who were walking the race, huddling together under an umbrella. "Go, go, go!"

Kate, who was standing next to her with the hood of her anorak cinched tight, chuckled playfully. "I don't think your cheering is going to get *them* to move any faster."

"Probably not," Hanna giggled as the middle-aged

women's portly butts disappeared around the bend.

"Why aren't you running this?" Kate pushed a half-peeled banana at a whippet-thin woman with iPod headphones in her ears. "I remember Mom making me cheer for you last year."

Hanna shrugged. Last year, she ran the race with Mike—and beat him by a couple of seconds. They'd celebrated with a big bowl of pasta at Spaghetti Heaven afterwards and were so inspired by their times that they'd registered for a few more races, which they'd run this summer. But Hanna hadn't gone running once since she and Mike broke up.

She gave Kate a sidelong glance. "Actually, the better question is why aren't *you* running?" Kate had been a champion on her cross-country team at her old school in Annapolis. Isabel never shut up about it.

Kate fingered her chestnut ponytail. "Because Naomi and Riley registered first. The race isn't big enough for all of us."

Hanna poured more water into cups, just to do something with her hands. "So you guys are still fighting?"

"Yeah." Kate clapped loudly for the passing runners. "The fight's just with Naomi. Not Riley."

Hanna gave Kate a strange look, hoping she'd elaborate. Was the fight still over her? Was Kate pro-Hanna, or anti-Hanna? But then Kate's phone rang, and she took refuge under the awning of the coffee shop behind them to answer the call. Hanna watched more people stream past. There were kids from Hollis College, their T-shirts plastered to their chests. There were gung-ho über-runner types in racing singlets and track shoes. Suddenly, two familiar figures appeared around the bend. Mike's blue-black hair was matted against his head, and he wore a white long-sleeved T-shirt, baggy black running shorts, and neon-yellow Nikes. His right hand was firmly entwined with Colleen's. They were wearing matching outfits—only Colleen's white tee was now see-through from the rain. It hurt to see that the Mike-and-Hanna hobby was now a Mike-and-Colleen hobby.

Hanna tried to duck behind the water table, but then Colleen spied her and broke into a huge smile. *Shit.* They trotted over, breathing hard. "Omigod, Hanna, it's so sweet that you're handing out water!" Colleen gushed, accepting a cup, gulping it down, and grabbing another. "Thank you!"

"Drink the whole gallon, why don't you!" Hanna said under her breath, wanting to stuff the paper cup down her throat. Then she turned to Mike and offered him a cup of water, too. "Having a good time?" she said in the sweetest voice she could muster, as if there were no hard feelings.

"Yeah." Mike downed the water, then selected a banana from the tray. "This race rocks. I'm loving seeing so many girls' butts in wet spandex."

"*Mike*," Colleen scolded, her eyebrows furrowing. Mike hung his head in apology, and Colleen rolled her eyes before jogging to a nearby trash can to toss in

her empty water cup. Hanna raised an eyebrow. Colleen
didn't put up with Mike's sex jokes? How did they even
have a conversation?

Mike looked at Hanna with curiosity. "I'm surprised
you're not running this year."

Hanna shrugged. "Nope, dad-duty calls." She showed
him the VOTE FOR TOM MARIN button she'd pinned on her
jacket. "I remember last year, though. After we finished,
we dove into the bushes and made out, still wearing our
medals."

Mike's lips twitched. "Uh, yeah . . ."

Hanna checked on Colleen. She was talking to one of
the other Tom Marin volunteers by the trash can. "And then
there was the 10k on the Marwyn Trail this summer, where
it was so hot we went skinny-dipping in that pond halfway
through. Remember how that old lady almost caught us?"

Mike's cheeks got redder. "Hanna, I'm not sure—"

"We should have done it that day, don't you think?"
Hanna interrupted.

Mike's Adam's apple bobbed. He opened his mouth,
but no words came out. He might have been uncomfortable, but he definitely didn't look disgusted. Maybe he
did want to have sex with her, after all.

Hanna wiped a droplet of water off Mike's cheek.
"You know, my dad's having a campaign party tomorrow
night," she murmured into his ear. "You should come."

Mike's lips parted again. There was an intrigued sparkle
in his eyes, and Hanna could tell he was considering saying

yes. Then a hand gripped his arm. "Hey, my two favorite people! What are we talking about?" Colleen asked.

Mike blinked hard, then stood up straighter. "Mr. Marin's campaign party," he mumbled.

Colleen's eyes lit up. "Omigod! Mike and I are *so* excited for that!"

Hanna glared at Mike, but he was pointedly avoiding her gaze. "Colleen got a really pretty dress," he muttered.

"*Yes,*" Colleen swooned. "It was from the bebe store at the King James. Do you know that place, Hanna?"

Hanna snorted. "Yeah. Only sluts shop there."

Colleen's face crumpled. Mike's eyebrows shot up, and then he grabbed his girlfriend's hand and pulled her into the crowd of runners. "That wasn't very nice," he said over his shoulder. And then he was gone.

What. The. *Hell?* As Hanna contemplated throwing cut-up bananas at the backs of their heads, a taunting giggle lilted through the air, and the hair on the back of her neck rose.

Ping. She glanced down at her phone, which was tucked in her jacket pocket. *One new text.* Disturbingly, it was from a jumble of nonsensical letters and numbers.

Think Colleen is as innocent as she seems? Think again.
Everyone has secrets . . . even her. —A

Hanna stared at the text for a long time. What the hell was A talking about?

"Hanna! There you are!"

Her dad stood behind her, clutching an enormous striped golf umbrella. Standing next to him was a tall, slender woman dressed in a rain hat, North Face top, straight-leg jeans, and furry boots. A Louis Vuitton bag was slung casually over her arm, a cell phone was in her hand, and she was looking at Hanna with a smirking expression. Hanna's stomach dropped to her feet for the second time in under a minute when she realized who it was.

Gayle.

"Oh." It came out like a croak. "H-hi." Hanna eyed the cell phone in Gayle's hand. The screen was lit up, as if the phone had just been used. Had she sent Hanna that text?

"Hanna, Ms. Riggs is going to help us campaign," Mr. Marin said. "Isn't that nice of her?"

Gayle waved her hand dismissively. "Please. Anything to help the Tom Marin cause." She slipped her phone into the pocket of her coat. "I'm sorry I got here so late, Tom. My husband and I were in Princeton for a dinner last night to celebrate the new cancer lab he funded, and we just got in."

"It's no problem at all." Mr. Marin peered into the crowd of runners. "I hate to make you stand in this weather, though. If you really insist on helping, maybe you'd prefer to make calls in the coffee shop instead?"

"Really, it's no trouble," Gayle said breezily. "I don't mind a little drizzle. And besides, I can get to know your lovely daughter!" She turned to Hanna, an ominous smile on her lips. "I really wanted to chat with you at the town hall meeting, but you disappeared, Hanna," she said sweetly. "I guess you wanted to hang out with your friends, huh?"

"Yes, several of Hanna's friends attended the town hall meeting," Mr. Marin said. "They've all been very supportive of the campaign."

"That's so nice," Gayle trilled. "Who was that girl with the reddish hair I saw you with?"

Hanna stiffened. "Ah, you must mean Emily Fields," Mr. Marin jumped in before she could stop him. "She's been Hanna's friend for a long time."

"Emily Fields." Gayle pretended to contemplate this. Mr. Marin turned to take a phone call, and Gayle inched closer. "Funny, she told me she went by Heather," she added under her breath.

Hanna bit down hard on the inside of her lip, feeling Gayle's hot, impatient stare. "I don't know what you're talking about," she mumbled.

"Oh, I think you do." Gayle gazed at the passing crowd. "I think you know exactly what I mean. Don't think I don't know what's going on. Don't think I don't know about *everything*."

Hanna tried to keep her expression neutral, but it felt like ping-pong balls were bouncing in her stomach. Was Gayle admitting she was A?

She thought back to the end of the summer. Right before Emily had her C-section, she'd gathered Hanna and the other girls at the hospital and explained that she needed them to help her sneak the baby out before Gayle could come and take her away.

She'd pressed a weighty envelope into Hanna's hands. "I need you to drive this to New Jersey and put it in Gayle's mailbox," she explained. "It's the cash from the check she gave me, along with a letter of apology. Just put it in the mailbox and drive away. Don't let her see you. If she realizes I've given her money back, she'll come to the hospital early, and our plan will be ruined."

Hanna couldn't say no. That afternoon, after the baby was born, she drove the fifteen minutes over the Ben Franklin Bridge to Gayle's enormous house. She'd rolled up to the curb, feeling shaky and sick. She didn't want to come face-to-face with a crazy woman. Not after what happened with Real Ali.

She winced as she rolled down her window and pulled the handle to open the mailbox. Her hands trembled as she dropped the envelope inside. A swishing sound rushed through her ears. Something moved in the trees beside the house. Hanna hit the gas fast, not slowing to buckle her seat belt until she was safely out of the neighborhood. Had she just blown Emily's cover? Had someone seen her? Did the property have security cameras?

A bunch of people next to Hanna cheered loudly, snapping her back to the present. Her dad was still chatting on his cell phone, and Gayle was standing so close to Hanna that their hips touched. She laid an icy hand on

Hanna's arm. "Listen up, and listen good," she whispered with clenched teeth. "All I want is what I'm owed. I don't think that's too much to ask. And if I'm not given it, I can—and *will*—go to great lengths to make sure I get it. I can play dirty—*very* dirty. Pass that message to your friend. Got it?"

Her lips curled into a cruel smile, and her fingernails dug into Hanna's skin. Hanna's jaw trembled.

"Gayle?" Mr. Marin hung up and appeared beside them.

Gayle immediately released Hanna's arm. She swiveled around and smiled brightly at Hanna's father. "My campaign manager is here," Mr. Marin said. "I'd love for you to meet him."

"Wonderful!" Gayle gushed. And just like that, she was gone.

Hanna shot to a nearby bench, sank down, and covered her face with her hands. Her pulse was vibrating so vigorously she could feel it in her palms. Gayle's words crackled in her ears. *All I want is what I'm owed. I can play dirty—very dirty.* There was so much Gayle could do. Expose all of them. Ruin them. Send them to jail. Destroy their lives. Ruin her dad's life, too.

She reached into her pocket for her phone and pressed the speed dial button for Emily. "Pick up, pick *up*," she whispered, but the phone rang and rang. She hung up without waiting for the beep, instead tapping out a text for Emily to call her as soon as possible. It was then that she noticed a little mailbox icon in the top corner of the screen. Another text had come in while she was typing.

Hanna looked around uneasily. Her father, Gayle, and Mr. Marin's campaign manager were standing near the coffee shop, talking. Gayle was pretending to pay attention, but her eyes were on her phone. For a split second, she glanced at Hanna, an eerie smirk on her face.

Shuddering, Hanna pressed READ.

Better do as you're told! You wouldn't want Daddy's campaign to go up in smoke. —A

17

SMILE! YOU'RE ON CAMERA!

Saturday afternoon, Aria stood in the Kahns' game room, a large, sectioned-off part of the basement, complete with a pool table, several pinball machines, and a large felt-covered poker table. Noel, Noel's parents, and his older brother, Eric, stood around the pool table with her, eyeing the balls in play. Mrs. Kahn chalked up her cue and sank the six into the corner pocket.

"*Yes,*" Mrs. Kahn said primly, standing back up and blowing off the tip of the cue as though it were smoking.

"Nice one, dear." Mr. Kahn nudged Noel and Eric. "I think the ladies have us beat."

Noel pouted. "That's because it's five against three."

Aria considered protesting, shooting a look at Klaudia, Naomi Zeigler, and Riley Wolfe, the third, fourth, and fifth members of the all-girl pool team. They hadn't taken one shot. Aria knew they were only here to make her feel uncomfortable.

"Klaudia?" Mrs. Kahn said sweetly. "Do you want to play?"

"That okay." Klaudia glanced at Aria. "I waiting for a call from my new boyfriend. He writer who live in New York."

"I think *you* know him, Aria," Naomi said, and Riley burst into giggles.

Aria gripped the pool cue hard, resisting the urge to javelin-throw it toward them.

Noel sauntered over to Aria, wrapped his arm around her, and gave her a long, passionate kiss. She sensed the girls shifting uncomfortably behind her, and when she opened her eyes, Klaudia was pointedly looking away. Aria slipped her hand into Noel's, grateful. "What did I do to deserve you?" she whispered.

"I'm sorry they're freezing you out." Noel rolled his eyes in their direction.

Aria shrugged. "I'm used to it."

It was Mr. Kahn's turn to shoot, and he rolled up the sleeves of his blue Brooks Brothers shirt, leaned over the table, and hit the cue ball with laserlike precision. It banked off the far rail and clonked against the number six, sending two more balls plopping into the pockets.

Mrs. Kahn golf-clapped. "Brilliant shot, dear! You've still got the magic touch."

Mr. Kahn looked at his kids. "Did Mom ever tell you I hustled pool one weekend in Monte Carlo?"

"You were so sexy," Mrs. Kahn purred, kissing Mr. Kahn's cheek.

"Guys, *gross*." Noel covered his eyes.

Mr. Kahn took his wife's hands and started waltzing her around the room. "We need to practice for the Art Museum Costume Gala next month."

"I can't wait," Mrs. Kahn lilted. "It's so lovely to dress up, isn't it, dear?" She glanced at the others. "We're going as Marie Antoinette and Louis the Sixteenth."

"We'll make a lovely pair." Mr. Kahn dipped his wife so low that the top of her head practically kissed the carpet. "I do love a good costume."

Aria was so startled she nearly swallowed her gum. But as she watched the Kahns swirl around the game room, she felt herself relaxing. No matter what Mr. Kahn did in his free time, this was a couple that loved each other. There was probably a logical explanation for why Mr. Kahn had dressed up as a woman at Fresh Fields. Maybe he was getting in character for his Art Museum Gala costume—people spent thousands of dollars on flamboyant disguises for that event. Or maybe he'd lost a bet with a business partner.

Aria grabbed Noel's hand and squeezed it tight, feeling victorious. She hadn't gotten a single text about this, which meant she'd beaten A at A's game. For once, *she* was in control of the information, not the other way around.

Mr. and Mrs. Kahn kept dancing, and the pool game continued. The boys sank the rest of the balls, edging them to victory. Afterward, Noel scooped Aria up in his arms. "Want to get out of here? Escape to a movie at the

Ritz, maybe?" His eyebrows rose up and down suggestively. Going to the Ritz was code for sitting in the back row and making out.

Just then, Mr. Kahn clapped his hands. "What does everyone say to gelato? There's that new place in Yarmouth I've been dying to try."

"Ooh, I heard that place was divine." Mrs. Kahn slid the pool cues back into the rack. "I'm in."

"I could go for that," Eric said.

Naomi made a face. "Gelato is, like, pure fat."

"I no like things that are cold—only hot," Klaudia said, making sexy eyes at Eric, who ignored her. Apparently he'd gotten the message that Klaudia was loony, too.

Noel glanced at Aria apologetically, probably thinking she wanted to get out of there, but Aria just shrugged. She didn't have time to go to the movies with Noel, anyway—she was meeting Emily at the Bakers' open house in about an hour and a half.

"I think gelato would be great," she said to Mr. Kahn.

"Fantastic." Mr. Kahn was already halfway up the stairs. "I'll go pick it up."

"The weather is so dreary, though." Mrs. Kahn peered through the door of the walk-out basement at the rain pounding on the brick patio. "I'd hate for you to drive all the way to Yarmouth."

"I don't mind," Mr. Kahn called over his shoulder. "Why doesn't everyone give me their orders?"

Noel, Aria, Eric, and Mrs. Kahn climbed the stairs

behind Mr. Kahn and waited as he dug the menu out of a leather file in the cabinet drawer. They selected their flavors, and Mr. Kahn made the call. As he was slipping on his rain jacket, Mrs. Kahn touched his arm. "Want me to go with you?"

Mr. Kahn kissed her lightly on the lips. "There's no use for us both to get soaked. I won't be long."

He shut the front door, and his car engine roared. Mrs. Kahn and Eric disappeared into the den, and Noel excused himself to the bathroom, leaving Aria all alone in the cavernous kitchen. The huge house was suddenly very still and overwhelming, the only sound the pounding rain against the roof. Suddenly thunder crackled, and the room went dark. Aria screamed. "Noel?" she called out, feeling along the walls.

Somewhere in the distance, someone—Naomi, maybe—giggled. Another clap of thunder sounded, shaking the pots and pans hanging over the island. Lightning lit up the room. For a split second, Aria was sure she saw a pair of eyes staring at her from outside the back window. She screamed again.

Then the lights snapped back on with a spark. The refrigerator hummed calmly, the recessed lights cast a peaceful yellow glow over the room, and the eyes at the window were gone. When Aria looked down, she saw that her cell phone, which was nestled in her pocket, was blinking. She grabbed it and swallowed hard. *One new text message from Anonymous.*

She pressed READ, dreading what she might see.

It was a picture of a blond-haired woman applying cherry-red lipstick in the front seat of a car. The woman wore a blue oxford shirt and an expensive gold watch—the same ones Mr. Kahn had worn during the pool game. Add in his telltale bushy eyebrows and straight mouth, and *anyone* would know it was him. The clock on the dashboard of his car said 1:35—three minutes ago. The tall, iron eagle on the post in the corner of the picture was the eagle at the Kahns' front gate. He'd put on the wig before he'd even left the property.

Aria ran to the window, certain she'd see someone lurking at the end of the driveway, but there was no one there. Sweat beaded on her forehead. *No.*

"Aria?" Noel called from the hall. "Are you okay?"

Aria dropped the curtain and whipped around. Noel was walking toward her. She fumbled for the ERASE button on her phone, not wanting Noel to see the picture, but her finger bumped the right arrow instead, bringing up a note that went with the picture. As Aria read it, her heart stopped dead.

Secrets are such a drag. Break up with your loving boy-friend, or this pic goes public. —A

18

THE HOME OF HER DREAMS

"Welcome to the open house!" a cheery realtor with a stiff black hair-helmet said as she ushered Emily and Aria through the open door of 204 Ship Lane. She thrust a square business card into each of their hands. "My name is Sandra. Have a look around!"

Emily turned the card over. *Let me find you the home of your dreams*, Sandra's slogan read. "Actually, I was wonder-ing—" she started, but Sandra was already attending to a new couple who had come in after them.

Shaking out her umbrella and pushing back the hood of her raincoat, Emily stepped into the foyer of the house she'd obsessed over for the past seven months. It was empty, and only a few hints of the Bakers remained. The air smelled like a peppermint candle and Windex. The walls were painted a cheerful blue, and in the open closet was a blue plastic wrapper for the *Philadelphia Sentinel*. There were tiny scratches in the golden wooden floor from dog

toenails, and someone had left a God's-eye string ornament hanging over the door.

Emily stared at the brass strip that separated the tiled
foyer from the wooden living room floor, afraid to step
any further into the house. Was she really ready to see
this place?

Aria turned to Emily, as if sensing her apprehension.
"Are you okay?"

"Uh huh," Emily said woozily. "Thanks for meeting
me here."

"No problem." An uneasy look swept over Aria's face,
but when she noticed Emily looking at her, she quickly
smiled again.

"Are *you* okay?" Emily asked.

Aria's jaw trembled. "I don't want to bother you with
it. You've got enough going on."

Emily rolled her eyes. "Come on. What?"

After a moment's hesitation, Aria leaned in closer, her
feather earrings brushing against Emily's cheek. "Well,
okay. I got a note from A about an hour ago."

Emily's mouth dropped open. "What did it say?"

Aria pressed her glossy lips together. "It doesn't matter.
Just some stupid stuff. But I was at Noel's house, and A
took a picture of something at the end of Noel's driveway.
A was *so close*, and I missed seeing who it was."

A shiver snaked up Emily's spine. "Remember the note
I got on my car at the covered bridge? The one with the
picture of me and Tabitha? A was close then, too."

Aria skirted out of the way of two more people who had come through the front door. "How is it that we keep missing A? And how does A always know where we are?"

"Ali would always know where we were," Emily said quietly.

Aria's shoulders lowered. "Em, A *isn't* Ali. There's no way."

Emily shut her eyes. She was so sick of having the same argument over and over. But she couldn't explain why she was convinced Ali wasn't dead—she'd have to confess that she'd left open the door in the burning house in the Poconos.

Aria stepped into the living room. The blue carpet had deep indentations from where the furniture had stood. "A is definitely Gayle, Em. Remember how weird she was that day at the café? She's totally capable of stalking us."

"But it makes no sense." Emily glanced over her shoulder to make sure an elderly couple in matching argyle sweaters wasn't listening. "Gayle has no connection to Jamaica. How could she know what we did?"

"Are you sure you didn't say anything to anyone?" Aria asked. "What about that friend of yours, Derrick? He worked for Gayle, right? Are you sure you didn't slip and tell him anything about Tabitha?"

Emily whirled around and glared at Aria. "Of course not! How could you even think that?"

Aria held up her hands in surrender. "I'm sorry. I'm just trying to cover all the bases."

Sandra's voice rang out in the other room, telling a potential buyer about the square footage and the kitchen upgrades. Emily tried to swallow her annoyance, knowing Aria wasn't trying to accuse her of anything. She wandered out of the living room and up the stairs to the second floor. The master bedroom was the first room on the right.

The room was painted a dusty gray and had wooden blinds on the windows. Emily could picture a bed on one wall, a dresser on another. But she couldn't picture the Bakers living within these walls. Were they late sleepers or early risers? Did they snack on cookies and potato chips in bed, leaving crumbs in the sheets? How many tears had they shed over not being able to have a child?

It was one of the first things the Bakers had told Emily when she'd met them—they'd been trying for over four years to no avail. "We both work with kids all day, and we'd love to have some of our own," Mrs. Baker had said earnestly. "We've always wanted to be parents." Mr. Baker's fingers gripped his wife's hand hard.

Now, Emily walked the perimeter of the room, touching the light switch, tracing a tiny crack in the wall, and poking her head into an empty closet. She could only imagine how overjoyed the Bakers had been when they'd found out she had chosen them as her baby's adoptive parents. They'd probably lain in bed at night, dreaming of their child, fantasizing about swimming lessons, vacations, and the first day of school. Then she imagined the

Bakers' shock when they found out Emily had changed her mind. She'd asked Rebecca, the adoption coordinator, to pass on the message—she'd been too chicken to tell the Bakers herself.

Rebecca had been confused. "So . . . you're *keeping* the baby?" she'd sounded out.

"Uh, I've just come up with another option," Emily said evasively, not wanting to admit that she'd found another adoptive parent—*or* that Gayle had offered her a lot of money.

The coordinator called back a little later and told Emily that the Bakers had been very gracious with her decision. "They want your baby to have the best home possible, and if you think that's somewhere else, they understand," Rebecca said. In some ways, it disappointed Emily: She would have rather they'd been furious at her. It was what she deserved.

Emily had thought about the Bakers a lot after she made the decision to give the baby to Gayle, especially after Gayle started calling Emily nonstop. Every time Emily's phone rang, it was Gayle, checking in. At first, Emily indulged her, rationalizing Gayle's rapid speech, her shaky laugh, her nervous questions. She was just excited, right? She tried to justify why she hadn't met Gayle's husband, the potential father, yet—Gayle said he was really busy, but he was one hundred percent on board. When her phone started ringing every hour, Emily let the calls go to voicemail, the uneasiness growing sharper and more acrid inside her. Something wasn't right. She began looking for ways to get out of the deal. She dreaded the day she'd have to give the baby up.

The final straw came two weeks before Emily's scheduled C-section. Derrick had asked Emily to pick him up at Gayle's house after work one Saturday; they were going to go to the Camden Aquarium. Emily hadn't told Gayle she was coming; she was too tired to deal with her. After parking the car in the long driveway, she'd walked up to the front door and looked through the window. Gayle was standing in the foyer with her back to Emily, talking on the phone. "Yes, it's true," she was saying into the receiver. "I'm having a baby. I know, I know, I've barely gained *any* weight, but I guess I'm one of those lucky pregnant people."

Emily had nearly tumbled off the porch. What kind of crazy person pretended *they* were pregnant when they really weren't? Was she going to try and pass off Emily's baby as her own? It left a horrible taste in her mouth. The Bakers had told Emily that the child would know she'd been adopted. They'd even tell her about Emily. What *else* would Gayle lie to the baby about?

She'd fled back to her car, revved the engine fast, and driven away, too upset to even leave a message for Derrick. Everything was so clear in that moment. There was no way Gayle was getting her baby. The money didn't matter. The privileged life the child might lead in Gayle's care didn't matter. And so, the next day, she called Gayle and told her that the doctor had rescheduled her C-section for two days later than originally planned. Then she'd called Aria, Hanna, and Spencer, asking for their help.

"Emily?" Aria called now. "Em, you have to come see this!"

Emily followed Aria's voice to a smaller bedroom down the hall. "Look!" Aria said, spreading out her arms.

Emily spun around. The walls were striped with green and yellow paint. On the far wall was a mural of a circus train, a lion, tiger, elephant, and monkey peeking out of the cars. Above the mural was a decal that said *Violet,* the *o* a smiley face, and the *t* sprouting a flower out the top.

"It was her room," Aria whispered.

Tears filled Emily's eyes. She remembered the Bakers telling her that they'd designed a nursery for the baby in gender-neutral colors, leaving a space on the wall for a boy name or a girl name. They hadn't told Emily their choices, though, saying they wanted to see what the baby looked like before they made a final decision. The name Violet, she thought, was perfect.

"It's so beautiful," Emily whispered, walking to the little window seat and settling on the cushion. There were still marks where the crib and changing table had stood. When the Bakers found the baby seat on their doorstep, had they brought her in here to sleep? No, Emily decided. Not that first night. They'd probably held the baby until the sun came up, amazed she was theirs. Scared, too. They'd probably made plans to move that very night to avoid questions and to make sure the baby wouldn't be taken away.

Suddenly, Emily knew something for sure: The Bakers had done everything they could for the baby. They'd uprooted their lives just to ensure they could keep her, her happiness meaning more than their community, their home. That was worth more than any amount of money. She had made the right choice giving her daughter—*Violet*—to them.

"Hey," Aria said soothingly, noticing Emily's tear-streaked face. She wrapped her arms around Emily and squeezed tight. Emily hugged back, and they remained that way for several minutes. She felt happy and sad at the same time. It was wonderful to know that the baby had such a loving home, but she hated that she still didn't know where the Bakers had gone.

Emily broke from Aria's embrace and started down the stairs to find the realtor, suddenly fueled with purpose. Sandra was in the kitchen, rearranging papers in a binder.

"Excuse me," she called. Sandra turned, a plastic smile frozen on her face. "The family that lived here before. Do you know what happened to them?"

"If I recall, they left in early September, I believe." Sandra flipped through a file folder containing information about the house. "Their names were Charles and Lizzie Baker."

"Do you have a forwarding address?" Emily asked.

Sandra shook her head. "Were you the one who e-mailed me about this?"

"E-mail?" Emily raised an eyebrow. "No . . ."

Sandra whipped out her BlackBerry and scrolled through it. "That's funny. I got an e-mail asking the same question. Someone else was eager to know where the Bakers went, too."

Aria, who had just arrived in the kitchen, coughed. "Do you remember who sent the e-mail?"

Sandra stared at her BlackBerry. "I swore I had it on here, but maybe I deleted it. It was a woman's name, definitely. Maybe it started with a G?"

"Gayle Riggs?" Aria blurted.

Sandra's face lit up. "Yes, I believe that's it! Do you know her?"

Emily and Aria exchanged a haunted look. Emily had never told Gayle who she'd originally chosen to give the baby to. The adoption agency would never have given out that information, either. What if she'd found out, somehow? What if A had told her? And what if—Emily's heart started to pound—Gayle was trying to track the baby down?

Suddenly, a *ping* sounded from inside Aria's bag. She pulled it out and looked at her phone. "Hanna says she's been trying to contact you, Em."

Emily reached into her pocket for her phone and studied the dark screen. "The battery's dead."

Aria's eyes were still on her phone. She hit a button and gasped. "Look at this." She passed it to Emily. *Tell Em it's urgent*, a text from Hanna said. *I think Gayle is after her baby. Call me ASAP.*

"Oh my God," Emily whispered.

Another *ping* sounded as a new message arrived on Aria's phone. The sender was a jumble of letters and numbers. Aria clapped her hand to her mouth. Emily's heart thudded fast as she read the words.

Guess Emily's not the only one looking for that little bundle of joy. Who's going to get there first? —A

19

SECRET AGENT HANNA

The thing about camo, Hanna realized, was that it was really ugly. There should be Louis Vuitton camo or camo that actually complemented one's skin tone. It wasn't like she was hiding out in the green and brown woods, after all. She was lurking in the King James Mall.

It was a little later on Saturday afternoon, and Hanna had just put on her first—and last—camouflage outfit to kick off Operation Figure Out If Colleen Is Hiding Something. She'd bought the outfit at the Rosewood Army/Navy, a terrifying store full of gas masks, grenade holders, unflattering combat boots, and other sundries she hoped to never see again, except maybe on CNN. She'd also picked up a field scope that had scratches on it (probably from some scary war), night-vision goggles, and a platoon helmet, just in case she had to do a commando roll or jump out of a moving car. Perhaps it was overkill to buy all that equipment to spy on a girl who'd probably be delighted if she knew Hanna had taken such an acute interest in her, but Hanna thought it would help her get in the mood.

Now, she was crouching behind a large fake plant in the middle of the esplanade and peering through the binoculars at Colleen and Mike strolling into Victoria's Secret. Hanna felt a moment of misgiving. Was it weird that she was doing this? It was sort of like she was becoming an A herself. But then, maybe Gayle was right—maybe Colleen had a secret she didn't know about. Everyone did.

Hanna checked her watch. She would give it another half hour, she decided, and then call Emily again. As for the Colleen thing, it wasn't like she and Gayle were on the same team or anything—A just had a good idea for once. All she needed to do was unearth some embarrassing secret of Colleen's to turn Mike off her for good and kick her back to dork-dom where she belonged.

There was only one problem: so far, Colleen seemed like an open book. Hanna had peeked in Colleen's car in the parking garage, but she kept it tidy and boring. She'd followed the couple to Otter, the best boutique in the mall, and watched as Hanna's favorite salesgirl showed Colleen a brand-new style of James jeans that had just come in—jeans that *Hanna* was supposed to see first. *Traitor*.

Now, Colleen approached the Victoria's Secret salesgirl and explained she was looking for some new lingerie. "What size are you?" the assistant asked. Hanna had learned how to lip-read when she was in fifth grade, mostly to decipher her parents' tense fights through the glass back-patio door. Colleen gave her the answer, and Hanna's jaw dropped. Colleen's boobs were even bigger than she had thought.

As the salesgirl searched for some styles Colleen might like, Mike wandered over to a table of satin bras, held an enormous pink one to his chest, and started striking exaggerated poses. Hanna snickered. Mike used to do that all the time when they went shopping together, and it never failed to crack her up. But when Colleen saw him, a disapproving scowl settled over her features. Mike pouted and dropped the bra back to the table, looking like a scolded puppy.

Hanna's phone chimed loudly, and she frantically patted her pocket to silence it. Aria's picture was flashing on the screen. "Did you get in touch with Emily?" Hanna whispered into the receiver.

"I'm with Emily, and I've patched in Spencer, too." Aria's voice echoed on speakerphone. "We're really freaked. I got a note today. A is *definitely* after Emily's baby."

Hanna sank down further into the bushes. "We have to prove Gayle is A. But how do we do that without going to the cops?"

"Gayle's psycho," Aria explained. "Just like Kelsey. The cops wouldn't believe anything she says."

"Yeah, but she has *money*," Hanna reminded her. "And

she's an adult. That holds some weight, don't you think?"

"Guys, I'm not so sure Gayle is A," Spencer's voice sounded far away. "I got a note last night, and I'm at Princeton. How could Gayle be in two places at once?"

Hanna watched as a bunch of kids from Rosewood Day passed. "Maybe she *can* be. At the race this morning, Gayle apologized for being late, saying she'd just come from Princeton. Her husband just donated some cancer lab."

Spencer made a small noise at the back of her throat. "Do you think she followed me to my party? Wouldn't I have noticed someone like her in a crowd of kids?"

"She was probably hiding in the bushes outside," Hanna said.

"That still doesn't prove Gayle is A," Emily protested. "But the important thing is, either way, she's after the baby. How are we going to find out where the Bakers went? We need to warn them."

"The realtor didn't have the information on where they moved," Aria added, sounding despondent. "They could be anywhere."

"Actually, I might be able to find them." Hanna moved the phone to the other ear. "My dad's campaign has voter registration information for people across Pennsylvania. If they stayed in the state, I can probably dig up their new address."

"Really?" Emily sounded hopeful. "How soon can you do that?"

"I'll look into it when I get home," Hanna promised. "It may take a few days, though."

"I still think Gayle's A," Aria said. "But how can we prove it?"

There was a pause on the line. "Well, A is following all of us, right?" Spencer said after a moment. "Maybe one of us could try to catch her in the act."

"Or one of us could try to steal her cell phone," Hanna piped up.

"That would be great, but we'd have to know her schedule and show up somewhere she's going to be." Aria sounded discouraged.

"I know somewhere she's going to be." Hanna ran her tongue over her teeth. "My dad's campaign party tomorrow. Maybe we could figure out a way to snag her phone and go through her texts then. You guys are all going to be there anyway, right?"

Emily groaned. "I never want to see Gayle again."

"We'll keep you safe," Hanna assured her. "But if Gayle does want to confront you, we could steal her phone while she's preoccupied. Then we'll prove she's A."

"But she might *not* be A," Emily moaned.

"Look at it this way," Aria said gently. "Even if she isn't A, maybe there's something in her phone about her search for the baby. Maybe A tipped her off or something. You want to know what she's up to, right?"

Emily agreed, and the girls promised to be on the look-out for anyone following them and get in touch as soon as they got another message from A. After she hung up, Hanna parted two of the leaves of the potted plant and gazed into Victoria's Secret. Mike and Colleen weren't there anymore. *Shit.*

Then she spied them walking hand-in-hand toward the exit. Shooting out of the plants—and getting strange looks from the passersby—she trailed them to the parking garage. They paused by Colleen's car and talked. Hanna ducked behind a VW Beetle to listen.

"Are you sure I can't come with you?" Mike was saying.

"It's probably better I go alone," Colleen answered, her hand on the driver's door.

"Come *on*." Mike brushed Colleen's bangs out of her eyes. "I bet it's going to be really hot."

Colleen kissed the tip of Mike's nose. "I'll tell you all about it when I'm done, okay?"

She slipped into the driver's seat and revved the engine. Mike waved until she'd rounded the bend. Hanna darted for her car, which was parked only a few aisles away. She needed to get a move on if she was going to follow Colleen to her secret rendezvous.

She caught up to Colleen on the little driveway out of the mall to Route 30, then trailed the car down a series of back roads. Strip malls gave way to old Victorian houses and the brick-and-stone school buildings of Hollis. One street was blocked off; there had been a fender-bender between a Jeep and an old Cadillac. Hanna averted her eyes, the old memories of her own car accident from the previous summer swarming back to her. Not that she'd stayed around to see the ambulance lights.

Colleen turned onto a side street and expertly parallel-parked at the curb. Hanna turned her car around in an alley, parked crookedly, and dove into a bush just in time to see Colleen walking up the front steps of an old, grand house on the corner. Colleen rang the bell and stood back, fixing her hair.

The door opened, and a graying man with crow's feet opened the door. "Great to see you," he said, giving Colleen an air kiss.

"Thank you so much for seeing me at such short notice," Colleen said.

"Anything for you, dear." The guy cupped Colleen's face in his hands. "You have such good bone structure. You're a natural."

Colleen tittered bashfully. "I'm so glad you think so."

A natural for what? Hanna pushed a branch out of the way. Was Colleen two-timing Mike with this geezer?

When the door slammed, Hanna scampered up to the porch and stared at a plaque next to the doorbell. JEFFREY LABRECQUE, it said. PHOTOGRAPHER.

Hanna snickered. So Colleen was getting professional photos taken. She knew just how *that* would go—if this Jeffrey character was anything like Patrick, her seedy photographer, he'd butter up Colleen and then convince her to take off her top. Mike's jealousy of Patrick—and Hanna's reaction to it—was what had broken them up.

It could be just the thing to ruin Mike and Colleen, too.

Hanna peered into the window, watching the photographer set up a bunch of lights around a black screen. He gestured for Colleen to sit on a stool, then perched behind his camera. The flash went off again and again, Colleen twisting her knees this way and that and making faces ranging from ecstatic to intense to brooding to sullen. After a few minutes, Jeffrey Labrecque walked toward Colleen and said something Hanna couldn't hear. He stepped away, and Colleen slipped off her cardigan sweater. Hanna leaned forward. This was probably the moment she was going to pose in her lacy black bra.

But when Jeffrey stepped away, Colleen was still in a T-shirt. She smiled for the camera, looking wholesome and sweet. Within minutes, the photo session was over, and Colleen rose from the stool, handed the photographer a check, and shook his hand.

"Unbelievable," Hanna muttered. Everything was so damn pure the whole vignette could have a halo over it.

Colleen headed for the front door, and Hanna skittered off the porch before Colleen saw her. As she rounded the corner, she almost ran smack into a black sedan chugging at the curb. The windows were tinted, but she could see a pair of eyes peering through the slightly open backseat window. Before she could see who it was, the car sped away. Hanna swung around and stared at the receding car, but it was too far away for her to see the license plate.

Beep.

Hanna's phone glowed at the bottom of her bag. The words of a new text assaulted her as soon as she looked at the screen.

You're close, Hanna. Keep digging. —A

20

A POT OF GOLD

That same afternoon, Spencer left the seedy Motel 6 on the outskirts of the Princeton University campus, where she'd been staying since the party disaster last night, and started toward the train station. The rain had abated and the sun had come out, making the sidewalks glimmer and the air smell like fresh flowers. People folded up their umbrellas and lowered their raincoat hoods. A couple of Ultimate Frisbee players straggled out of the dorms and resumed their games. On any other day, Spencer would have taken the opportunity to sit on one of the benches and just gaze at the splendor that was Princeton University. But today, she just felt exhausted.

Starting almost immediately after the police had hauled Harper away from the party, Spencer had texted Harper with several profuse apologies, but Harper hadn't responded. Neither had Quinn or Jessie or anyone else whose numbers she'd gotten before the big drug bust.

Spencer knew staying at the Ivy House—or anywhere else on campus—wasn't an option, so she'd Googled local motels in the area and stumbled into the Motel 6 room at almost midnight. All she wanted to do was get some sleep and forget about everything that had happened, but she'd been kept awake almost all night by the techno music coming from the adult bookstore next to the motel. Her hair was greasy from the motel shampoo, her skin itched from the cheap cotton sheets, and her head was spinning from just how badly she'd ruined her chances at getting into Ivy.

She was ready to go home.

A group of adults in business attire swept past, looking honored and important. Hanna said Gayle had been on the Princeton campus. It was obvious Gayle had spied on her the other night and had called the cops on Harper. Spencer understood this woman was angry about Emily not giving her the baby, but what lunatic went to such extremes to mess with kids half her age?

A blonde sitting on a bench swam into view, and Spencer stopped short. There, reading a D. H. Lawrence novel and nursing a large Starbucks coffee, was Harper.

"Oh," Spencer blurted. "H-hey!"

Harper looked up, and her features settled into a scowl. She returned to her book without a word.

"I've been trying to reach you," Spencer rushed to the bench, dropping her duffel at her feet. "Are you okay?"

Harper flipped a page. "If you wanted to get me in

trouble, you're out of luck. The cops couldn't find any pot on me. They let me go with a warning."

"*I* didn't want to get you in trouble!" Spencer cried. "Why would I do something like that?"

"You were the only person at the party who I don't know really, really well, and you seemed pretty uncomfortable with me smoking." Harper still didn't look up.

A flock of pigeons landed close to them, fighting over a pizza crust. Spencer wished she could tell Harper about A, but A would wreak havoc if she did. "I have some skeletons in my closet, so I'm skittish about getting caught again," she admitted in a low voice. "But I would never rat you out."

Harper finally met Spencer's gaze. "What happened?"

Spencer raised one shoulder. "A friend and I were into study drugs last summer. We were caught with it on us."

Harper's eyes bugged. "Did you get in trouble?"

"I was let off with a warning." Spencer stared at her duffel. There was no use getting into the Kelsey stuff now. "It freaked me out. But I promise I didn't narc on you. Please give me another chance."

Harper saved her page with a tasseled bookmark and shut the text tight. She stared at Spencer for a long time as though trying to opine her thoughts. "You know, I really *do* want to like you, Spencer," she said. "If you want to make it up to me, there's an Ivy luncheon tomorrow you can come to. But there's a catch: You have to bring a dish."

Spencer blinked. "I have to cook something? Where

am I supposed to find a kitchen?"

"That's for you to figure out." Harper slipped the book into her bag and stood. "Everyone has to bring a dish. It's a *potluck*."

"Okay," Spencer said. "I'll figure something out."

The corners of Harper's mouth slowly curled into a grin. "See you at the Ivy House tomorrow at twelve sharp. Bye!"

She strode down the sidewalk, her hips swinging and her bag bouncing against her butt. Spencer shifted from foot to foot, puzzled. A potluck? Seriously? That sounded like something Nana Hastings would've done for the Women's League she once chaired. Even the term *potluck* sounded weirdly 1950s, conjuring up images of garish, Technicolor macaroni salads and Jell-O molds.

The words clanged in her head again. *Potluck*. Harper had winked at her like they had a double meaning. Spencer laughed out loud, something clicking. It was a potluck—*literally*. Harper wanted her to bake pot *inside* a dish. It was Spencer's chance to prove she wasn't a narc.

The clock bells chimed the hour, and the pigeons lifted off the sidewalk all at once. Spencer sank into the bench, thinking hard. Even though she hated the idea of buying drugs again, she was desperate to get back in Harper's good graces—and into Ivy. Only, how was she going to get her hands on pot? She didn't know anyone here besides the people she'd met at the party, and they probably wouldn't help her.

She sat up straighter, hit with a bolt of brilliance. *Reefer.*

Hc lived near Princeton, didn't he? She rifled through her purse, looking for the slip of paper he'd given her at the Princeton dinner. Blessedly, it was tucked into a pocket. *What a long, strange trip it's been*, the note said.

You're telling me, Spencer thought. Then she held her breath as if plunging into a room with a nasty smell and dialed his number, hoping she wasn't making a huge mistake.

"I knew you were going to call," Reefer said as he opened the door to a large Colonial house in a neighborhood a few miles from the Princeton campus. He was dressed in an oversize Bob Marley T-shirt, baggy jeans with a pot-leaf patch on the knee, and the same hemp sneakers he'd had on at the dinner at Striped Bass. His longish hair had been tucked into one of those hideous, brightly colored Jamaican hats that every druggie Spencer had ever known loved to wear, but he'd at least shaved the goat beard. He looked a million times better without it—not that she thought he was cute or anything.

"I appreciate you taking the time to see me," Spencer said primly, straightening her cardigan sweater.

"*Mi casa es su casa.*" Reefer was practically salivating as he escorted her inside.

Spencer's heels rang out in the foyer. The living room was long and narrow with beige carpet and leather couches and chairs. Volumes of an aging *World Book Encyclopedia* from the eighties lined the bookshelves, and a gilded harp stood in the corner. Next to the living room was the kitchen, which had swirly, psychedelic wallpaper and a cookie jar in the shape of a leering owl. Spencer wondered if Reefer hung out in there when he was high.

She sniffed the air. Strangely, the house didn't smell like pot, but of cinnamon candles and minty mouthwash. What if Reefer didn't smoke at home? Even worse, what if he was one of those kids who only *pretended* he was stoned all the time but really was afraid of the stuff?

"So what can I do for you?" Reefer asked.

Spencer placed her hands on her hips, suddenly unsure. She'd bought drugs last summer, but that involved secret passwords and back-alley deals. She doubted getting pot was the same. She decided to be blunt and precise: "I'm wondering if I could buy some marijuana from you."

Reefer's eyes lit up. "I knew it! I knew you smoked! You can totally score some! We can even smoke together if you want!"

Well, that answered that. "Thanks," Spencer said, feeling relieved. "But it's not for me. It's for this potluck hosted by the Ivy Eating Club. Basically, they want everyone to bring a dish that has pot baked into it. So I need some pot . . . and a recipe. It's really important."

Reefer raised an eyebrow. "Does this have anything to do with you getting that chick in trouble at the party last night?"

Spencer's shoulders tensed. "I didn't get her in trouble! But it's because of that, yes. Harper is really influential at

Ivy, and I want to make sure I get in."

Reefer plucked a string of the harp. "Ivy hosts pot parties? I didn't realize they were so cool."

What do you *know?* Spencer thought, annoyed. "Well, do you have pot for me or not?"

"Of course. This way."

He walked up the stairs to the second level. They passed a small bathroom with a nautical theme and a guest bedroom containing several pieces of exercise equipment and finally entered Reefer's bedroom. It was bright and big, with a queen bed, white bookshelves, and a white Eames chair and ottoman. Spencer had expected a stinky drug den with weird optical illusion posters on the walls, but this looked like a bedroom out of a boutique hotel in New York City. Of course, he probably hadn't decorated it.

"So you're vying to get into Ivy, huh?" Reefer walked to the closet at the far end of the room.

Spencer snorted. "Uh, *yeah.* Isn't everyone?"

Reefer shrugged. "Nah. It's a little stuffy for me."

"An organization that supports a drug potluck is *stuffy?*"

"I'm just not into organizations." Reefer put *organizations* in air quotes. "I don't like being put into one category, you know? It's so stifling."

Spencer burst out laughing. "Isn't that the pot calling the kettle black?"

Reefer stared at her blankly, leaning against the bureau.

"I'm just saying. Aren't *you* putting yourself into a

category?" Spencer waved her hands up and down Reefer's body. "What about the whole Rastafarian thing you've got going on?"

A half-smile crept onto Reefer's face. "How do you know I'm not more than just this? You shouldn't judge a book by its cover." Then he turned to his closet. "Why do you care so much about getting into Ivy, anyway? You don't look like the kind of girl who'd have trouble making friends."

Spencer bristled. "Uh, because being part of an Eating Club is a huge honor?"

"It is? Says who?"

Spencer wrinkled her nose. What planet did this guy live on? "Look, can I just see the pot?"

"Of course." Reefer opened his closet doors and stepped away. Inside was a tall, clear plastic cabinet with at least thirty pullout drawers. Each drawer was labeled with things like Northern Lights and Power Skunk. Inside, Spencer could see a small, greenish-gray clump that looked like a cross between a wad of moss and a dreadlock in each one.

"Whoa," Spencer whispered. She'd figured Reefer would have his stash in a dirty sock under his bed, or rolled up in a bunch of Socialist newspapers. The organizer was pristinely clean, and the same amount of pot was in each one, as though compulsively weighed on a mini scale. On the left side of the cabinets were pot varieties like Americano, Buddha's Sister, and Caramella.

On the very right side, at the bottom, was a variety called Yumboldt—Spencer assumed there wasn't any pot that started with Z. It was in alphabetical order. Spencer smiled inwardly. If she were a pot fiend, she'd probably organize her drug stash just like this.

"All this is yours?" she asked.

"Uh huh," Reefer looked proud of himself. "Most of it I grew using hybridization and genetic recombination techniques. It's totally organic, too."

"Are you a dealer?" She suddenly felt nervous. Was it dangerous to be here?

Reefer shook his head. "Nah, it's more like a collection. I don't deal—except to gorgeous girls like you."

Spencer lowered her eyes. What did Reefer see in her, anyway? A Lilith Fair–going, eyebrow-pierced, bohemian hell-raiser seemed more his type. "So what kind is good for baking?" she asked, changing the subject.

Reefer opened a drawer and selected a greenish clump. "This stuff is super-mellow and really fragrant. Smell."

Spencer backed away from him. "It's not like it's wine."

Reefer gave her a condescending look. "In some cultures, distinguishing different brands of pot is much more refined than having a good palate for wines."

"I guess you're the expert." Spencer brought the wad of pot to her nostrils and breathed in. "Ugh." She turned her head away, assaulted by the familiar skunky odor. "It smells like butt."

"Novice." Reefer chuckled. "Keep sniffing. There's

more to it than just that. It's a secret that's locked just underneath."

Spencer gave him a wary look, but then shrugged and moved in for another sniff. After getting over the stale, icky, pot smell, she began to notice another scent just beneath it. Something almost . . . fragrant. She looked up, surprised. "Orange peels?"

"Exactly." Reefer smiled. "It's a hybrid of two different kinds of pot that have really fruity characteristics. I created the blend myself." He turned and pulled out another bud and waved it under Spencer's nostrils. "What about this one?"

Spencer closed her eyes and breathed in. "Chocolate?" she said after a moment.

Reefer nodded. "It's called Chocolate Chunk. You have a really good nose."

"If only there were a career in pot-sniffing," Spencer joked. But deep down, she couldn't help but feel pleased. She liked when someone pointed out she was good at something.

She dared a smile at Reefer, and he smiled back. For a moment, he looked really cute. His eyes were such a disarming golden color. If he just got rid of those stupid clothes, he'd be gorgeous.

Then Spencer forced the corners of her lips down, startled by her thoughts. The pot fumes were probably getting to her. "So you can bake these into brownies?" she barked.

Reefer cleared his throat and stepped away, too. "Yep.

I've got a great recipe you can borrow, too." He pulled out a binder from an organized bookshelf, extracted an index card, and handed it to her. *Magical Mystery Brownies* read the heading at the top.

Spencer put the card in her pocket. "What do I owe you?"

Reefer waved his hand. "Nothing. Like I said, I'm not a dealer."

"I want to give you *something*."

Reefer thought for a moment. "You can answer me something. Why do you want to be part of Ivy?"

Spencer bristled. "Why do you care?"

Reefer shrugged. "I just don't understand Eating Clubs. It seems like most people use them to feel better about themselves, but do you really need a stupid club to tell you that you're cool?"

Spencer's face turned hot. "Of course not! And if you ask anyone who belongs to them, I'm sure that's not why *they're* part of them, either."

Reefer snorted. "Please. I heard those Ivy girls at the party. They name-dropped like crazy. I guarantee you the only reason they're part of the club is to impress their parents or one-up their siblings or because it gives them an automatic clique. It's so . . . *safe*."

Spencer's mind reeled. "I assure you that's *not* what they're thinking. That's not what I'm thinking, either."

"Okay." Reefer crossed his arms over his chest. "Tell me what you *are* thinking, then."

Spencer opened her mouth to speak, but no words

came out. Infuriatingly, she couldn't think of a single reason Reefer would understand. Even worse, maybe he was right—maybe she *did* want an automatic clique. Maybe she wanted to impress her parents, Mr. Pennythistle, Amelia, Melissa, and everyone at Rosewood Day who didn't believe in her. But Reefer had made it sound like wanting those things was shallow and unadventurous. He painted her as an eager, insecure little girl, only wanting to make Mommy and Daddy happy, not thinking for herself.

"Where do you get off?" she sputtered, facing Reefer. "What makes you so high and mighty? What about Princeton itself? They only admit a few people while rejecting plenty of others. You have no problem with being part of *that*!"

"Who says I don't have a problem with it?" Reefer said quietly. "You really shouldn't—"

"Judge a book by its cover, I got it," Spencer snapped angrily. "Maybe you should listen to your own advice." She fished in her wallet and flung two twenties at Reefer for the pot. He stared at them as though they were coated in anthrax. Then she marched out of the house, slamming the front door behind her.

The cold air was a welcome greeting on her hot skin. Her jaw hurt from clenching it so tightly. Why did she even care what Reefer thought? It wasn't like they were friends. Still, she glanced up at his bedroom window. The blinds weren't parted and Reefer wasn't looking forlornly out, begging her forgiveness. *Jerk.*

Rolling back her shoulders, she stomped down the steps and pulled out her cell phone to call the cab company to take her back to the motel. Her eyes watered, and she drew back and sniffed the phone's leather case. It smelled like the pot Reefer had given her. She wrinkled her nose, cursing the odor. It no longer smelled of sweet, tangy orange peels. Maybe it never had.

21

A FRIENDLY REUNION

On Saturday evening, Emily scurried down the street in Old Hollis, the commercial district next to the college that boasted bars, restaurants, funky T-shirt shops, and a psychic who read tarot cards. A neon sign in the shape of an ice cream cone swung from an awning ahead, and her stomach did a nervous flip. She was on her way to hang out with Isaac again, and even though her secret weighed heavily on her, the buzzy, giddy feeling she'd had since she last saw him hadn't ceased.

She couldn't stop thinking about Isaac since their dinner. The way he'd hung on her words, the way he'd stood up for her in front of his mom—he seemed older, somehow, really mature.

"Emily?"

She stared across the dark street. A figure in a blue checked coat was waving at her from Snooker's, a college bar with Eagles pennants and Pabst Blue Ribbon lamps.

He had a wrist brace on his hand and spiky dark hair. When he called her name again, Emily recognized the voice immediately. It was Derrick, her closest friend from the summer.

"Oh my God," Emily yelped, crossing the street. A driver honked angrily as he swerved to avoid her. "What are you doing here?" she called gleefully to Derrick.

"Taking some classes at Hollis." Derrick grabbed Emily and engulfed her in a huge hug. He looked her up and down. "Man, you look a little different since I saw you last. What happened to you, anyway? You fell off the face of the earth! We were supposed to hang out back in the summer, but you never showed. Never called, either."

Emily stared down at her sneakers, feeling ashamed. She'd ditched Derrick the day she'd overheard Gayle saying that *she* was the one who was pregnant. She'd meant to call him later with an update, but she hadn't gotten around to it. She thought she'd see him at the restaurant, but their schedules had never matched up. A week passed, then another, and suddenly it felt weird to call him. Too much had happened. There was too much to explain.

Derrick leaned in closer, giving Emily a concerned look. "How did everything go with the baby?"

"*Shhh.*" Emily looked around, terrified one of the passersby on the busy street might hear. "No one knows about that. Especially my parents."

Derrick's eyebrows shot up. "You *still* haven't told them?"

Emily shook her head. "I didn't have to."

"So I guess you didn't keep it, then." Derrick twisted his mouth. "And I *know* you didn't give it to Gayle." He looked wounded. "You know, I *should* be mad at you. You got me in some deep shit with that woman."

Emily shivered at the sound of Gayle's name. "What do you mean?"

"About two weeks after you ditched me, she found me in her garden shed and told me you went back on your word. She was unhinged. She thought I had something to do with it, helped you escape or something. She started throwing stuff at me—a bag of birdseed, a rake, then a shovel. She broke a window—it was insane. I tried to tell her I had no idea what she was talking about, but she didn't believe me." He bit his lip. "I'd never seen her so . . . violent."

Emily covered her mouth with her hands. She thought of A's last note, which all but spelled out how Gayle was searching for the baby. What did Gayle have planned when she found her? Was she going to take her away from the Bakers? And exactly what role was A playing in it all?

Emily felt a presence beside her and looked up. Standing opposite Derrick, with a strange look on his face, was Isaac. "H-hey," he said cautiously. His eyes flickered to Derrick, then back to her.

"Oh!" Emily blurted a little too loudly. "Isaac! Hey!" She gestured to Derrick. "This is my friend, Derrick. Derrick, this is, uh, Isaac."

Derrick's eyes widened. *"Isaac?"* Emily remembered that one night last summer, she'd admitted Isaac's name to Derrick.

"W-we should get going," Emily said, inserting herself between the two boys. She knew Derrick wouldn't say anything, but this was just too weird.

"We should finish catching up sometime," Derrick said, patting Emily on the shoulder. "I've missed you."

"Uh huh," Emily said quickly, taking Isaac's arm and hurrying down the street. "Great to see you, Derrick! Bye!" She felt bad for ditching Derrick again, but she didn't dare turn around.

They passed a retro toy store, a bank, and an empty storefront before Isaac cleared his throat. "So who was that?"

"Derrick?" Emily chirped innocently, pushing into the ice cream shop. The bells on the door chimed cheerfully. "Oh, he's just a friend I met last summer in Philly."

Then she gazed hard at the menu board above the counter and started to ramble. "So what are you going to get? I hear the cherry vanilla is really good. Or, ooh, look! Organic rocky road!" If she kept talking, she figured, Isaac wouldn't be able to get a word in edgewise.

"Emily."

She looked up guiltily. In the bright light of the ice cream parlor, Isaac's eyes looked bluer than ever. He fiddled with a string bracelet around his wrist. "Are you sure you're all right? You seem really freaked."

"Of course I'm all right!" Emily said, knowing her voice sounded high-pitched and strange.

"Don't take this the wrong way," Isaac said, "but did that Derrick guy do something to you? It seemed like you couldn't wait to get away from him."

Emily searched his face. "Oh my God, *no.*" It was so funny that she burst out laughing. If *only* it was that simple.

The line shifted, and Emily and Isaac moved closer to the register. "I care about you, that's all. I don't want to see you get hurt."

Emily kept her gaze fixed on the chrome ice cream scoops behind the counter, her heart breaking from Isaac's kindness. She *wanted* him to care about her. "He's just an old friend I confided in a lot about Ali—that's probably what you were sensing," she said haltingly. "There's nothing weird going on. I promise."

"Are you sure?" Isaac asked, grabbing Emily's hands.

"Positive." She peered at their entwined fingers. They looked so nice together. Did the baby's hands look like a combination of theirs? Did the baby have Isaac's smile, Emily's freckles? A lump formed in her throat.

"Okay, well in that case, there was actually something I wanted to ask you about," Isaac said, looking serious.

Emily swallowed hard, suddenly worried he could read her thoughts. "Yeah?"

Isaac looked into her eyes. "Do you want to go with

me to Tom Marin's fund-raiser ball tomorrow? It sounds fun, and my dad's company isn't catering it."

"Oh!" Emily said, unable to hide her surprise. She'd intended on going to the fund-raiser alone, especially since she was only going in order to help the girls steal Gayle's phone. Bringing Isaac would be tricky. What if Gayle said something? What if she took one look at Isaac and knew, somehow, he was the father?

But Isaac was looking at her nervously, like he'd be crushed if she said no. And before she could stop herself, she blurted out, "Yes!"

"Great!" Isaac said, looking relived. "It's a date."

Emily forced a bright smile on her face. She'd never felt so many things at once. Freaked, definitely. Pleased, too—she did want to see Isaac again. But she also hated herself for everything she wasn't telling him. She was playing a very dangerous game.

It was their turn to order, and they stepped up to the counter. A motorcycle engine revved, and she glanced at the street out the window. There, across the wide avenue, backlit by the neon sign of the Hollis Liquor Store, stood someone in a black hood, staring at her. At first, she thought it might be Derrick, but this person was smaller, thinner. Emily shot away from Isaac and wound around the tables to get a closer look, but by the time she was at the glass, the figure was gone.

22

THE TOUGHEST DECISION EVER

Aria stood at the window of Ella's house in Rosewood, peering out at the dark street. She felt a hand on her shoulder and smelled Ella's familiar patchouli perfume. Her mother wore a paint-spattered artist's smock and chopsticks in her hair. She'd recently gotten inspiration for a new painting series, and between her new boyfriend, her job at an art gallery in Hollis, and her time in the studio, Aria barely saw her.

"What are you and Noel up to tonight?" she asked, perching on the paisley wing chair she and Byron had bought at a flea market a million years ago. "That's who you're waiting for, right?"

A lump formed in Aria's throat. Truthfully, she was hoping Noel wouldn't show up for their date. That way, Aria wouldn't have to break up with him.

A's note had tortured her all day, and she'd debated saying something versus keeping quiet. If she kept the secret, she'd have to end things. On the other hand, if she outed Noel's father, Noel would hate her and probably break up with her anyway. And how the hell had A found out? How did A know everything?

Aria had no doubt that A would spill Mr. Kahn's cross-dressing secret if she didn't act soon. It was bad enough that she still felt like she'd ruined her own family—she couldn't ruin Noel's, too. Only, could she really dump Noel after all they'd been through? She loved him so much.

She looked up at her mom and took a deep breath. "Do you still blame me for what happened between you and Byron?"

Ella blinked hard. "What do you mean, *still*?"

"I kept it a secret. If I would have said something to you, maybe you could have . . ."

Aria's mother sank further into the chair cushion. "Honey, your father put you in a horrible position. You should have never had to make the decision to tell or not to tell. Even if you had told me sooner, it wouldn't have changed anything in the end. It's not your fault." She laid a hand on Aria's thigh.

"I know, but you got so mad at me for not saying anything," Aria mumbled. Ella had kicked her out of the house, and she'd had to live with Sean Ackard, her then-boyfriend.

Ella cradled a knitted throw pillow between her hands. "I shouldn't have reacted like that. I was just so blindsided, and I had to lash out at someone." She looked up. "I'm sorry, too, honey. You shouldn't dwell over this. Things happen. And we're all happier and healthier now, right?"

Aria nodded, feeling a knot in her stomach. "But if we were to do it all over again, would you rather I told you sooner?"

Ella thought about this for a moment, running her finger over her bottom lip. "Maybe not," she said. "I think I needed to be in the dark, at least for a little while longer. I needed to get strong enough to know what I wanted and realize that I was capable of living on my own. Moving to Iceland, figuring out a new country, that really helped me, but it was because of your father that we went there. So, actually, Aria, if I had known earlier, I never would have gotten that experience. In a weird way, I'm glad I found out when I did."

Aria nodded, working this over in her mind. "So you're saying that if you know a secret about someone, but you also know that someone else isn't ready to hear it, you should keep it to yourself?"

"I guess it depends." Ella wrinkled her brow, looking suspicious. "Why? Do you know a secret about someone?"

"No," Aria said quickly. "I was just speaking hypothetically."

Her mom's cell phone rang, saving Aria from having to explain further. But then she peered out the window and saw Noel's Escalade parked at the curb, and her stomach clenched. Ella's advice made perfect sense, but that meant she had to break up with Noel.

Swallowing hard, she waved good-bye to Ella, zipped up her denim jacket, and stepped out the door. Her heart broke when she saw Noel's smiling face through the window. "You look gorgeous, as usual," he crooned when she opened the door.

"Thanks," Aria mumbled, even though she'd worn her ugliest jeans and a big, bulky sweater that was one of her first knitting projects. She wanted to seem as unattractive as possible to soften the blow.

"So where do you want to go?" Noel shifted into drive and pulled away from the curb. "Williams-Sonoma for cooking supplies? I hear next week we're making popovers."

Aria stared at the passing streetlamps until her vision blurred, keeping her mouth shut. She was afraid that if she said anything, she'd burst into tears.

"Okay, not in a Williams-Sonoma mood," Noel said slowly, turning the steering wheel. "What about that cool coffee bar we found in Yarmouth? Or hey, we could go back to that psychic shop by the train station. Where it all began." He nudged Aria playfully. He was referring to how they'd bonded at a séance at the shop last year.

Aria fiddled with the zipper on her jacket, wishing Noel would just be quiet.

"Last-ditch effort," Noel said cheerfully. "How about we go to Hollis and just get really drunk? Play some darts and beer pong, act like idiots . . ."

"Noel, I can't," Aria blurted.

Noel came to a stop at a light adjacent to a big strip mall. "Can't what? Drink?" He grinned. "C'mon. I saw you drink plenty in Iceland."

She winced. Iceland just twisted the knife more painfully—it was yet another secret she was keeping. "No, I can't do . . . *this.*" Her voice cracked. "Me and you. It's not working."

A frozen smile appeared on Noel's face. "Wait. What?"

"I'm serious." She stared at the glowing red clock numbers on the dashboard. "I want to break up."

The light turned green, and Noel wordlessly swerved into the other lane and turned into the strip mall. It was one of those monstrous shopping plazas that contained a Barnes & Noble superstore, a Target, a warehouse-size wine shop, and a bunch of upscale salons and jewelry boutiques.

Noel pulled into a parking space, shut off the engine, and looked at her. "*Why?*"

Aria kept her head down. "I don't know."

"You've got to have *some* reason. It's not Klaudia, is it? Because I can't stand that girl, I swear."

"It's not Klaudia."

Noel ran his hands over his forehead. "Are you into someone else? That Ezra guy?"

Aria shook her head vigorously. "Of course not."

"Then *what*? Tell me!"

There was an imploring, desperate expression on his face. It took everything in Aria's power not to throw her arms around Noel and tell him she didn't mean it, but A's note was branded in her mind. She wouldn't be responsible for wrecking his family. She needed to get as far away from Noel as possible. She was poison to him.

"I'm sorry, but it's just something I have to do," she whispered. "I'll come by tomorrow and get the stuff I left at your house." Then she reached for the door handle and swung her legs to the pavement. The cold air assaulted her senses. The aroma of brick-oven pizza wafted into her nostrils, turning her stomach.

"Aria." Noel leaned over and caught her arm. "Please. Don't go." Aria bit back tears, staring blankly at the shopping cart corral. "There's nothing more to say," she said in a dead voice. Then she jumped out of the car, slammed the door hard, and started walking blindly toward the closest store, a Babies "R" Us. Noel called her name again and again, but she kept walking, staring at her boots, breathing in and out, and making sure no cars ran her over. Finally, the Escalade's engine revved, and the SUV backed up and gunned toward the exit.

Beep.

Aria's phone sounded from the bottom of her bag. The screen was lit up as she pulled it out. A new text had come in.

Kudos, Aria. No pain, no gain, right? Mwah! —A

Aria threw her phone back in her bag, hard. *You win,*

A, she thought, blinking through tears. *You win every god-damn time.*

She was at the curb of the Babies "R" Us by now. A stroller display took up the whole window, and banners of happy, giggling babies decorated the store. Pregnant women cruised the aisles, buying baby bottles, onesies, and diapers. All the happiness she saw felt like a kick in the stomach. She felt the urge to ram a shopping cart into the window and watch the glass shatter around the blissful scene.

The automatic doors swished open, and a woman in an expensive-looking black wool coat pushed a cart full of shopping bags down the ramp. She looked just as joyful as the others, though there was something about her expression that looked a little strained. Aria squinted hard, her pulse racing.

It was Gayle. But what was she doing here? Stocking up on stuff for when she kidnapped Emily's baby?

Without breaking her stride, Gayle met Aria's gaze. Her eyebrows shot up, and she winked, seeming pleased with herself. Probably because she'd been the one who'd written the note demanding that Aria and Noel break up. Probably because she saw Aria's tear-streaked face now and understood that Aria had gone through with it.

Because she was A, and she was pulling all the strings.

23

LADIES WHO LUNCHEON

Spencer rang the bell at the Ivy House, then stepped back and examined her reflection in the glass next to the door. It was Sunday afternoon, a few minutes after Harper had told her to arrive for the potluck, and she was ready. She'd managed to blow-dry her hair with the shoddy hair dryer at the motel and had done her makeup in the cracked mirror. The iron had worked to press the wrinkles out of the dress she'd brought, and, most importantly, she was holding three pans of gooey, chocolatey pot brownies in her hands.

The door flung open, and Harper, dressed in a polka-dotted sheath and high patent-leather heels, gave her a cool smile. "Hi, Spencer. You made it."

"Yep, and I brought brownies." Spencer proffered the foil pans. "Double chocolate." *With a sprinkling of pot*, she wanted to add.

Harper looked pleased. "Brownies are perfect. C'mon in."

Spencer figured the potluck would be filled with *only* desserts—pot brownies, specifically. But when Harper led her into an enormous, state-of-the-art kitchen, complete with a huge, eight-burner Wolf oven, a massive fridge, and an island bigger than the Hastings' dining room table, there were all sorts of dishes spread out. Quinoa casseroles. Quiche. Baked ziti, steam rising from the tray. There was a large punch bowl full of reddish liquid with apple chunks floating on top. A cheese platter was piled high with Brie, Manchego, and Stilton.

She gaped at the spread. How had everyone managed to smuggle drugs into all this stuff? It had been a struggle for Spencer to simply *bake* the brownies; the oven in the motel's kitchen had been a godsend. She'd begged the guy on night desk duty to let her use it, mixing up the brownie batch in her ice bucket and crumbling in the pot at the last minute. She'd fallen asleep on the pleather couch in the lobby while they were cooking, waking up only when the buzzer went off. She had no idea if they'd be good or not, but it didn't matter—she'd done it.

Reefer's admonishing words rushed through her head. *Do you really need a stupid club to tell you that you're cool?* But he'd probably said all that disparaging stuff about Ivy because he knew he'd never get into something so prestigious. *Loser.*

"Plates and silverware are that way." Harper gestured to a table.

Spencer hovered over the food, amazed that every

single item contained an illegal substance. She didn't want to eat any of it. She muttered something about not being hungry and followed Harper into the parlor.

The room was packed with well-dressed boys in ties and khakis and girls in dresses. Classical music played in the background, and a waitress was wandering around with flutes of mimosa. Spencer overheard conversations about a composer she'd never heard of, nature versus nurture, foreign policy in Afghanistan, and vacationing on St. Barts. *This* was why she wanted to belong to Ivy—everyone spoke in such smart, informed, adult voices about sophisticated topics. Screw Reefer and his judgmental attitude.

Harper had joined Quinn and Jessie. The girls looked at Spencer with surprise, but then gave her a cautious smile and a cordial hello. Everyone sank into a leather couch and resumed their conversation about a girl named Patricia; apparently, her boyfriend had gotten her pregnant over the holiday break.

"Is she going to keep the baby?" Harper asked, forking a bite of macaroni salad.

Jessie shrugged. "I don't know. But she's terrified of telling her parents. She knows they're going to freak."

Quinn shook her head sympathetically. "Mine would, too."

It was disconcerting that the girls were talking about an issue that was so close to Spencer's heart. Looking at Emily's situation objectively, it *was* crazy that Emily had hidden her pregnancy from almost everyone she knew. It was even crazier that she'd smuggled the baby out of the hospital and left it on someone's doorstep. Even worse, A—Gayle—had figured out exactly what happened. Was Gayle going to tell? Not just about that, but about everything *else* they'd done?

She stared down at her empty plate, wishing she had something to do with her hands.

"Spencer, these are really good," Harper said, pointing to a brownie she'd cut from one of Spencer's pans. "Try."

She shoved the brownie toward Spencer's mouth, but Spencer recoiled. "That's okay."

"Why? They're amazing!"

Quinn narrowed her eyes. "Unless you're anti-sugar, too?"

The girls were all staring at her so quizzically that Spencer began to feel insecure. She wondered if it was a *requirement* to eat the food, like an Ivy rite of passage. Maybe she had no choice. "Thanks," she said, accepting a bite. Harper was right: The brownie was gooey and delicious, and Spencer couldn't even taste the baked-in pot. Her stomach rumbled in response; she hadn't eaten since last night. One little brownie wouldn't hurt, would it?

"Okay, you convinced me," Spencer said, rising from her seat to get a brownie square for herself.

When she returned, having eaten almost the whole brownie by the time she sat down again, the girls were talking about how they wanted to make a film to enter into the Princeton Student Film contest. "I want to make one about toy tops, just like Charles and Ray Eames did," Quinn said.

"I was thinking of making a movie about Bethany. Remember how I told you about her? The really fat girl who sits in front of me in Intro to Psych?" Jessie rolled her eyes. "It could be called *Girl Who Eats Donuts*."

Spencer took a bite of brownie and wished she was brave enough to tell Jessie she wasn't exactly a sylph. For some reason, the word *sylph* suddenly struck her as funny. The oversize freckles on Jessie's cheeks were kind of funny, too. Jessie looked at her strangely. "What?"

"Uh, I don't know," Spencer said, taking another nibble of the brownie. A few crumbs fell onto her lap, reminding her of gerbil poops. She started laughing again.

Harper stood, giving Spencer a *you're hopelessly weird* look. "I'm going to get another brownie. Girls, you in?"

"Grab me one," Quinn said. Jessie nodded too.

The brownies. That was why Spencer found everything so funny. She'd only smoked pot twice before, both times at parties at Noel Kahn's house, but the familiar sensations rushed back. Her pulse slowed. Her normally obsessive tendencies began to fade into the background. She leaned back and grinned at the beautiful kids around her, marveling at their brightly colored dresses and silk ties. Her eyelids felt heavy, and her limbs relaxed into the couch.

Suddenly, she roused herself. A couple was making out across the room, their hands all over each other, their tongues flailing. Another couple was kissing by the grand piano. They were so into it that they leaned on the keys, a tinkle of sounds ringing out. There was a clump of kids staring at a glass-paned china cabinet in the corner, remarking on how amazing the plate patterns were. Quinn was standing in the doorway, telling a story about how her housekeeper always said *acrossed* instead of *across* in a snotty, cleaning-people-are-*such*-lower-class-citizens voice. Jessie's eyes were glassy and red, and she was wiggling her fingernails in front of her face like they were amazing.

Spencer rubbed her eyes. How long had she been out?

"Streaker!" someone yelled, and a guy in a Princeton beanie and nothing else ran through the parlor, a half-eaten brownie in his hand. A couple of kids stripped off their clothes and followed him down the hall.

Harper appeared above Spencer and pulled her to her feet. "Let's join in, sleepyhead!"

Spencer woozily pulled her cotton dress over her head, feeling naked in her slip. They followed a string of students through the library, the dining room, and then the kitchen. There were pots and pans all over the floor in the kitchen, an upturned tray of nachos on the table, and, for some reason, a roll of toilet paper was strung around the chandelier over the prep island. Her tray of brownies was almost empty. Spencer grabbed the last square and popped it into her mouth.

When they got back to the parlor, even more kids were

making out, and a group was playing a version of Strip Twister, using the large rug in the center of the room as the board. Spencer flopped back on the couch. "Is it me, or has this party suddenly gotten really wild?" she asked Harper.

"Isn't it awesome?" Harper's eyes gleamed. "Everyone is flying high, right?"

Uh, isn't that the point? Spencer wanted to say, but Harper had already whipped around and was staring at the windows. "Hey, you know what I want to do?" she said excitedly. "Make myself a dress out of the curtains just like Scarlett O'Hara did in *Gone with the Wind*!"

She leapt onto the windowsill and ripped the curtains from the poles before anyone could stop her. Then, grabbing a letter opener from the nearby desk, she slashed the fabric into long strips. Spencer half-giggled, half-winced. Those were probably valuable antique curtains.

Quinn pulled out her cell phone. "This is amazing. It should be our film for the festival!"

"And I want us all to be the stars!" Harper said sloppily, stumbling over the syllables. She looked at Spencer. "Can you record us on your phone?"

"Okay," Spencer said. She called up the video function on her iPhone and started recording. Harper yanked down more curtains and pulled the stuffing out of the pillows on the leather couch, looking crazed.

"Yeah!" Daniel, the boy who'd hosted the party on Friday, grabbed a swath of curtain fabric and wrapped it around his naked body—he'd been part of the streaking parade—like a toga. A few other guys followed suit, and they all marched around in a circle chanting "To-*ga*! To-*ga*! To-*ga*!"

As they paraded past, Spencer caught a glimpse of a guy with longish dark hair. Was that *Phineas*? She hadn't seen him since before her run-in with the law at Penn last year. But when she blinked, he'd vanished, like he'd never been there at all. She pressed her fingers to her temples and made several slow circles. She was *so* high.

Spencer turned back to Harper. She had seemingly grown bored of ruining the curtains and was now lying on the carpet with her legs up in the air. "I just feel so . . . *alive*," she trilled. Then she eyed Spencer. "Hey. I have something to tell you. You know that guy, Raif—Reefer? He has a crush on you."

Spencer groaned. "What a loser. How'd he get into Princeton, anyway? Is he a legacy?"

Harper's eyes grew wide. "You don't know?"

"Know what?"

Harper put her fingers to her lips and giggled. "Spencer, Reefer is, like, a *genius*. Like Einstein."

Spencer snickered. "Uh, I don't think so."

"No, I'm serious." Suddenly Harper looked dead sober. "He got a full scholarship. He invented some chemical process that, like, converts plants into renewable energy really cheaply. He received a MacArthur Genius Grant."

Spencer snorted. "Um, are we talking about the same person?"

Harper's expression was still serious. Spencer leaned back on her elbows and let this sink in. Reefer was . . . smart? *Ridiculously* smart? She thought about what he said yesterday at his house. *Don't judge a book by its cover.* She started to laugh. The giggles came so fast and furious tears started to stream from her eyes and she could barely breathe.

Harper started laughing, too. "What's so funny?"

Spencer shook her head, not even sure. "I've had one too many pot brownies, I think. I'm a lightweight."

Harper frowned. "Pot brownies? Where?"

The muscles in Spencer's mouth felt gummy and loose. She studied Harper carefully, wondering if this was a hallucination, too. "I baked pot into the brownies I brought," she said in an isn't-it-obvious voice.

Harper's mouth made an *O*. "No *way*," she whispered, slapping Spencer five. "That's the best idea *ever*." She started to laugh for real. "No wonder I feel so bubbly! And here I thought someone spiked the punch with absinthe!"

Spencer laughed nervously. "Well, it's not *necessarily* my brownies, is it?" Harper had eaten all kinds of other dishes, after all. Who knew what *they* had baked into them.

When she noticed the puzzled look on Harper's face, everything turned upside-down. Maybe none of those other dishes had illegal substances inside them. What if Spencer's brownies were what was making everyone so crazy?

She looked around the room. In one corner, a girl

was feeding another girl a bite of something gooey and brownie-like. Two guys by the window chowed down on the brownies like they were their last meal. The brownies were everywhere. On plates left on side tables. In people's hands as they swigged back sips of punch. On cheeks and under fingernails and ground into the fibers of the carpet. A half-eaten tray sat on the coffee table. Another tray was balanced on the radiator. Spencer peeked into the kitchen. Her three trays of brownies were still there, the bottoms scraped clean. Had someone *else* brought brownies, or had she brought five instead of three? Her mind felt so cloudy right now she couldn't think clearly at all.

Her skin prickled. Harper seemed thrilled by the pot-brownie prank. But it was one thing if her brownies were one of many illegal foods at the party, and another for them to be the singular secret potion that made everyone act insane.

The walls felt like they were closing in on her. "I'll be back," she murmured to Harper, pushing to stand. She wove around a bunch of kids making snow angels on the carpet and two guys dueling with antique swords pulled from hooks on the wall and grabbed her coat from a pile near the kitchen. Ahead of her was a heavy door that led to the backyard; she pushed through it and stood in the crisp, late-winter air. To her surprise, only a thin strip of sunlight gleamed through the trees. Hours must have passed since she'd arrived.

Spencer stepped off the patio, taking deep breaths of

cold air. The university buildings shone on the horizon. A billboard cut through the sky, bearing a picture of a newborn baby and the words CHOOSE PRINCETON HOSPITAL FOR YOUR MOST PRECIOUS MOMENTS.

It made Spencer think of the day she'd met Emily at the hospital for her C-section. By the time she got there, still flummoxed by Emily's news, Aria and Hanna were standing by her side. Spencer's jaw had dropped at the sight of Emily's swollen belly. Her heart had picked up speed when she saw the shadowy image of the baby on the fetal monitor screen next to Emily's bed. This was *real*.

"Emily?" a nurse had said, popping her head into the room. "They're ready for you. It's time to have your baby."

There was no question whether Spencer and the others would be there for Emily's surgery. They dressed in blue scrubs and followed the gurney into an operating room. Emily was freaking out, but the three of them held her hands the whole time, telling her she was strong and amazing. Spencer didn't have the guts to peek over the curtain to watch as the OB cut through Emily's midsection, but within minutes, he let out a happy whoop. "A healthy baby girl!"

The doctor lifted a tiny, perfect creature over the partition. She had red, wrinkled skin, tiny, closed eyes, and a big screaming mouth. Tears welled in all of their eyes. It was amazing and sad, all at the same time. They squeezed Emily's hands hard, so grateful they'd been able to share this with her.

206 ♦ SARA SHEPARD

Luckily, the baby didn't need to be in the NICU, which meant the girls could follow through with their plans of sneaking mother and baby out of the hospital that very night. At midnight, when there was a nurse shift change, the girls helped Emily out of bed and into her clothes. They dressed the baby as quietly as they could and tiptoed out of Emily's room. The maternity ward was silent and still. Nurses were tending to newborns in the nursery. When a doctor rounded the corner, Spencer distracted her by asking for directions to the cafeteria. The others spirited Emily and baby into the elevator. Once they were on the main floor, no one looked at them twice.

They crept to the parking garage, the lights of Philadelphia blazing all around them. But as they were getting into Aria's car, a flutter of activity behind one of the concrete beams caught Spencer's eye. Nerves streaked through her belly. Was checking a baby out of the hospital before it was discharged illegal? She stood very still for a few moments, waiting for whomever it was to reveal herself, but no one did. She figured she was just tired, although now she wasn't sure. Maybe A had been there. Maybe A had seen everything.

Snap.

Spencer returned to the present with a start. Dark trees surrounded her. Branches scratched her skin. The bark on the trees spiraled psychedelically; the stars were huge and garish in the sky, like a Van Gogh painting. What the hell was in this pot, anyway?

There was a whooshing sound of someone crunching through leaves. Spencer rubbed her eyes. "Hello? Who's there?"

No answer. The crunching sounds grew louder and louder. Spencer blinked, searching for the path back to the Ivy House, but her vision was distorted and blurred. "Hello?" she cried again.

A hand clapped on her shoulder, and she screamed. She flailed her arms, trying to see who it was, but her senses were too muddled, the night too dark. Her legs gave out from under her, and she felt herself falling, falling, falling. The last thing she remembered seeing was a dark shape standing next to her, glaring. Maybe wanting to hurt her. Maybe wanting to get rid of her forever.

And then everything went black.

24

HANNA BRINGS HER A GAME

Hanna knew she was supposed to be in the stretch limo with her father, Isabel, and Kate, heading to the fund-raising ball, not balanced on her four-inch Louboutin platform heels outside the familiar Victorian house in Old Hollis that was home to Jeffrey Lebrecque's photo studio. But here she was, like it or not. Ready to nail Colleen once and for all.

The porch light was on, throwing golden light onto Hanna's professionally made-up face. The front parlor window was all lit up, too, which meant the photographer was home. Just before Hanna climbed the steps, her phone chimed. It was Richard, one of her dad's campaign assistants. *Just wanted to let you know the voter registration records database is back up*, he wrote.

Perfect, Hanna replied. That meant she could search for where the Bakers had moved. The site had been down, and she'd had to resort to asking Richard about it, but she didn't dare ask him to look up the family himself.

Then, rolling her shoulders back, she rang the bell. There were footsteps, and the door creaked open and the same graying man she'd seen the day before answered.

"Hello?" Jeffrey Lebrecque looked Hanna up and down, from the big ringlets in her hair to her navy chiffon dress to the faux-mink shrug around her shoulders she'd picked out for the ball. There was a gaudy gold ring on his pinkie finger, and he had the top two buttons of his shirt unbuttoned, exposing quite a bit of chest hair. *Ick.*

"Hi!" Hanna said brightly. "Are you Mr. Lebrecque?"

"That's right." The man furrowed his brow. "Do we have an appointment?"

"Actually, I'm here to pick up photos for Colleen Bebris," Hanna said in her most innocent voice, batting her eyelashes at him. "I'm her best friend, and she asked me to do it. She got held up at an exercise class. She's a pole dancer, did you know that?"

The photographer frowned. "I'm not sure I can do that. Ms. Bebris didn't say someone else was going to pick them up. Maybe I should call her." He reached into his shirt pocket and pulled out a cell phone.

"No need!" Hanna said quickly, whipping out her own phone and showing him a text on the screen. "See?" The sender was Colleen Bebris, and the text asked if Hanna could pick up her photos. Of course it wasn't *really* from Colleen—Hanna just used her mom's phone to send the

text, temporarily changing her mom's contact information to Colleen's name.

Jeffrey Lebrecque read the text, and his caterpillar-
esque eyebrows knitted together. "There's also the matter
of payment."

"Oh, she told me to pay for it and then she'd pay me
back," Hanna piped up, proud she'd thought to raid her
emergency cash shoebox before coming.

The photographer peered at Hanna, and for a moment,
she was afraid he was going to call her bluff. Did Mona-
as-A and Real Ali-as-A worry they were going to get caught
when they skulked, stole, and lied to get top-secret information on Hanna and the others? Was it wrong of her
to do this? It wasn't like she was ruining Colleen's life,
though. All she wanted was her boyfriend back.

"Follow me," Mr. Lebrecque said, turning and heading down the hallway and into his studio. Slides and
printouts covered a work desk, and a large-screen Apple
monitor glowed in the corner. A fluffy white cat padded
lazily through the room, and a calico preened itself on the
windowsill. The place smelled like a mix of dust and cat
litter and seemed sketchy in a way Hanna couldn't quite
put her finger on. She hunted around for telltale signs
that this guy was running a covert Internet-porn operation, though she wasn't entirely sure what she should be
looking for. *Playboy* magazines? Blackout shades? Bottles
of Cristal, like they drank in hip-hop videos?

Mr. Lebrecque shuffled to a table at the back of the

room, sorted through a pile of envelopes, and pulled one out. "I picked these up from the printer today. Tell Colleen that I printed all of them, just like she asked, but if she wants more copies it'll cost her extra." He punched some numbers into a calculator. "So . . . that'll be $450."

Hanna gritted her teeth. Couldn't Colleen have chosen a slightly cheaper photographer? Begrudgingly, she traded the cash for the envelope of photos and bid the photographer good-bye, scurrying out of the apartment as fast as she could. Her eyes were starting to itch from all that cat hair.

Her phone chirped when she stepped onto the porch, but it was just her father—he, Isabel, and Kate were at the event space, and he was wondering where Hanna was. *Be there soon*, Hanna typed back before slipping her phone into her bag and excitedly ripping open the envelope. She wondered if the various As had sometimes felt like this, too, when they'd gotten their hands on valuable evidence. There *was* something satisfying about it.

She stared at the stack of photos under the street lamp. The first was of Colleen looking fresh-faced and oh-so-sweet, like an actress on a Disney Channel show. The next shots were pretty much the same, just with slightly different facial expressions and camera angles. Hanna flipped through the stack, gazing at Colleen looking elated, then brooding, then bookish. Before she knew it, Hanna was looking at the last photo, a shot of Colleen winking at the camera from over her shoulder. She riffled through them once more just to make sure she hadn't missed any, but she hadn't.

They were exactly the same shots she'd seen from the window the day before. Nothing from a previous photo session, nothing she'd missed. They were all perfectly kosher and professional, and worse, Colleen looked really amazing in a lot of them, far more photogenic than Hanna was. Hanna kicked the streetlamp post. Why the hell had A told her to follow this stupid lead? Just to mess with her? For her to lose some cash? She should have known A was going to screw her over, not help her.

Someone coughed across the street, and Hanna shot up. It was only a college-age couple walking hand-in-hand down the sidewalk, but she felt nervous all the same. She tottered to her Prius, her ankles already aching, wrenched the car door open, and tossed the envelope inside so hard that it careened off the door and landed in the footwell. Groaning, she slid into the driver's seat and reached for it, but she grabbed the wrong end and all of the pictures spilled out onto the carpet.

"Damn it." Hanna leaned over and shoved the photos back into the slightly-too-small envelope once more. Her fingers grazed something behind the last photo. It didn't feel glossy, like the photos, but more like a piece of computer paper.

She pulled the paper from the envelope and held it to the light. *Colleen Evelina Bebris*, it said at the top in plain font, listing her address, e-mail, Twitter name, and blog.

Below that was what looked like a list. *Dramatic experience*, it said in bold. There were descriptions of the various school plays Colleen had been in, culminating with her part in *Macbeth* last week. It was a resume, presumably for when Colleen went on auditions. *Boring.*

Then, something at the bottom caught her eye. *Commercial experience*, a heading said. There was only one entry below it. *Visiem Labak, Latvia*, it said. *Starring role in Latvian commercial for an important dietary supplement.* According to the resume, the commercial had run last year on the most popular Latvian TV station.

Rifling through her bag, Hanna grabbed her phone and punched *Visiem Labak* into Google. *All better*, a translation came up. A bunch of what she could only assume were Latvian websites also popped on the screen, and a few showed a smiling person eating yogurt. A YouTube link appeared at the bottom of the first search page. *Visiem Labak Commercial*, it said. There was a still shot of Colleen's face.

Hanna clicked the link. The commercial started with three girls sitting around a table at a café, drinking coffee and laughing. The camera then focused on Colleen, who rattled off something in a language Hanna couldn't even begin to decipher, then clutched her stomach miserably. The other girls handed her a cup of yogurt, which Colleen began to eat with gusto. Next Colleen shut herself in the coffee bar's bathroom, putting up a sign that surely said OCCUPIED in Latvian. Happy music played, there was a voice-over in Latvian, and Colleen emerged from the bathroom looking victorious. She held up a pot of the yogurt and grinned maniacally. The commercial ended with another shot of the yogurt.

"Oh. My. *God*," Hanna whispered. This was just like those stupid commercials where Jamie Lee Curtis pimped out Activia to bloated, constipated women. And here Colleen was, playing the Latvian girl who needed a yogurt laxative to get her regular again. No *wonder* she hadn't bragged about it. Hanna guessed she hadn't told anyone.

"*Yes*," she whispered, placing the resume and envelope into the glove compartment. After all this went down, she'd charge Colleen for the pictures, if she still wanted them. It wasn't like Hanna needed them anymore. Those pictures didn't tell a story. But a certain video did.

25

SECRETS, OPEN AND CLOSED

As dusk was falling, Aria pulled into the circular driveway at Noel's house and shut off the engine. The house was dark, with only one of the porch lights lit. She checked the text on her phone again. *Come at six*, Noel had said—and it was six on the dot.

She stepped out of the car and walked toward the door, careful not to trip in her high heels. She was going to Mr. Marin's fund-raising ball after this, an event she and Noel were supposed to attend together. Obviously, that was off. Aria wasn't sure if Noel was planning to go anyway. A lot of kids from Rosewood Day would be there, after all.

Footsteps sounded from inside after she rang the bell. Noel opened the door quietly, not looking her in the eye. Aria almost gasped at his appearance. His face was puffy and red, his eyes bloodshot. His hair looked like it hadn't been washed that morning, and he had the exhausted, heavy-lidded look of someone who hadn't slept.

"I got your stuff together," Noel said woodenly, turning and heading toward the den. Aria followed. The house was unusually quiet and still, with no TVs blaring or music playing or Patrice humming jovially in the kitchen.

"Where is everyone?" she asked.

Noel sniffed, walking stiffly to a cardboard box that was sitting on the couch. "My mom went to that fundraiser. My dad's . . . somewhere." He eyed her. "Why do you care, anyway?"

Aria flinched. It was weird to see Noel angry, especially at her. "I was just making conversation," she said sheepishly. She grabbed the box and hefted it into her arms. "I'll go, okay?"

"That's probably a good idea," Noel growled.

But then he awkwardly swallowed. Aria turned around and met his gaze. She stared at him for a long moment, trying to convey that breaking up was the only way she could make things right.

Noel looked away. "I'll walk you out," he said, heading downstairs. He held the door open for her, and Aria mumbled good-bye and scuttled out. As she stepped off the porch, the box slipped from her grasp and spilled onto the brick path. She scrambled to pick up the spilled CDs, books, and T-shirts, and then felt a hand on her arm.

"Here." Noel leaned down, his voice softening. "I'll get that."

Aria allowed him to gather up her things and load them back into the box. When she stood up, she saw something move at the back of the Kahns' property. Someone was skulking around by the guest house. At first, she feared it was A, but then a spotlight beamed down on the figure's tall blond hairdo, frilly dress, and clunky heels.

The figure turned in the light, revealing her face. Aria tensed. It wasn't Mrs. Kahn . . . it was Noel's father. In drag. At *home*.

Aria gasped before she could stop herself and, as if in slow motion, watched Noel's head turn in the direction she was looking. "No!" she shouted, throwing herself in front of Noel to obstruct his view.

"What are you doing?" Noel asked.

"Um, I was . . ." Aria peeked over her shoulder. Mr. Kahn was gone. "I, um, thought I saw a bat swoop for your head."

Noel stared at her like she was nuts. A long, tense few seconds passed. Shrugging, he helped put Aria's stuff in the back of her car, then turned toward the house. At the same time, the front door creaked open. Mr. Kahn had gotten through the house and to the front door, and now he stood on the porch in his lipstick and dress. He gawked at Noel, then Aria. The blood drained from his face.

"D-Dad," Noel stammered.

"Oh," he croaked, his voice gruff and deep. "I-I thought no one was home."

Mr. Kahn did an about-face and marched back into the house. Aria covered her face in her hands. But surprisingly, Noel was making no noise at all. No gasps, no violent freak-outs, *nothing*. She peeked at him through her fingers. Instead of staring at the front door, which Mr. Kahn had just gone through, he was gaping at her.

"You blocked my way," he said. "You were trying to stop me from seeing my dad, weren't you?"

Aria shifted her weight. "Well, yeah."

Noel studied her for a long time. His eyes widened. "You *knew*, didn't you? Before just now, I mean. You knew about how my dad dresses like . . . *that*. And you thought I *didn't* know. You were keeping it from me."

Aria felt heat creep to her cheeks. "It wasn't like that!" she cried. Then she stepped back. "Wait. *You* knew?"

"Well, yeah. I've known for years." Noel's eyes blazed. "How long have *you* known?"

Aria's chin wobbled. "Only a few days. I saw your dad at Fresh Fields last week. I was afraid to tell you."

"So you decided to break up with me instead?" Noel's mouth was tight, and his eyes were wild. "Or was there some *other* mysterious reason why you did that?"

"Of course not!" Aria protested. "Please calm down! We can talk about this, can't we?"

Suddenly, she was filled with hope. Maybe there was a silver lining to this. If Noel already knew about his dad, if this wasn't some big, ruinous, earth-shattering revelation, A had nothing on her. It was just a bluff. "I've changed my mind. I was confused. I want to stay together."

Noel barked out a cold, sinister laugh, the likes of which Aria had never heard before. "That train has left the station. I knew something was on your mind, Aria. I asked you a million times about it, and you told me you were fine. Just days ago I begged you to be honest with me about everything, and instead you lie?"

"You lied, too!" Aria said, grasping at straws. "You never told me that your dad . . . *you* know!"

Noel's eyes narrowed, as though he didn't particularly like this shift of gears. "You never asked me. And, for the record, I was *going* to tell you. I just didn't want to do it when we were at my house, and lately you've seemed so distracted, and . . ." He trailed off, his mouth dropping open. "Do you think it's *weird*? Is *that* why you broke up with me?"

"Noel, no!" Aria cried, grabbing for his hands.

Noel wrenched away from her, a horrible twist of anger on his face. "And here I thought you were open-minded." He spun around and went back inside, slamming the door so hard the house shook. A dreadful silence followed.

Aria stared at her shaking hands, questioning if what had just happened was real. She waited for Noel to come back, but he didn't. How had this happened? She thought she'd done the right thing, when she'd just made things a million times worse.

And then it hit her: Maybe A had *meant* for things to play out this way. Maybe A had known that Mr. Kahn's cross-dressing was an open secret all along but led her to believe it would destroy Noel's family. After all, the only thing that was worse than A ruining a relationship was Aria sabotaging it all on her own.

26

OD-NO SHE DIDN'T

"Spencer. Psst! Spencer!"

Spencer opened her eyes. She was lying on a small cot in the middle of a room that smelled pungently of anti-septic. Her limbs felt welded to the mattress, and she was certain someone had stuffed a torch down her throat. As her vision cleared, she saw a pretty girl with blond hair and big eyes standing at the foot of the bed. She was wearing a familiar yellow dress and had a knowing smile on her face.

Spencer shot up, recognizing her instantly. *"Tabitha?"*

Tabitha spread out her arms. "Nice to see you again. How are you feeling?"

Spencer touched her forehead. It felt wet, as though covered in sweat—or blood. "Not great. Where am I?"

Tabitha giggled. "Don't you remember what happened?"

Spencer tried to think, but her mind was a deep, black hole. "I don't remember anything."

Tabitha's heels rang out on the cold, hard floor as she stepped closer to Spencer. Her skin smelled like the same vanilla soap Ali used to use. "You're here because of what you did," she whispered, her breath hot on Spencer's face. "What *all* of you did. She told me you'd pay for this, and she was right."

"What do you mean, *she*? Who?"

Tabitha pretended to zip her lips and throw away the key. "I swore I wouldn't tell."

"What happened to me?" Spencer tried to move her legs under the covers, but they were strapped down with thick leather belts. "Where am I?"

Tabitha rolled her eyes. "Do I have to spell everything out for you? I thought you were smart. You got into Princeton, after all. Not that you'll be going there now."

Spencer's eyes widened. "W-why not?"

Tabitha's smile was crooked and strange. "Because you're *dead*." And then she leaned over and touched Spencer's eyes, as if to close them. "Say good-bye!"

Spencer shrieked and fought to keep her eyes open, kicking against the leather restraints. When she opened her eyes again, she was in a different room. The walls were green, not pink. An IV pole and a bunch of whirring machines stood next to her bed, measuring her blood pressure and pulse. Just within reach was a small tray table containing a yellow plastic pitcher, her cell phone, and three round white pills. When Spencer looked at the cotton gown she was wearing, it was printed with the words PROPERTY OF PRINCETON GENERAL HOSPITAL.

Tabitha's voice reverberated in Spencer's mind. *It's because of what you did. What* all *of you did. She told me you'd pay for this, and she was right.* Was Tabitha talking about Gayle? But how did she and Gayle know each other? Or did she mean Real Ali?

More importantly, what the hell was she doing in a hospital? All she remembered was wandering to Ivy's backyard and hearing something in the woods. There had been footsteps . . . someone had grabbed her . . . and then what?

Her monitor chirped. As if on cue, a nurse wearing blue scrubs and a terry-cloth headband entered the room. "Ah, you're up." The nurse looked at the machines, then shone a light in Spencer's eyes. "Your name's Spencer Hastings, right? Your driver's license says you're from Pennsylvania. Do you know what day it is?"

Spencer blinked. Everything was moving too quickly. "Um, Sunday?"

"That's right." The nurse wrote something down on the clipboard she was holding.

"W-what happened to me?" Spencer squeaked.

The nurse placed a blood pressure cuff on Spencer's arm. "You overdosed on a dangerous mix of drugs. We had to pump your stomach about an hour ago."

"What?" Spencer sat up in bed. "That's impossible!"

The nurse sighed. "Well, your blood tested positive for marijuana, Ritalin, and LSD. The tox screen for the twenty-six other kids at the same party also tested positive for those substances, but they keep telling me they didn't do any drugs, either." She rolled her eyes. "I wish one of you would have just admitted it when we brought you in. It would've made our lives a lot easier."

Spencer licked her lips, which were so dry they hurt. More people from the party were here? "Is everyone okay?"

"Everyone's fine, but you all had a serious scare." The nurse wrote something down on her clipboard, then patted Spencer's leg. "You rest now, okay? Your body has been through a lot."

The door clicked closed, and Spencer was alone once more. She shifted around in the bed, making sure her legs weren't strapped to the bed like they were in her dream. How did all of those other drugs get into her system? Not just hers, but twenty-six other kids, as well?

Spencer closed her eyes and thought of the bizarre debauchery that had taken place at the potluck. How so many kids had paired up and disappeared upstairs. Straight-A students had stripped off their clothes and run naked through the house. Harper had started to trash the place, and others had followed. Even Spencer had done things she wouldn't normally do. The whole experience was so . . . unhinged. Bizarre.

"Oh my God," Spencer blurted, a crack suddenly

opening in her brain. Could it have been because of the brownies? They were the only thing she'd eaten. She pictured Reefer proffering her an enormous clump of pot, claiming it was really mellow and perfect for baking. He'd smiled at her, as though completely guileless and honest, then said all that stuff about Ivy. Maybe this was his idea of civil disobedience. He was sticking it to those old-fart-y institutions for being so staid, boring, and exclusionary.

Spencer twisted her body to reach the cell phone on the little table and dialed Reefer's phone number. It rang a few times, and then Reefer picked up, letting out a cautious hello.

"You almost killed us," she growled.

"Um, excuse me?" Reefer said.

"We're all in the hospital because of you! Do you really hate Ivy that much?"

There was a pause on the line. "What are you talking about?" Reefer sounded confused.

"I'm talking about the LSD and Ritalin that was in your *mellow* pot," Spencer said through her teeth, noting that her pulse on the monitor was rising. "You spiked it to screw with us, right?"

"Whoa, whoa, whoa!" Reefer interrupted. "I don't *do* that stuff. And I certainly wouldn't lace it into my pot. I gave you the tamest thing I had, Spencer. I swear."

Spencer frowned. Reefer sounded blindsided by the accusation. Was he telling the truth? Could someone else have tampered with the brownies? The food at the party was out in plain sight, though—it would have been difficult for someone to stealthily sprinkle various poisons into the brownie dish. And Spencer hadn't let the pot or the brownies out of her sight since she'd baked them the night before.

She widened her eyes. Actually, she *had* let them out of her sight—she'd fallen asleep while they were baking. Was it possible someone could have crept into the motel at that very moment and sabotaged her dish? There had also been more pans at the party than she remembered bringing—were some of the brownies smuggled in and passed off as hers?

"Spencer?" Reefer's voice came through the line.

"Uh, I'll call you back," Spencer croaked, then hung up. Suddenly, it was so cold in the room that her skin broke out in goose bumps.

Her cell phone, which she was still holding, let out a bloop. She looked at the screen. Her vital signs on the monitor spiked again. *New message from Anonymous.*

Talk about a bad trip, huh? That's what you get for leaving your potluck goodies unattended. —A

27

STALKER FILES

"Are you *sure* there isn't anything we can do to help?" Hanna asked her father as he restraightened his tie in the lobby of the Hollis Gemological Museum, the site of the fund-raiser ball. It was a huge, beautiful space with marble floors, mosaic-tiled walls, and tons of display cases full of priceless diamonds, rubies, sapphires, emeralds, meteorites, and geodes. The place was immaculate and gorgeous, with white linens on the two dozen tables set up around the room, massive bouquets of flowers everywhere, and a silent auction area featuring a Fabergé egg, a vintage Louis Vuitton sable coat, and a three-month-long sailboat charter around the world.

"Yes, Tom, *please* let us do something." Kate, dressed in an aubergine gown and black velvet strappy heels, began preening in front of the mirror, too.

Mr. Marin smiled at the girls. "You two have done so much." He thought for a moment, then raised one finger.

"You *could* show Ms. Riggs a good time. You used to come to this museum all the time, didn't you, Hanna? You could point out the displays."

Hanna bit back a grimace. It was true she used to go to the museum with Ali in sixth grade, but playing tour guide with Gayle was just about the last thing she wanted to do. But it would give her an opening to steal Gayle's phone and prove she was A. Now, there was even more of a reason to do so: Spencer had called on the way over, telling Hanna she was in the hospital—A had drugged her and a bunch of kids at Princeton, and if they could prove A was Gayle and that Gayle definitely spiked the brownies, they could put her away for a long time.

"So she's coming?" Hanna tried to sound nonchalant.

"Of course." Mr. Marin checked his Rolex. "Actually, I'm surprised she's not here yet. I know she wants to talk to you, Hanna, before the festivities begin."

"A-about what?" Hanna croaked. The idea of alone time with Gayle sounded terrifying.

"I was surprised, too." Mr. Marin raised an eyebrow. "One of her charities is helping get teenagers involved in community activities. She said something about how she's really impressed by your involvement in the campaign—especially organizing that flash mob. I think she wants to pick your brain."

Hanna's stomach churned. She was sure picking her brain wasn't all Gayle wanted to do. She'd met Liam at the flash mob, and A—Gayle—knew that.

She threw back her shoulders, took a deep breath, and glanced at her phone again. *Plan of attack*, Aria had written in an e-mail to her and Emily. *Hanna, you distract Gayle by talking about the campaign. If that doesn't work, Emily, you walk by and look Gayle straight in the eye. When she's not paying attention, I'll sneak up and grab her phone. We rendezvous at my car, check her messages, and download everything to our phones.*

Hanna could only hope it was that easy.

The doors swung open, and people began to arrive. Hanna glued her I'm-a-politician's-daughter smile on her face and greeted the VIPs. Rupert Millington, who was always in the society pages because his great-grandparents once owned half of Rosewood, walked over and shook Mr. Marin's hand. Fletch Huxley, Rosewood's mayor, gave Hanna a kiss on the cheek. A bunch of ladies from local charities and horse-riding clubs air kissed and fake hugged. She looked around for Gayle, but she still hadn't arrived. Neither Aria nor Emily had, either. Then, gliding through the double doors like royalty, was a familiar black-haired boy in a fitted tuxedo and a girl in an annoyingly pretty pink bebe dress that didn't look slutty in the slightest. It was Mike and Colleen, deep in conversation.

Hanna's heart started to pound. There was something else she had to do tonight. She ducked behind a column to listen in.

"I don't know what could have happened to those pictures," Colleen was saying. "The photographer said someone picked them up for me, but that's impossible!"

Hanna bit the inside of her cheek. She really didn't want to own up to the fact that she'd stolen Colleen's photos. Maybe she could just send them back anonymously and chalk up the money she'd paid for them as the price she had to pay for getting Mike back.

On cue, Mike turned his head and noticed Hanna behind the column. Hanna looked away, but then Colleen saw her, too, and she let out a happy squeal. "Kiss kiss!" she said ecstatically, running over and kissing Hanna on both cheeks before Hanna could stop her. "This is *so* amazing. Thank you so much for inviting me!"

Hanna sniffed. "I *didn't* invite you," she said, the words like bile in her mouth.

Colleen's face fell. Mike gave Hanna a withering look, then shrugged and drifted over to a bunch of guys on the soccer team, who'd no doubt spiked their ginger ales with vodka from someone's flask.

Colleen watched Mike go, then turned back to Hanna. Her eyes widened slightly. "Uh, Hanna?" She leaned forward. "You have something stuck to your shoe."

Hanna's head shot down. A long piece of toilet paper was affixed to her back heel. Heat shot through her body. How long had it been there? Had she really greeted the mayor of Rosewood like this? Had Mike seen it?

Hanna bent down and pulled the piece, which was disgustingly soggy, off her foot. When she looked up again, Colleen had joined Mike at a table with his friends. She felt more infuriated than ever.

As the room filled and the volume swelled, Hanna ducked down a hallway that featured carved banded agate from Brazil and reached for her phone. She pulled up the yogurt commercial and watched it once more, smirking at Colleen's constipated face. *Priceless.* Then she copied and pasted the link into a new text and selected everyone in her Rosewood Day address book as the recipients.

Once that was finished, Hanna's finger hovered over the SEND button. She looked into the room, watching as the band set up and partygoers schmoozed. Colleen and Mike were sitting at a table with Mike's lacrosse buddies. Mike was deep in conversation with the goalie, who Hanna always called Frankenstein because of his square head. Colleen was sitting next to him, sipping her sparkling water and looking a little lost. *The perfect little actress doesn't know how to socialize*, she thought with satisfaction. *I guess insta-popularity is a little harder than it looks, huh?*

But suddenly, Colleen's fish-out-of-water expression sparked a memory. Hanna saw herself and Mona sitting at the best table in the cafeteria. Colleen came up and asked if she could join them, and both of them laughed. "We don't sit with girls who wear Hobbit shoes," Mona said, pointing to the square-toed Mary Janes on Colleen's feet. And Hanna crooned, "The *cir*-cle of life," because Colleen had carried a *Lion King* lunch bag to school until eighth grade.

For a split second, the hurt was obvious on her face, but then she shrugged and chirped, "Okay! Well, have a fun lunch, guys!" Mona and Hanna had collapsed into giggles when she walked away.

The thing was, not that long before that, Hanna had laughed at Mona when she was in Ali's clique. And not long before *that*, Real Ali had laughed at Hanna. At the way her rolls of fat spilled over her jeans. At how she couldn't do a cartwheel in gym. Hanna remembered how humiliated and ashamed she'd felt. And yet, when it was her turn to wear the Queen Bee crown, she'd teased people so effortlessly, like she'd never been on the other side.

Popularity had turned Ali, Mona, and Hanna into remorseless bitches. It hadn't affected Colleen at all, though—even dating Mike, she'd remained exactly the same girl as before. And now Hanna was being tormented by the worst popular bitch of all—A. Did Hanna really want to do that to someone else?

Her phone suddenly beeped, shrill and loud in the quiet hall. A new text envelope appeared on the screen. Frowning, Hanna exited out of the text she was planning to write and opened the new one. The sender was a series of jumbled letters and numbers.

C'mon, Hanna. Send that video. You know you want to.

Hanna's stomach felt like it was on fire. *Did* she want to? She missed Mike desperately. She wanted him to be *her* date here, not Colleen's, and for them to go on runs and sneak into the movies and play hours and hours of *Gran Turismo* like they used to. But could she live with herself if the only way she accomplished that was to send around the video? It reminded her of the way she felt when she wore a pair of shoes or a bracelet she had shop-lifted: It was amazing to have a Tiffany toggle around her wrist, but something about it made her feel a little dirty, too. Colleen might have been annoying, but she didn't deserve her own personal A.

Hanna returned to the text with the video link, took a deep breath, and pressed DELETE. Doing so felt cleansing. Almost . . . *good*. Like she'd beaten A at A's game.

A high-pitched giggle swirled from one of the corners, and she whipped around. Footsteps rang out behind her. Suddenly, Naomi Zeigler and Riley Wolfe sauntered up to Hanna, their phones in their hands.

"You've outdone yourself this time, Hanna," Naomi snickered.

"Nice one," Riley added, pushing a lock of bright-red hair behind her ear.

"What are you talking about?" Hanna snapped.

"That video." Naomi waved her phone back and forth. "It's priceless."

Hanna's stomach plummeted to her feet. *Video?* Did Naomi mean what she thought? But Hanna had deleted the text! Had A sent it out anyway and just *said* it was from Hanna? "It wasn't me," she blurted.

Riley gave her a crazy look. "Uh, this sure as hell *looks* like you."

She shoved her cell phone in Hanna's face. Hanna stared at it, fully expecting to see Colleen in the Latvian yogurt commercial, but her own image popped up instead. The first part of the video was Hanna at the pole dancing class. Her skimpy top rode up and her shorts rode down, showing off a strip of her lacy underwear. Her hips looked huge as she did circles and rolls, and when she tried to climb that pole she looked like a deranged monkey. The camera caught an unfortunate shot of her crotch as she tumbled to the ground.

"What?" Hanna whispered.

The video kept going. The next part showed Hanna skulking through the bushes at the King James Mall, staring into Victoria's Secret with binoculars. The camo made her skin look red and blotchy and her waist so much bigger than it really was. And when she emerged from the bushes, she had a couple of leaves on her butt. The camera zoomed in on them as she followed Mike and Colleen down the concourse.

Hanna peered at the girls, her heart thudding faster. "I don't understand."

"Doing some spying, were you, Hanna?" Naomi giggled.

The video continued. Next was a clip of Colleen walking into the photographer's studio, Hanna sneaking up behind her, looking desperate and ridiculous. And then it showed Hanna just a few hours before, retrieving Colleen's photos, looking through them angrily, and tossing them into her glove box. The final frame was a message in bold, red type. *Hanna Marin, desperate stalker!*

"Oh my God." Hanna's stomach sank.

Naomi snickered. "I always thought you were a loser for going out with a younger guy, but spying on him after he dumps you? That's a new low, even for you. And now everyone knows."

"Everyone?" Hanna croaked.

She stared into the ballroom and got her answer. A bunch of Rosewood Day kids gaped at their phones, then raised their heads en masse and gawked at Hanna. "Looking hot in camo, Hanna!" Seth Cardiff said. "Hey, Mike, you've got a secret admirer!" Mason Byers chuckled.

Mike. Hanna found him and Colleen near the window, staring at his phone. Hanna could pinpoint the exact moment when Colleen got to the part in the video where Hanna stole her photos. She covered her mouth with her hand and then turned to Hanna with a betrayed look on her face. Mike's head shot up and he stared at her, too, his eyes burning. Colleen turned and fled into the lobby. Mike followed.

Hanna took a few crooked steps backward, almost tripping over a long curtain that separated the main room from a little hallway. How had this happened? Who had been following her around? Who had sent that video to everyone?

Of course: A. *This* was A's reason for encouraging her to spy on Colleen: to throw it back in her face and make sure she lost Mike for good.

28

TIME IS RUNNING OUT

"They went all out, huh?" Isaac said as he and Emily walked into the Hollis Gemological Museum.

"Seriously," Emily whispered, looking around. She'd never been to a political fund-raiser ball before, but this one was amazing—*way* better than prom. Tons of white balloons hugged the arched ceiling. A live band was playing a jazzy song, and a few couples in tuxedos and gowns were slow dancing. Emily had never seen so many diamonds—and she wasn't talking just about the ones under glass. A jewel thief would have a field day just slipping rings off rich women's fingers at this party.

Ali had brought Emily, Spencer, Hanna, and Aria to this place. They had sometimes spent whole afternoons at the museum, fantasizing about what it must be like to wear enormous diamonds to fancy parties. "When I'm older, I'm going to have an engagement ring as enormous as that one," Ali said, pointing to the ten-carat stone on display. "No one's going to stop me." Emily wondered if she meant *Real* Ali. She'd probably assumed she'd keep her twin's charmed life forever.

"This place is gorgeous," Emily murmured.

"But *you're* the most gorgeous thing here," Isaac said, squeezing Emily's hand.

Emily gave Isaac a wobbly smile, trying to admire his handsome tuxedo, brushed-back hair, and shiny shoes. But she couldn't really enjoy being here. The black maxi dress with beading at the bodice felt binding around her ribs, and her feet wobbled in the high heels she'd found in the back of her closet. She'd practically drawn a messy red line across her face while applying her lipstick, her hands were shaking so hard.

The idea of coming face-to-face with Gayle terrified her. Gayle would tell everyone about her pregnancy . . . and then Isaac would know. He'd ask why they'd hung out three times now and Emily hadn't said anything. He would hate her, and he'd tell his mom, her parents, everyone.

She knew that going to the gala was part of the plan to get Gayle's cell phone and determine whether she was A, but as soon as Isaac had shown up at Emily's door, she'd felt like this was a huge mistake. But if she bolted, Isaac would ask questions she didn't know how to answer.

She scanned the crowd, looking for her friends—it was important that Aria and Hanna were here, too, otherwise the plan wouldn't work. A bunch of kids were laughing at something on their phones. Mason Byers and Lanie Iler were giggling over a plate of pasta. Sean Ackard was talking animatedly to Nanette Ulster from the Quaker school. A tall blonde in an expensive-looking red gown emerged from the bathroom. Emily stiffened, suddenly alert. *Gayle?*

She grabbed Isaac's tuxedo sleeve and ushered him back into the lobby. They stopped under a giant piece of rose quartz that was suspended from the ceiling, and Emily caught her breath. As much as she'd prepared for this moment, actually being faced with the possibility terrified her.

"What's going on?" Isaac asked, confused.

"Um, I just wanted to . . ." Emily peered at the woman in red again—she accepted a cocktail from a passing waiter and turned toward them. Her face was lined, and her nose was thin and pointy, not small and round like Gayle's. *Oops.*

Of course, that might mean Gayle was walking through the front entrance at this very moment—and they would be the first thing she saw. "I changed my mind. Let's go dance." Emily yanked Isaac into the main room again, nearly trampling a bunch of uppity-looking Main Line women wearing VOTE FOR TOM buttons.

Isaac laughed nervously as he stumbled behind her. "Are you okay?"

"Of course!" Emily knew she must seem insane. She wrapped her arms around Isaac and began a slow waltz to the Sinatra song the band was playing. The dance floor had a good view of every table, the bar, and the silent auction booth. Tons of people she recognized from the Marins' parties stood around chatting. Several photographers circled the room, snapping pictures.

Isaac spun Emily. "It's fun being a guest instead of a caterer."

"How'd you convince your mom to let you go to this with me, anyway?" Emily asked idly.

"I told her the truth, actually. She's coming around to the idea of us together again, believe it or not."

Emily *couldn't* believe it, but she didn't have time to dwell on it. Her gaze flicked from the front entrance to the emergency exit to a little nook by the bathrooms. Noel Kahn's mother glided across her field of view, wearing a tiara. Hanna's dad was holding court in the corner, talking to a bunch of wealthy-looking businessmen.

"I've really missed you," Isaac went on.

Emily pulled back, feeling bad. Isaac deserved her full attention. It felt good to be wrapped in his arms, but she was so scared that any minute, the delicate house of cards that was her life would topple over.

She couldn't help but scan the crowd again. Mr. Marin stood up and strode across the room to someone who'd just emerged from a side entrance. Emily craned her neck to see, but her view was blocked.

"So what do you say?" Isaac asked.

Emily blinked stupidly. Isaac had been speaking this

whole time and she hadn't heard a word. "What was that?"

Isaac licked his lips. "I wanted to know if we're dating again."

Emily's mouth opened, but no words came out. Despite her distraction, despite the fact that she was keeping something huge from Isaac, the words felt welcome.

"There's only one thing," Isaac interrupted before Emily had a chance to speak. "Something is bothering you. Something you think you can't talk about. But you *can*, Emily. Whatever it is, I'm here for you. If it's something with that guy we saw at Hollis the other day, don't be afraid to tell me."

Emily shut her eyes. "It doesn't have anything to do with Derrick."

"But it *is* something?"

The trumpets blaring on the stage were starting to make Emily's head hurt. "It's nothing."

"You seem so stressed." Isaac's voice was pleading. "I just want to help."

Emily concentrated on the dance steps, delaying her answer. Isaac cared and wanted to make everything better, which made her feel relieved and terrible at the same time. She wanted him to like her. She wanted him to want to get back together with her. But what did *she* want for herself?

"Breaking up was a huge mistake, Emily," Isaac said, staring deeply into Emily's eyes. "I want to start over. What do you think?"

"I . . ." Emily started, but then she noticed another blond figure at the edge of the dance floor. She was the right height and build, and Mr. Marin was talking to her happily and graciously. Emily ducked, her heart jackhammering again. "Oh my God," she whispered.

She grabbed Isaac once more, pulled him off the dance floor, and escaped around the corner to a small alcove that held a variety of meteorites behind glass. Isaac crossed his arms over his chest, looking fed up. "Are you going to let me in on what's going on with you tonight?"

The woman talking to Mr. Marin turned slightly. Only a few more degrees, and she'd see Emily and Isaac. Thinking quickly, she grabbed the sides of Isaac's face and planted her lips squarely on his. Isaac's eyes widened for a moment, but then they fluttered closed, and he passionately kissed her back. Emily felt her pulse pounding firmly in her fingertips and her lips. The kiss felt good, but she knew it was only a means to an end. She felt like the worst person in the world.

Isaac pulled back for a moment and smiled crookedly. "So I guess that's a yes?"

Emily swallowed hard, feeling like she'd just done something she couldn't undo. She wasn't acting like herself at all. She glanced again into the ballroom. The woman who'd been talking to Mr. Marin was gone.

Beep.

Her phone was glowing through the flimsy mesh fabric of her silver clutch. Emily stared at it in horror. "It looks like you have a text," Isaac said, sounding relaxed and happy.

242 ◆ SARA SHEPARD

A lump formed in Emily's throat. She pulled out the phone and peeked at the screen. Her blood ran cold.

"Isaac, I have to go," she whispered.

"*Go?*" The content look on Isaac's face vanished. "What are you talking about?"

Emily took a few frantic paces back into the ballroom. Mr. Marin was still talking to the woman, and though Emily was almost positive she was Gayle, her face was still turned away. Emily looked around the rest of the room. It was even more crowded than a few seconds ago. Where the hell was Hanna? Why didn't she see Aria? There was no time to waste.

"Emily?" She felt a hand on her sleeve. Isaac was staring at her, his mouth a straight line. "Who just texted you?"

The band finished its song, and everyone on the dance floor clapped. Emily stared into Isaac's open, caring face. She knew what walking away without explaining looked like. But she didn't know what else to do.

"I'm sorry," she whispered, and then turned and fled across the dance floor.

"Emily!" Isaac called after her, but Emily kept going, weaving through the crowds until she reached the lobby. She dug inside her clutch, pulled out her cell phone, and read the horrible note once more. Just looking at the words made her stomach lurch. This couldn't be happening.

I've got your baby. If you want her to be safe, come to 56 Mockingbird Drive. Ticktock! —A

29

FRIENDS DON'T LET FRIENDS
GO ALONE

Aria pulled into the Gemological Museum lot, fluffed her hair, and checked her makeup in the rearview mirror. She'd done a fair job of cleaning up the tear-streaked mess she'd been after her argument with Noel, but she still looked stressed and tired. Then again, she didn't have anyone to impress at this party.

After she parked, she pulled out her phone and composed a text to Noel. *Please let me explain*, she wrote. *Everything that happened . . . it was kind of out of my control. Someone forced me to break up with you. Someone is threatening me and controlling my life.*

Then she hit DELETE fast. The text gave away too much. She couldn't tell Noel about A.

Swallowing a sob, she slammed the door and walked toward the entrance, which was lit on either side by glowing Japanese lanterns. A gust of wind kicked up, rolling an empty Coke can down the sidewalk. Aria heard a whisper and whirled around, staring at the line of parked cars.

After a few seconds of peering into nothingness, sensing no movement, she pressed on. A few kids were clustered by the front hedges, staring at something on their cell phones. "*So* desperate," Riley snickered.

"She is loser, no?" Klaudia shivered in her strapless, barely-there black dress.

Aria peeked at the cell phone screen over Riley's shoulder. There was a picture of Hanna wearing army fatigues and hiding in the plastic bushes at the mall concourse. Aria had no idea what it was all about, but before she could ask any questions, Emily barreled out of the double doors, grabbed her shoulder, and pulled her to the other side of the walkway.

"Thank God I found you," Emily said, her voice full of fear. "I need your car."

"What happened?" Aria asked. "Did you get Gayle's phone already?"

"No, but this is much more important."

Emily held her phone in Aria's face. *I've got your baby,* said the screen. Aria clapped a hand over her mouth. "Do you think it's true?"

"I'm not waiting around to find out." Emily started toward the parking lot, then noticed Hanna trudging out the door with an ashamed look on her face. She waved her over. "You have to see this."

Hanna looked pained, like she didn't feel like dealing with anything right now, but she walked over and inspected the text. Color drained from her face. "*Shit.* How could this happen?"

"I don't know. But I have to save her." Emily's eyes darted back and forth. "If Ali has her, who knows what she'll do?"

"Em, it's not Ali who has Violet," Aria whispered. "Don't you see? It's Gayle. I saw her going into Babies "R" Us last night with a huge, weird smile on her face. She was getting ready for when she found your baby."

Emily frowned, then peered at the hulking museum behind them. "But isn't Gayle here? I thought I saw her talking to your dad, Hanna."

Hanna bit her lip. "Actually, I haven't seen her all night."

"Of course she's not here," Aria said. "She's at this house on Mockingbird Drive!" She looked at Hanna. "You're with me, right? You think this is Gayle?"

A conflicted look crossed Hanna's face. "I *think* so. But why would Gayle tell us she has Violet if she wants to keep her for herself? It sounds like a setup."

"I don't care!" Emily grabbed Aria's car keys from her hands. "This is my daughter's life we're talking about! I'm sorry, Aria, but I'm going to that house, even if I have to go alone!"

Aria set her jaw. "We're not letting you go alone."

"We're not?" Hanna squeaked.

Aria gave Hanna a look. "Of course we're not." She

snatched the car keys back from Emily, marched across the parking lot, and slid into the driver's seat. "C'mon, Em. Let's go. You too, Hanna."

The girls got into the car and slammed the doors. Aria kicked off her high heels, gunned the engine, and cranked the heat up high. As she pulled out of the parking lot, she looked behind her and saw a perfectly round, eerily yellow moon reflected in the museum windows. And there, next to the moon's reflection, was a person in silhouette. Watching. Maybe even laughing at what fools they were.

Aria breathed in sharply, the hair on the back of her neck standing on end. But when she looked at the window again, only the moon was there, bright and full, filling up the expanse of the glass.

30

THE GIRL IN THE PHOTO

Twenty-five minutes and three wrong turns later, the girls pulled onto Mockingbird Drive, a twisting street on the other side of Mount Kale. "Whoa," Hanna mumbled, staring through the fog, which had rolled in heavily. Every estate was on a massive plot of land. Winding driveways led to faux castles, French estates, Tudor manors, and buildings that looked like a cross between the Capitol and a Frank Gehry masterpiece. Ferraris sat in driveways. Tennis court lights twinkled in backyards. Hanna was used to luxurious houses like Noel's, Spencer's, and even her dad's new place, but people who lived in this neighborhood had more money than they knew what to do with, and they didn't mind flaunting it.

The next mailbox bore the number 56 in Gothic script, and Aria rolled slowly up the long drive. Tall, imposing trees made a canopy over the road, creating a spooky tunnel. They passed a huge, six-car garage and a horse stable, and then came upon the house, an imposing mansion with columns and huge arched windows. It was positioned a bit cockeyed on the lot, probably angled so that it got the best morning sun. Not a single light was on in the windows.

"Um, now what?" Hanna whispered as Aria cut the engine.

"Come on." Emily opened her car door and jogged up the front walk. Hanna and Aria scrambled after her. When Hanna heard a whispering sound, her heart began to thud. What if A had led them straight into a trap?

"Where do you think Spencer is?" Emily said over her shoulder. "She hasn't responded to my texts." They'd sent Spencer messages about what was going on and demanded that she meet them here.

"Maybe it took a while for her to get released from the hospital," Hanna whispered.

"Or maybe she got as lost as we did." Aria stepped up on the porch and stared at the doorbell. "What are we supposed to do, ring? 'Hey, A, we're here!'" She looked at Hanna. "You do it."

Hanna's eyes bulged. "No way!"

"*I'll* do it." Emily touched the door, and it opened with a creak that sounded exactly like a haunted house entrance. Hanna shivered. What kind of person left their front door open in the middle of the night?

Emily pushed past them and walked into the foyer. "Hello?" she called out.

Hanna followed her. The foyer smelled oddly of nail polish remover. A single lamp on a console table was lit, showing a double staircase, an impressive crystal chandelier, and a wall full of black-and-white paintings of undulating sand dunes, animal skulls, and possessed-looking vultures. Heavy curtains hung on the windows in the room to the right; thick wool rugs decorated the floors. The coat closet door was ajar, and several jackets swung from hangers. The place had a museumlike stillness, as though it were a movie set, not someone's actual house.

"Hello?" Emily said again.

There was no answer. Emily peered up the stairs. Aria wandered toward the kitchen. Hanna picked up a stone rabbit on the table next to the front door and set it down again. It was so quiet, she began to hear noises that might not have been there. A nervous swallow. A slight rustle. A joint crack.

"Something doesn't feel right," Emily whispered suddenly, pushing a lock of hair behind her ear. "Where's Violet?"

"I told you this was a bad idea," Hanna whispered.

"Guys." Aria's voice was as thin as a pinched wire. She was standing next to a table in the living room, an envelope in her hand. "Look at this."

Hanna squinted at the words. At the top left corner was a logo for Pennsylvania Electric Power. In the center was the address, 56 Mockingbird Lane. Then her gaze fell on the recipient's name.

"Oh my God," Hanna whispered. *Gayle Riggs.*

Aria set the envelope down, her eyes wide. "Guys, this is Gayle's *house*. I *told* you."

Emily blinked rapidly. "What does this mean?"

"It means we should get the hell out of here," Hanna snapped. "Gayle doesn't have your baby. She just used that to get us here because she wants to hurt us."

She walked back toward the door, taking in every shadow, every dark crevice. A sculpture of a willow tree looked dangerous and alive. The coat rack reminded her of a hunched, crazy old man. A series of photographs were lined up across the mantle like crooked teeth in a ravenous mouth. In the dim light, she could make out a wedding photo of Gayle and her husband. Next to it was a snapshot of the two of them on vacation, and then a family portrait of Gayle and her husband and a smiling blond girl. Maybe this was the daughter Gayle had spoken about to Emily, the one she said she'd lost. Hanna squinted, trying to see what she looked like, but the picture was too small, the features too difficult to make out.

Until she looked at the photo next to it, an 8 x 10 in a wood frame. It was a school headshot of a pretty blond teenager. As soon as Hanna saw her cunning blue eyes and devious smile, the taste of metal filled her mouth. She'd recognize that smirk anywhere.

Hanna stopped short. "Oh my God." She pointed a shaky finger at the picture. Emily walked over and followed her gaze, and then sank down, her knees going weak.

"Is that . . . ?" Emily whispered.

Aria just let out a terrified gasp.

Hanna picked up the photo from the shelf. This explained everything—how Gayle knew everything and why Gayle didn't just want them to suffer . . . but to *die*.

"Tabitha's her daughter?" Emily's voice shook uncontrollably.

"How did you not know that?" Hanna demanded. "Didn't you ever meet the husband? Didn't you ask for the daughter's name? Didn't you find out what happened to her?"

Emily shook her head dazedly. "I never met the husband—and it wouldn't have mattered anyway, since we didn't know what he looked like until Tabitha's body was found. Plus Gayle goes by Riggs, not Clark. She never told me any details of what happened to her daughter, either, just said she disappeared. And none of this ever came up on a Google search!"

Hanna ran her hands down the length of her face. "Why didn't she turn us in?" She could barely get the words out she was breathing so hard.

Emily bit her lip. "Maybe she *doesn't* know for sure. Maybe this is her way of drawing us out and making us confess. She's trying to drive us crazy, make us tell the truth."

"So do you *still* think Ali's A, Em?" Aria snapped.

Emily looked terrified. "I guess not."

They all turned and peered at the photograph again. For a split second, it looked like Tabitha was winking at them. *Gotcha!* It was the same expression Ali used to have when she'd pressured the girls into doing something they didn't want to do.

And then, clear as day, came a keening, desperate wail. The girls whipped around. Hanna grabbed Aria's hand, and Aria grabbed Emily's. The wail persisted, growing louder and more urgent.

"A baby," Hanna whispered.

"Violet!" Emily screamed.

She shot down the hall, running blindly toward the sound. Aria ran after her, and Hanna brought up the rear, her heart pounding. They zipped past an office, a powder room, and an enormous, immaculately clean marble kitchen that smelled like fresh lemons. The sound seemed to be coming from just beyond a set of French doors on the other side of the island. Emily twisted the lock and flung one of the doors open.

They walked onto a massive brick patio. The fog had grown even denser since they'd been inside. The mewling cries echoed through the air, but there were no signs of a baby anywhere.

"Violet?" Emily spun around, tears in her eyes.

Suddenly, the noise ceased. The silence was deafening. Hanna looked up at her friends, the fog curling around their faces. She thought the worst: Was the baby *dead*?

Snap.

Hanna stood up straighter, staring at the garage and the trees through the fog. Even though she couldn't see anything, she sensed a presence. Then she heard it: footsteps.

"Guys." Her voice quivered.

"Maybe it's just Spencer," Emily said bravely. Her phone's screen glowed in the darkness. "She just texted me that she's here."

"Then where's her car?" Aria gestured to the driveway. Besides Aria's Subaru, there was no other vehicle there.

Emily bit her lip. "Maybe she parked it at the bottom of the hill and is walking up."

Hanna marched across the patio toward the driveway. "Someone's out here, and it's not just Spencer. We need to warn her."

She was halfway past the garage when she heard the sound of something metal—car keys, maybe—dropping on the blacktop. She froze and looked around, but all she could see was fog. Footsteps followed, and then tense whispers, a conversation back and forth that she couldn't hear. Finally, there was a boom so loud it made Hanna's teeth hurt.

She swung around and stared at her friends. They stood paralyzed on the patio. Then she turned back and peered at the driveway again. When she saw a blurry figure lying splayed out near one of the flower beds, she screamed. Whoever it was wore a heavy coat with a hood that covered her turned face; the only part of her Hanna could see was a small, delicate hand.

"Is that Spencer?" Aria shrieked.

Hanna groped through the mist toward the figure. Tears streamed down her face uncontrollably. Didn't Spencer have a down jacket just like that? Didn't she own pointy leather boots? Suddenly, Hanna stopped. Was the murderer lurking nearby? Were they next?

"Spencer?" Emily came up behind Hanna. "Spencer?" She looked at Hanna in horror. "Do you think she's . . . ?"

Hanna reached out to touch the down-filled hood, but then drew her hand away. She was terrified of what she was going to see. Spencer's face, frozen in a scream? Half of Spencer's brains collected inside the hood?

A car passed on the road, its headlights momentarily illuminating their bodies. When the beams bounced off the figure on the ground, Hanna noticed something wasn't right. The few strands of hair peeking out from under the hood were paler than Spencer's. The hand looked veiny and older. There was an enormous diamond ring on the fourth finger.

"Who *is* that?" Aria whispered.

Drawing in a breath, Hanna pulled back the figure's hood. Aria screamed. Emily covered her eyes. And just as the sound of sirens filled the air, Hanna peered down. The two eyes were closed, the lips parted just so. It looked like the person was sleeping, save for the horrible gash just above her right temple. She took in the whole face, and then realized. She sank to her knees, feeling relieved, horrified, and confused at the same time.

The figure on the ground wasn't Spencer. It was Gayle.

31

THE TRUTH COMES OUT

Emily stared at Gayle's inert features, her pale skin, and the blood seeping out of her head. A shrill noise rang in her ears, and it took her a few seconds to realize it was the sound of her own screams. She spun around and bent over, dry-heaving on the grass.

The sound of sirens roared closer, and a car purred up the drive. It was Spencer. She slammed the door and took a few steps toward them, a confused look on her face. Then she saw Gayle's figure on the ground and stopped short. Her face registered a series of emotions—surprise, horror, fear—in a split second. "Oh my God," she screamed. "Is that . . . ?"

"Gayle," Emily croaked, her voice quavering.

Spencer looked like she was going to be sick. "What *happened*?"

"We're not sure." Tears ran down Aria's face. "We came out into the courtyard because we heard a baby crying, there was all this fog, we heard footsteps, and then something that sounded like a gunshot, and then . . ."

Police cars blazed up the street, and the girls froze. The vehicles sped up the driveway and screeched to a stop behind Spencer's car. Hanna's mouth dropped open. Spencer instinctively raised her hands in surrender. Emily took a big step away from Gayle's body.

The doors to the police cars opened, and four cops jumped out. Two of them rushed to the fallen body, requesting for backup, while the other two stalked over to Emily and her friends. "What the hell is going on here?"

Emily stared up at the cop who'd spoken. He had spiky blond hair, acne scars, and wore a shiny gold Lieutenant's badge that said LOWRY. "We didn't do this!"

"We can explain!" Aria shouted at the same time.

Lowry twisted around and stared into the darkness beyond the police cars. "Where's the person who called this in?"

"I'm here," a voice responded.

Another figure emerged through the fog. Emily presumed it would be a neighbor, but then she noticed the guy's black tuxedo, shiny shoes, and shoulder-length brown hair. Her stomach dropped to her feet. It was Isaac.

"W-what are you doing here?" Emily sputtered.

Isaac stared at her. "I followed you—I was worried about you. Then I heard the gunshot, so I called the cops."

Emily's head whirled. "You had no right to follow me! This is private!"

"If you would have told me what was going on I wouldn't have!" Isaac's voice cracked. "I was afraid you were in trouble!" His gaze fell to Gayle's body, and his mouth wobbled.

Lowry snatched his walkie-talkie from his belt and checked in on the backup and ambulance. Then he looked at the girls. "Do you know who this woman is?"

"Her name is Gayle Riggs," Aria said in a small voice.

Lowry stared, chewing his gum hard. "Were you trying to rob her?"

"Of course not!" Emily cried. "We were just . . . here! Someone else did this!" She looked at Isaac. "Tell him I wouldn't do something like this."

Isaac rolled his jaw. "Well, I didn't actually see what happened—the fog was too thick. But Emily *wouldn't* do something like this, Officers. She's not a killer."

The guy who was holding Spencer snorted. "People can surprise you."

Lowry chomped on his gum and stared at Emily. "You want to explain what you *are* doing here?"

Emily glanced guiltily at Isaac. The whirling lights on top of the cop car cast blue and red lights across his face. He was still looking at her with loving concern. "It's personal."

Lowry looked annoyed. "If you can't explain why you're here, we'll have to bring you into the station as suspects."

Her friends gasped beside her. Emily's stomach

clenched. Could she seriously allow them to be accused of a crime they didn't commit just to keep her secret?

She cleared her throat. "I'm here because I thought my baby was in danger. I thought she'd been kidnapped. We didn't know Gayle Riggs lived here—we just got a tip that the baby was at this address."

Isaac's eyes bugged. "*What* baby?"

Lowering her eyes, Emily took the deepest breath ever. "I had a baby girl this summer." She said the words very fast.

Isaac looked stunned. "You *did*?"

She nodded. "She's yours, Isaac."

For a moment, everything in the world went still. Isaac scrunched up his face. "Uh . . . *what*?"

"It's true." Emily's voice trembled. "I found out several months after we broke up. I hid in Philly last summer and looked into giving the baby up for adoption. I met Gayle, and she was interested in adopting the baby, but I decided that I wanted to give the baby to someone else. Afterward, Gayle made threats that sounded like she might try to steal the baby from the new family. So when I got the tip that the baby was here, I dragged my friends along to see if it was true." Emily figured this was as close to the truth as she could get. "And we really thought she *was* here—we heard a baby crying. But then it . . . stopped. We didn't do anything to hurt Gayle, though," she added. "And don't punish my friends. It's because of me that they're here."

When she was finished, her throat was raw and she felt

like she'd just swum the English Channel. Isaac's expression morphed from disbelief to confusion to anger all in the matter of a few seconds. "A . . . *baby*?" he squeaked out, his voice cracking. "A girl?"

"Yes." Emily felt tears in her eyes.

Isaac ran his hand over the top of his head. "Unbelievable." He took a step to the right, then a tottering lurch to the left. All of a sudden, he turned around and staggered toward the other two cops, his posture stiff. Emily stepped forward to go after him, but Hanna touched the small of her back.

"Leave him alone," she whispered.

Seconds later, more police cars, an ambulance, and a fire truck roared up the drive. Cops leapt from the cars and set up a perimeter around the crime scene. A detective in a gray jacket pulled out a camera and took photos of Gayle's lifeless figure. A man in a coat that said CORONER on the back examined the body, making sure she was indeed dead. Police dogs yapped on their leashes, saliva dripping off their jaws. The sirens blared relentlessly, giving Emily a headache.

The cop next to Aria, a big burly guy with a bald head, turned to Emily. "You really expect us to believe your story?" he asked.

"It's the truth." Emily felt defeated. "You can look up my medical records from Jefferson Hospital."

"Why didn't you come to the police when Ms. Riggs allegedly made these threats?"

Emily glanced at her friends. Spencer cleared her throat. "She didn't want her parents to know she was pregnant," she said. "She thought she could handle things herself."

"And what about this tip you received, saying the baby was here? Who wrote that?"

Emily's stomach flipped. The last thing she wanted to do was tell the cops about A. "I guess it was a hoax. Someone messing with us."

"So why is Ms. Riggs dead?" Lowry snapped.

"I have no idea," Emily whispered.

"So you don't know where that came from?" Lowry pointed at something on the ground.

Emily followed his finger. Lying next to Gayle's elbow was a black gun. It blended in with the dark pavement. She jumped away from it as though it were a rattlesnake. "Oh my God."

"We heard that go off," Aria said.

"Did you see who shot it?" Lowry asked.

Everyone exchanged a helpless look. "The fog was too thick," Emily said. "All we heard were footsteps."

"I saw someone run in front of my car," Spencer offered, "but I didn't see a face."

Lowry snatched the gun with two gloved fingers, placed it into a plastic bag, and handed it to one of the detectives. The man tapped something into a laptop. Emily shivered next to her friends, trying to convey what she was thinking without speaking. *How had this happened?*

And who killed Gayle? Was it completely unrelated to us or the baby?

Or, Emily thought with a shiver, what if the killer was *absolutely* related? Was it possible Gayle *wasn't* A after all? Was it possible that *A* had killed Gayle?

But why?

After a few torturous minutes, the detective returned to the girls. "Okay. The weapon was registered to a Gayle Riggs. According to the records, it hadn't been stolen. Whoever shot it must have taken it from her house."

The cop holding Aria jutted a thumb into the darkness. "Isaac saw you girls go into the house. Coincidence?"

"Yes," Aria said weakly. "It was someone else."

Lowry glanced at Gayle's body on the ground, which was now covered with a sheet. "We'll run fingerprints on the gun. The results should take a few hours." Then he glanced at the girls. "Until then, you four are coming with us."

32

CONFESSION TIME

The last time Spencer had been at the Rosewood police station was when Darren Wilden brought her and her friends in a year ago—the cops had accused the girls of helping Ian Thomas escape police custody, as well as aiding and abetting in Ali's murder. The precinct had changed since then, having gotten a fresh coat of paint, new front windows, one of those fancy coffee machines that also made cappuccino and hot chocolate, and a marginally nicer interrogation room. Instead of the banged-up wooden table with the graffiti all over it, there was a shiny new metal one.

Not that any of it made Spencer feel more comfortable being here.

She and her friends sat silently around the table. Hanna bit relentlessly at her thumbnail, which was still stained from fingerprinting ink. Aria kept bursting into tears, her mascara streaking down her cheeks. Emily was sucking so hard on her lip it looked like it might disappear. Spencer leapt up and began pacing around the room, the gnawing feeling in her gut too much to bear. What if they were accused of Gayle's murder? What if they were put away for life?

She stopped pacing. "Guys, maybe we should just tell them that A gave us that tip to go to Gayle's house. They're probably going to ask about it again anyway."

Aria's eyes widened. "You know we can't do that. A will tell on us."

Spencer sat back down in the chair. "But what if A is Gayle's murderer?"

Hanna frowned. "But I thought Gayle *was* A."

"Seriously?" Spencer stared at her. "After what we just witnessed?"

"It doesn't seem likely." Emily leaned forward on her elbows. "What if A planned all this? Luring us to Mockingbird Drive, everything? It's possible there wasn't a baby at her house at all. Maybe it was a recording."

Aria squinted. "But why would A kill Gayle?"

"To frame us, maybe." Spencer thought for a moment. "Or maybe A meant to get to us first, but Gayle got in the way. Wasn't she supposed to be at the fund-raiser?"

She shut her eyes and thought about those terrifying seconds when she'd pulled up the driveway on Mockingbird Lane. A figure had run in front of the car, then darted across the street into the woods. Whoever it was wore all black and had a hood cinched tight—Spencer hadn't been able to tell if it was a guy or a girl.

Hanna cleared her throat. "But Gayle is Tabitha's mom. She was out to steal Violet. She was at Princeton when Spencer was, she infiltrated my dad's campaign, she threatened me at the race. It makes so much sense that she's A."

"I agree," Aria said.

"So why is Gayle dead now?" Spencer demanded.

The door swung open, and everyone jumped. Lowry walked through and made a motion for the girls to stand up. There was a pinched look on his face, and he was holding a steaming cup of coffee in his hand. "Well, none of the prints on the gun matched any of yours."

Spencer stood up abruptly. "Whose prints *were* on the gun?"

"Ms. Riggs's." Lowry sipped his coffee. "And a set of prints we don't have on record. They could be her husband's. He just arrived from New York, and I want all of us to talk together."

Spencer exchanged a terrified look with the others. Gayle's husband was Tabitha's *father.*

Before they could say a word, a tall, thin man entered the room. Spencer recognized him from the news stories about Tabitha, the mourning father who'd do anything to have his daughter back. His eyes were tinged red, and he had a look on his face as though he'd just been struck by lightning. She folded in her shoulders, terrified that he'd know what they'd done to his daughter, but Mr. Clark seemed too catatonic to notice them.

Lowry curled his hands over the back of an empty chair. "Mr. Clark, I'd like to clear up a story Ms. Fields told us about your wife." He glanced at Emily, then at Tabitha's father. "I apologize that we have to do this so soon after her death, but it's important for our investigation."

He repeated what Emily had told him about Gayle wanting to adopt her baby this summer, ending in how Emily was worried that Gayle had stolen the baby tonight—they'd heard a baby crying on the back porch. Mr. Clark stared at Emily, looking startled. "She never told me about wanting to adopt a baby last summer," he said faintly.

Spencer squinted at him, hardly believing what she was hearing. How could Gayle not have told her own husband?

"She said you knew," Emily said. Spencer was amazed at her ability to speak—if she was the one being questioned right now, she'd probably hide under the table. "She said she was going to put you on the phone, but she never did."

"Probably because I told her very clearly I didn't want to adopt." Mr. Clark rubbed the top of his head. "So what happened? Why didn't you give her the baby?"

Emily's throat bobbed. "I chose another family. That's all."

Mr. Clark blinked rapidly. "Was it because you never spoke to me? Was it because you thought we weren't a good match?"

"It's hard to explain," Emily mumbled, staring at her high heels.

Mr. Clark's eyes were vacant and hollow as he stared past the girls at the wall. "Sometimes Gayle gets ideas in her head that she can't let go of. She can be very determined—even pigheaded—to get what she wants."

He blew his nose. "I assure you, though, we didn't kidnap any children. We hadn't told anyone yet, but Gayle had just taken a pregnancy test last week. It was positive, and she was overjoyed." He shook his head. "We'd worked so hard to get pregnant. This was our fifth round of fertility treatments. We'd been through so much pain." His shoulders started to shake. "This can't be happening. First Tabitha, now Gayle."

Tabitha. Just hearing her name was torture. Spencer reached over and took Emily's hand. Hanna and Aria looked like they were going to explode.

Emily shifted her weight. "I'm very sorry about your daughter. That must have been so hard for you two as parents."

Mr. Clark's eyebrows lowered as he turned toward them. "Well, Gayle was Tabitha's stepmother. It was hard on her, of course, especially since they had some . . . problems. Tabitha had behavioral issues. Gayle pushed to have Tabitha sent away, and I finally relented."

Spencer exchanged a covert, startled look with Emily and the others. *Stepmother?* That would explain why she was never on the news and had a different last name.

Mr. Clark put his head in his hands. "I shouldn't have given into Gayle's pressure to send Tabitha away. And I made so many mistakes with Gayle, too. I shouldn't have nagged her about all the boards she was on, all the money she spent on parties. I shouldn't have yelled at her for that money that went missing last summer. I just want her back. I *need* her back."

He let out a low moan. Lowry stood and shooed the girls out of the room, following them out. Once they were far enough away, he put his hands in his pockets and jingled loose change. "I don't think we need to ask him any more questions about whether he kidnapped your baby, Ms. Fields. I just got a text that the police are done with their search of the house, too. They didn't find any clues, and they certainly didn't find any children."

Emily's throat bobbed as she swallowed. "Okay," she said quietly.

Lowry frowned. "Do you know who might have sent you to Ms. Riggs's house, even as a joke?"

Emily shot a nervous look at the others, then shook her head. "I don't. But I don't think whoever sent it meant anything by it—or had anything to do with Gayle's murder. We're the Pretty Little Liars. People send us fake notes all the time, and this was all just a terrible coincidence."

Her lips trembled. Spencer could tell she hated lying. She almost jumped in to tell the cop everything about A, but then restrained herself.

Lowry let out a frustrated, *why are you wasting my time*

sigh. "You girls are free to go. But don't think you're off the hook. You were still on someone's property without permission, and you were still witnesses to a murder. If there's anything you aren't telling me—like about who sent this text—you'd better come forward. And those of you who are under eighteen, I'm going to have to call your parents about this."

Emily flinched. "And tell them what?"

Lowry stared at her. "That you were trespassing. That you witnessed a murder. Personally, Ms. Fields, I think you should tell them the whole truth. But I can't make that decision for you."

With that, he opened the front door and let Spencer and the others out. The digital clock outside the bank across the street said it was almost three in the morning. Not a car was on Lancaster Avenue. Spencer pulled her coat around her and stared long and hard at her friends. "Okay. Did I just hear what I *thought* I heard?"

"I'm having a hard time believing it, too," Hanna whispered.

"That was why I saw her at Babies "R" Us," Aria murmured. "I thought it was to get ready for *your* baby, Em, but she must have been shopping for her own."

"But she threatened me," Hanna said in a small voice.

Spencer tapped her lips thoughtfully. "What exactly did she say?"

"That she wanted what she was owed. Meaning the baby."

"What if Gayle wasn't talking about the baby? What if she was talking about the *money*?" Spencer gestured in the direction of the police station. "Mr. Clark just said he was really hard on Gayle for losing some money over the summer. What if it was the money that she gave to Emily for the baby?"

"I gave that money back," Hanna protested.

"You put it in Gayle's mailbox. Someone could have easily stolen it," Spencer pointed out. "What if Gayle thought Emily scammed her? What if she's been pissed all this time because she thought you took her money and ran?" She blinked hard, the puzzle pieces suddenly snapping together in a different way. "It could make sense. What if A stole the cash from Gayle's mailbox to make her angry, which would make her look like she was out to get us? What if A took advantage of the situation and cast suspicion on someone innocent, just like what happened with Kelsey?"

"But . . ." Aria bit her fingernail. "Gayle's Tabitha's *mom*."

"*Step*mom," Spencer corrected. "It sounded like there wasn't any love lost between them, either."

"A could have lured us to Gayle's house, trying to trap us, just like you said, Spence," Emily said. "Maybe A hadn't expected Gayle to be there tonight—she was supposed to be at the gala. But then she was. Maybe she took A by surprise. So A killed her."

Spencer nodded, thinking the same thing. Had Gayle

inadvertently saved their lives? If she hadn't been at the house, would A have killed them instead?

Aria and Hanna shifted, but didn't say anything. A long silence followed. A lone Honda Civic rolled through a stop light without waiting for the light to turn green. A neon sign blinked across the avenue.

"Do you think it's true?" Hanna's skin was pale. "Do you think we were wrong *again*?"

Spencer shivered, staring into the distance. "Maybe," she whispered.

And someone else was dead because of it.

33

ARIA'S CONFIDANTE

The next morning, Aria sat cross-legged on the living room floor at her dad's house, trying to meditate. *Let go of all of your stress*, a soothing voice said through her headphones. *Breathe in and out and picture it all slowly floating away . . .*

It was easier said than done, though, because the image of Gayle's ashen, bloodless face kept leaping into Aria's mind. The news had talked about nothing but Gayle's murder all morning, and everyone was hysterical that another Rosewood killer might be on the loose. Miraculously, Aria and the others weren't mentioned in the story. Last night, when Spencer's dad found out the girls had been taken to the police station for questioning about Gayle's murder, he'd immediately left his apartment in Philadelphia, driven to Rosewood, and had a long talk with Lieutenant Lowry, who happened to be the son of one of his best friends. Because there was no evidence that the girls had actually *done* anything, because the girls had been through so much media scrutiny the previous year, and because Mr. Clark wasn't pressing charges for trespassing, the cops had agreed not to release the girls' names to the press.

There was a lot of speculation in the press about who Gayle's killer might be—someone after Gayle's money, or an enemy of her husband's, or a partner from a business deal gone sour. No one had guessed that the Pretty Little Liars were involved.

The idea that Gayle *wasn't* A and that A had set a trap for them at Gayle's house terrified Aria—whoever they were dealing with was diabolical and brilliant. And they still didn't know what had happened to Emily's baby, if anything. None of them had received a message from A since the one that appeared in Emily's inbox at the benefit, so maybe the whole thing—including the crying baby sounds—was a bluff. One good thing had happened: Early that morning, Aria received a text from Hanna saying she'd finally tracked down the address of the family who had adopted Violet, using her dad's voter records. *They live in Chestnut Hill*, the text said. *Em wants to drive by the house, and she wants us to go with her.* They arranged to drive there later that night. Hanna had added that she'd asked to borrow Kate's car—it might be good to take one that people didn't associate with any of them. Aria understood why without Hanna having to explain: An unrecognizable car meant A was less likely to follow them. If A was on the loose—and had no

trouble killing people—they couldn't run the risk of lead-
ing A straight to Violet.

Now move into downward-facing dog, said the lilting
voice in Aria's headphones.

Aria placed her hands on the carpet and pointed
her butt in the air. She heard footsteps and looked up.
Meredith leaned against the doorjamb, her fingers worry-
ing an apron around her waist. "I thought you said you
weren't into yoga."

Aria sat up quickly, feeling caught. "Uh . . ." She trailed
off, not able to find an appropriate excuse.

Meredith sat down on the edge of the couch and
flicked the tassels on one of the pillows. "It was really nice
to talk to you about that stuff between me and your dad
the other day."

Aria's mouth twitched. "Um, yeah," she mumbled, not
sure if she meant it.

"I've never been able to tell anyone about how hard
things were," Meredith went on. "I realize you weren't the
right person, and I understand that you probably don't
care if things were difficult for me or not. But I do know
that I hurt you. And I want you to know that I never
meant to. I didn't want to break up your family. I feel terrible about that every day."

"Think about how *I* felt," Aria said, feeling a rush of
anger. "*I* felt like I would break up my family if I didn't
keep the secret. But I also felt like I was betraying my
mom for not saying anything."

"I know," Meredith said earnestly. "And I'm sorry about that. But after things were out in the open, did you feel better?"

Aria arched her back, examining the wooden pendant light hanging from the ceiling. "It was awful hiding it. The anticipation of getting found out was even worse than people knowing the truth. I guess I did feel better eventually."

Meredith twisted the promise ring Byron had given her around her finger. "Can I ask you something? Did you ask me all that stuff because you were curious about me, or because you were dealing with a secret of your own? Something you didn't want to tell anyone?"

Aria's head shot up, and for a moment, she feared A had sent Meredith a message, telling her everything. But Meredith's expression was innocent—caring, even. Like it mattered to her what happened to Aria. For a moment, she almost felt like—well, not a mother, exactly, but family.

"Something like that," Aria mumbled into her chest.

"Are you okay?"

Aria shrugged, not answering.

Meredith sighed, then touched Aria's knee. "I'm really sorry. Secrets can eat you alive. They break down your soul. It's always better to have things out in the open."

Aria nodded, wishing Meredith would have told her that a few days ago instead of blathering on about how keeping secrets was sometimes in one's best interest. *No more secrets*, Noel had said to Aria last week. Of course he had a right to be furious with her—she'd kept something huge from him, something he deserved to know. How could she expect to have a real relationship with him if she didn't share her most intimate feelings, those things that either made or broke a couple? It was what Noel wanted. It was what Aria wanted, too—with him.

All of a sudden, a door opened in her mind. She checked her watch. Noel probably hadn't left for school yet. With any luck, she could catch him . . . and try to fix things.

Noel's telltale stomping footsteps sounded from the other side of his front door. "What are you doing here?" he said gruffly when he opened it and saw Aria.

Aria fiddled with the mohair scarf wound around her neck. "I came to apologize and explain."

Noel turned away. "Save your breath."

He was about to shut the door on her, but Aria caught it. "Hear me out, okay? I'm sorry I didn't tell you what happened with your dad. I was afraid of what it would do to your family. I hated the idea of us being together with me knowing a secret about you, so I thought it would be better if we were apart."

The Kahns' phone rang inside the house, letting out a couple of shrill peals. "Noel, can you get that?" Mrs. Kahn called. But Noel's gaze remained on Aria. He didn't say anything, just stared.

"I was trying to protect you." Aria went on, filling the

silence. "I had already hurt my family because of a secret. I didn't want to do that to your family, too. I care more about you than I do about us, if that makes any sense. And I knew family means everything to you. That's why I did it."

She closed her mouth, her heart racing. Even though it wasn't the whole truth, it was as close as she could come without telling him about A. Because there was no way she could do that—not with A on the loose, not with A so willing to murder people. Aria loved Noel too much to put him in danger.

There was a long pause. Noel stared at his feet, seemingly weighing his emotions. Aria sucked in her stomach nervously. What if he slammed the door in her face? What if he didn't care?

But suddenly, Noel stretched his arms wide. "The thing is, Aria, I care more about *us* than I do about *me*. No matter what you have to tell me, you just have to say it, okay?"

Aria fell into him, and they held each other for a long time. By the way his arms circled tightly around her, as if he never wanted to let her go, it was clear he'd forgiven her.

"I'm so sorry," she whispered into his ear.

"I know," Noel said. "I'm sorry, too. *I* should have told you about my dad instead of letting you discover it for yourself. I kept something from you, too." He pulled away and touched the tip of her nose. "Can you forgive me?"

"Of course," Aria said, hugging him even tighter. She'd never felt so connected to Noel, to *anyone*, in her whole life. But as she nuzzled her nose into his chest, she heard something across the yard and looked up. It sounded like someone was clearing her throat. She scanned the trees for a sign of life. The guesthouse windows were shuttered. A bird sat on the fence, raising and lowering its tail.

No one's here, she told herself, and tried to swallow the fear as best she could. But it got stuck in her throat, leaving a bad taste in her mouth.

A was still out there, after all. And it was very possible A was close, listening. But A had taken so much from her. A wasn't getting Noel, too.

A SURPRISE STALKING SIDE EFFECT

Later that Monday morning, Hanna steered into the parking lot of Rosewood Day. The clouds hung heavy and low in the sky, matching her mood. Kate, who was riding next to her, had set the radio to WKYW news. The local newscaster was recapping Gayle's tragic murder. "Ms. Riggs was a great benefactor to the Philadelphia Art Museum, the Camden Aquarium, and Big Brothers Big Sisters of New Jersey," the reporter said, the news ticker clacking in the background. "She will be greatly missed. The funeral is tomorrow morning, and record crowds are expected to attend. Ms. Riggs is survived by her husband, though she recently lost a stepdaughter, Tabitha—"

Hanna switched the radio off abruptly. "This is so horrible," Kate murmured, picking at her manicure. "You really didn't see who killed her?"

"*Shh*," Hanna hissed, even though they were the only people in the car. When she'd left the police station last night, she'd called her dad and told him as much of the story as she was willing to explain—that she'd gone on a wild goose chase with Emily, that she hadn't known it was Gayle's house, and that she was stunned to find Gayle dead in the driveway. Naturally, her father had been horrified, and he called his campaign manager and press secretary for advice on how best to spin the news. Kate had been privy to the conversation, but instead of looking at Hanna like she was a freak of nature—or a crazy killer—she'd been sympathetic. "That must have been awful," she'd said, a concerned look on her face.

Luckily, Spencer's dad had finagled a way to keep the Rosewood PD from telling the press that the girls were on Gayle's property, and everyone else who knew swore not to talk, too. But Hanna's father still gave her a stern lecture in the privacy of her bedroom. "Those photos you told me about were bad enough," he said through clenched teeth. "What were you doing trespassing? You could have gotten killed!"

Hanna hated to see her dad disappointed in her and more or less promised not to leave the house until the elections were over. But when her dad pressed her about what she was doing on Gayle's property to begin with, she fumbled for an excuse. There was no way she could tell him about Emily's baby or A.

Hanna pulled into a parking space and climbed out of the car. She trudged toward the side entrance, and Kate headed for the art wing, where she had homeroom.

A few kids paused to look at Hanna as though she were on fire. "Loser," muttered Devon Arliss, pulling ski team gear from the back of her car. Kirsten Cullen stopped texting on her phone and burst out laughing. Phi Templeton and Chassey Bledsoe nudged each another by the knoll where all the smokers hung out, and Lanie Iler and Mason Byers stopped making out long enough to whisper "*Psycho stalker*" in voices just loud enough for her to hear. Hanna would have thought a local murder would have trumped that stupid video of her, but she guessed wrong.

The torture didn't stop when she reached the halls, either. Everyone sitting at Steam, the school's coffee shop, raised their heads and whispered about the video they'd all received last night. Even a few teachers glanced at her with raised eyebrows. Hanna put her head down and darted for her locker as fast as she could, but the nasty laughter felt like barbs in her skin. Her nose began to twitch, but she could *not* let anyone see her cry. Being the loser of the school was bad enough.

She yanked open her locker and took out a handful of books without looking to see if they were the right ones for her classes. Then, a familiar figure at the end of the hall caught her eye. Mike was standing next to Colleen, his hand on her shoulder. Hanna turned away, willing them to disappear. She couldn't deal with seeing their smiling faces right now.

She closed her eyes, counted to ten, and then checked the hallway again. They were still standing there. But when Hanna looked closer, she saw tears in Colleen's eyes. Mike was holding out his palms. Then he lowered his head, patted Colleen's arm, and headed down the hall. Straight. Toward. Hanna.

Shit. Hanna slammed her locker shut and shoved her books into her bag as fast as she could. Mike's gaze was on her as he zigzagged around a bunch of freshmen horsing around in front of one of the chemistry rooms. It was clear he was going to chew her out for spying on Colleen and stealing her photos. On one hand, Hanna really didn't want to face him, but on the other, she knew she deserved it. Wouldn't *she* want to scream at New A if they ever came face-to-face?

"Hanna," Mike said when he got close.

"I'm sorry," she blurted. "I'm the biggest jerk ever, and I should never have followed Colleen around. I have her photos. She can have them back, and I'll even pay for them."

Hanna braced herself, but then felt the unexpected sensation of Mike's hand slipping into hers. There was an expression on his face she couldn't read. "I'm sure Colleen would like to hear that, Hanna. But, actually, I think what you did was kind of . . . amazing."

At first, Hanna thought that the classical music that was pumped through the hallway speakers was messing with her brain. "Excuse me?"

Mike's eyes gleamed. "You followed Colleen around because you wanted to see what she had over you, right? Why I was going out with her instead?"

Hanna bit the inside of her cheek. "Well, *kind* of . . ."

"You wanted me back *that* bad." Mike hitched his backpack higher on his shoulder. "No one's ever liked me that much."

"Colleen likes you that much," Hanna mumbled.

Mike glanced over his shoulder at the students clogging the halls. "I know. I feel bad. But . . . she's not for me." He inched closer. "You are."

A muscle in Hanna's jaw twitched. She smelled Mike's familiar piney, smoky scent. She always used to tease him for smelling like a ski lodge. She'd missed it so much.

But then she made a face. "So wait. You sleep with Colleen, then break up with her a week later? That's a pretty shitty thing to do, Mike."

Mike gave her a crazy look. "What gave you the idea Colleen and I were sleeping together? I know I'm a stud and everything, but we'd only been going out for a couple of weeks."

"But Mason and James . . . I overheard them saying . . ." Hanna ran her tongue over her teeth. "Wait. Is this just a guy thing? Do guys just assume everyone's doing their girlfriends?"

Mike shrugged. "I guess." He gave her a sweet, vulnerable smile. "Honestly, Hanna? I'm saving myself for you."

Fireworks went off in Hanna's head. "Well, it's your lucky day," she murmured. "I'm saving myself for you, too. Remember what I said about the Marwyn Trail? I'm game if you are."

Mike leaned into her again, and Hanna savored every second of their kiss. Then Mike pulled away and poked Hanna's side. "So, Ms. Stalker. What did you dig up on Colleen, anyway? Anything good?"

The between-classes music stopped, and when Hanna looked around, she realized that most of the students had cleared out of the halls. She licked her lips, considering spilling the beans, but suddenly, it didn't matter that much. Exposing a secret was only important when you felt threatened by someone—when they made you feel insecure or had something you wanted or made you scared—and Colleen didn't make her feel any of those things anymore. She wasn't like A, looking for revenge.

"Nah, nothing good at all," she chirped, taking Mike's hand and pulling him down the hall. It felt freeing to no longer be Colleen's A.

The only thing that would make everything perfect was if *her* A was gone, too.

35

ANY CLUB THAT DOESN'T WANT
SPENCER AS A MEMBER . . .

That afternoon, Spencer sat at the kitchen table with her parents. Her dad was staring at his phone, and her mother was sipping a glass of iced tea. It was almost like old times, when her parents were still together. But Mr. Pennythistle was there, too, leaning against the kitchen island, his arms crossed over his chest.

"I can't thank you enough for what you've done, Peter," Spencer's mom said, twisting a napkin between her hands. "The last thing this family needs is more scandal."

"I'm glad I could help," Mr. Hastings said. "I wanted to protect all of us, and Spencer's spot at Princeton." Then he gave her a stern look. "I still don't understand what you were thinking, though. Someone had a *gun*, Spencer. What if you'd been caught in the crossfire?"

"Haven't you been through enough?" Mrs. Hastings jumped in. "What do we have to do, lock you in your room until you go off to college so that you don't get in any more trouble?"

"I said I was sorry," Spencer mumbled. She'd gotten this same lecture three times now.

The doorbell rang, startling Mrs. Hastings so much that she nearly dropped her coffee mug. "Who could *that* be?" she grumbled.

"I'll get it." Spencer rose from her seat, zipped up her sweatshirt, and padded for the door, praying it wouldn't be that cop with more questions. A blond head moved back and forth behind the window. Spencer halted in her tracks. Was that . . . *Harper?*

She pulled the door open. Cold air swirled into the hall. Harper had her coat buttoned up to her neck, and the tip of her nose was bright red. Her eyes were red, too, as though she'd been crying nonstop. The corners of her mouth turned down, and for a few long seconds, she didn't say a word, just glared.

"Uh, why aren't you at Princeton?" Spencer asked cautiously.

Harper's eyes blazed. "Because I'm on academic probation. Because of *you.*"

Spencer glanced over her shoulder to make sure her mom wasn't listening. "What do you mean?"

Harper sank into one hip. "Isn't it obvious? The disciplinary committee blamed me for throwing a party with drugs." A sinister look washed across her face. "Funny, though. I recall you telling me about bringing a batch of brownies that had a few special ingredients in them. You seemed pretty proud of yourself, in fact."

Spencer held up her hands in a *whoa* gesture. "I didn't spike them with acid! It was someone else!"

An ugly snort came out of Harper's mouth. "*Right.* You're going down. I'm going to make sure you won't be welcome at Princeton next year."

Spencer's stomach twisted into knots. Going to Princeton seemed like it would be an amazing new start, an escape from Rosewood, and she'd been so excited about her friendship with Harper and the other girls. But as long as A was in her life, she'd never be able to move on. A would follow her wherever she went. Those text messages, photos, and videos would still come fast and furious, even if she went to China. Even if she went to the moon.

Videos. Suddenly, a light flipped on in her head. "Don't go yet. I have something you should see."

Spencer marched into the foyer and found her iPhone in her bag. Then she marched triumphantly back to the open door. Harper was still standing on the porch, looking annoyed.

Spencer shoved the phone into Harper's face and pressed PLAY. The clip of Harper trashing the Ivy House came into view. First she yanked the curtains off the walls and slashed them up. Next she pulled the stuffing out of the pillows. She knocked books off shelves, smashed a vase, and decorated a painting with a mascara wand.

288 ◆ SARA SHEPARD

Harper's face contorted. "This isn't me."

Spencer scoffed. "Nice try." She snatched the phone from Harper before she could delete the clip. "I don't want to do this, but if you tell on me, I'll tell on you. I doubt Ivy looks kindly on vandalism. And you don't have any solid proof about my brownies being spiked, only what I told you when we were high. *I*, on the other hand, have this video. You could get in worse trouble than you're already in."

The confident look on Harper's face faded. She opened and closed her mouth a few times, and her face turned purple. "Fine," she finally spat. "But don't you *dare* think you're getting into Ivy. I may be on probation, but I still have pull there. And I'm going to make sure they stay far, far away from you."

"I don't really care," Spencer said, trying to sound as nonchalant as she could even though Harper's words hurt her. "I don't like any of you, anyway."

Then she slammed the door in Harper's face, feeling tears well in her eyes. Everything felt so screwed up and wrong; the perfect plan for her life had fallen to pieces. She was supposed to join Ivy. It was supposed to be her hookup to an amazing future. The Ivy girls and guys were supposed to be her instant friends, people she'd know forever. Now, the only person at Princeton who'd speak to her was Reefer.

She shifted her weight. But maybe that wouldn't be so bad. She thought about how goofily into her Reefer had been at the Princeton dinner. How excited he'd gotten when he made her smell his homegrown pot. She didn't have to put on airs when she with him. She didn't have to compromise her principles to win him over.

Reefer was the nicest person she'd met at Princeton so far. If she was really honest, those Ivy kids were kind of . . . bitchy. And snobby. And superficial. Did she really want to hang out with them?

Spencer wiped away a tear and started back toward the kitchen, feeling strangely content. She'd be okay on her own. Maybe Reefer was right about Eating Clubs being stupid and elitist. Not that Reefer was right about everything. And not that it meant she liked him.

As she passed her dad's old office, she smiled to herself. Okay, maybe she liked Reefer a *little*. At the very least she owed him an apology. And who knew, maybe she'd even accompany him to an upcoming Occupy Philly rally or something, too. Just to be nice.

36

SAFE AND SOUND

"Okay, GPS says five hundred more feet to the exit." Emily glanced at the media console in the unfamiliar Audi sedan. "Turn here, turn here!"

"Em, I saw it coming from a mile away." Hanna steered the car off the highway at an exit marked CHESTNUT HILL and gave Emily a worried smile. "You okay?"

Emily slid down in her seat and picked at the skin around her thumb. It was a few hours later on Monday evening, and they'd all piled into Hanna's stepsister's car to go to the Bakers' new house together. Needless to say, Emily was jittery. What if she got there and the Bakers had moved again? What if she got there and the baby was gone?

It was the worst thing Emily could think of. A could still have Violet. She could still be living a nightmare.

Could A be Real Ali, after all? Had *she* set up Gayle to look like the villain, stealing the cash from Gayle's mailbox, sending Spencer texts when she was at Princeton, maybe even steering Gayle toward Hanna's dad's campaign? Had Real Ali lured the girls to Gayle's house in hopes of hurting them? Did Ali really have such little respect for human life?

Of course she does, a little voice in Emily's head said. All of a sudden, her blood began to boil. This wasn't a tragic story of a messed-up girl Emily could rescue—it was a story about a psycho bitch who wanted to get Emily any way she could, even if it meant harming an innocent child. If Real Ali *was* A, then Emily would do everything in her power to bring her down.

It was a weird revelation. On one hand, Emily felt empty inside, like someone had just stolen a vital organ from her. On the other, she suddenly felt clear-eyed and steady, as if she'd gotten LASIK and could see everything properly for the first time. It made her feel even worse for setting Real Ali free, though. Maybe she'd brought all this on herself.

The light turned green, and Hanna passed a Barnes & Noble and a Starbucks. Emily's phone beeped, and she jumped. A text from Isaac had come in. *I've thought about things, and I want to talk,* it said.

Emily stared at the words as they pulled up to a stop sign. Was this a good message . . . or an awful one? Isaac's angry, disgusted expression at Gayle's house had lingered with her. He *had* to be mad, right? Had he already told his mom? Had Mrs. Colbert already told everyone else?

Was she going to become the shame of Rosewood in mere days—hours?

Then again, it was going to come out sooner or later. The police had already tracked Emily's parents down in Texas, telling them she had witnessed a murder. The first flight they could get was tomorrow morning, and they'd be back by the time Emily returned from Gayle's funeral. Even though the cops hadn't revealed Emily's secret, her parents would ask questions. Maybe it would be better if this secret was out in the open. She had to be the one to tell them. All she could hope was that they didn't murder her.

"Em, this place is adorable," Aria murmured. Emily looked out the window. They were driving down Main Street in Chestnut Hill. It was full of funky bakeries, quaint restaurants, antique furniture stores, and upscale boutiques. A huge library with a big children's display in the window was on the left, several old stone churches were on the right, and side streets boasted beautifully restored old houses with station wagons and swing sets. Families walked strollers and dogs up the sidewalks. Kids raced around a baseball field.

A hopeful smile crossed Emily's face. This place *did* seem nice.

"Turn right, and you will have reached your destination," the GPS proclaimed. Hanna put on her turn signal and pulled into a parking space on the street. The girls got out and started down the sidewalk, looking at each of the old houses as they passed.

"There it is," Aria said halfway down the block, pointing at a house across the street. "Number 86."

Emily swallowed hard and dared to look. The house in question had white siding, black shutters, and a big front porch. There was a green watering can on the steps, daffodils peeking up in the flower beds, and a fruit wreath on the door.

"It's really nice, Em," Spencer breathed. "Nicer than the old place, even."

And then Emily saw something that made her heart leap. There, through the split rail fence in the backyard, was a detached garage. Its door gaped open, revealing two plastic trash cans, a ten-speed bicycle, and a running stroller. There was a kiddie swimming pool in the shape of a frog propped up against the wall. Emily pressed her hands to her mouth, feeling tears come to her eyes. *Kid things.* Could her baby still be here?

As though in cosmic answer, the front door to the house swung open. Emily yelped and ducked behind Spencer. A familiar man with a thin build and sandy hair came out first. "You got her?" he said to someone just behind him.

"Uh huh," a woman's voice said.

Emily peered around Spencer's shoulder just in time to see Lizzie Baker step onto the porch and pull the door shut. Lizzie looked fresh-faced and happy, wearing black yoga pants and Nike sneakers. In her arms was an apple-cheeked, bright-eyed, grinning seven-month-old girl in a pink corduroy dress and black patent Mary Janes. She waved a rattle around in her hand and let out a loud coo. Her hair was the exact reddish-blondish shade as Emily's.

"Oh my God," Emily said, tears coming to her eyes. It was her baby. Violet. Looking beautiful and happy and better than she ever imagined.

"Em," was all Aria said. Spencer grabbed Emily's arm and squeezed. Hanna leaned into Emily's shoulder and let out a happy sniff.

Violet was safe—*safe!* It was all that mattered. She could handle her parents. She could handle Isaac. She could handle everyone else in Rosewood, too. Everything was going to be—well, not okay, but manageable. If something had happened to the baby, she would have never forgiven herself.

She turned to the others. "I'm good now," she whispered. "Let's go before they see us."

They moved to leave, when suddenly Mrs. Baker stopped short, noticing Emily. Instinctively, she held Violet a little tighter. Her husband turned to see what his wife was looking at, then paled too. Swallowing hard, Emily held up her hand in a tentative, I-don't-mean-any-harm wave. After a moment, the Bakers waved back. Then they said a few things Emily couldn't hear. After a moment, Mrs. Baker crossed the street toward Emily, Violet in her arms.

"What are you doing?" Emily cried, panicking. When

she looked up, Spencer, Aria, and Hanna were drifting away. "Don't leave!"

"You'll be fine," Spencer encouraged, scampering around the corner.

Emily turned back and watched as Mrs. Baker stepped up on the curb and hitched Violet higher on her hip. The two of them stared at each other for a beat. Emily had no clue what Mrs. Baker might say. *How dare you? Get the hell out of here?*

"Wow," Mrs. Baker blurted. "Heather. Hi."

"It's Emily, actually," Emily said. "Emily Fields."

Mrs. Baker laughed nervously. "I know. I saw you in an old copy of *People* at the pediatrician's office. I couldn't believe I didn't realize it was you." Then she picked up Violet's hand and made her wave. "I guess you know who this is. We named her Violet."

"Hi, Violet." Emily almost couldn't get the words out. "She looks wonderful. Is she . . . happy?"

Mrs. Baker pushed a piece of hair behind her ear. "Well, she can't talk yet, but we think she is. We're happy, too." A bashful look came over her face.

"You moved," Emily pointed out.

Mrs. Baker nodded. "Yes. Shortly after—well, you know. We thought people might ask questions. We decided it was better if we moved someplace where no one knew us." When she raised her head and looked at Emily again, there were tears in her eyes, too. "We don't know why you changed your mind, but we can't thank you enough. We hope you know that."

296 + SARA SHEPARD

It felt like she'd injected Emily with sunlight. She wiped away a tear, looking again at Violet's goofy, gummy smile. "I can't thank *you* enough."

A double *beep* of a car unlocking sounded across the street, and Mrs. Baker turned and signaled to her husband, who was loading up a Honda SUV. "I'm telling everyone about the baby," Emily blurted. "But I'll never tell them about you."

Mrs. Baker nodded. "We'll keep your secret, too."

They gave each other a meaningful look. There were so many other things Emily wanted to ask about Violet, but maybe it wasn't her place to know. She'd given up the right to be Violet's parent. All she could hope for was that the Bakers gave her baby the best life possible. All of the money in the world couldn't have made a better life for Violet than the one the Bakers were giving her.

Emily kissed the top of Violet's fuzzy head. "Keep her safe, okay? Keep her locked up every night. Never let her out of your sight."

"Of course we will," Lizzie said.

"Good," Emily said. And then she awkwardly turned and walked as quickly as she could back to the girls, afraid that if she didn't get away fast, she'd never be able to leave Violet's side again. She looked back once, watching as Lizzie made Violet wave again. A sob rose in her throat. She thought about A looming somewhere close, just waiting to snatch Violet away. She couldn't bear the thought.

Swallowing hard, she stared at the traffic on the main

road. *If the next car that passes is blue, Violet will be okay*, she thought. *If it's red, A will do something horrible to her.*

She heard a growl of an engine and shut her eyes, afraid to see what the future might hold. She'd never cared so much about anything in her life. Just as the car was passing, she opened her eyes and saw a Mercedes hood ornament. She let out a long sigh, tears coming to her eyes once more.

The car was blue.

37

A STRANGER IN THE CROWD

The Rosewood Abbey was an old stone building in the middle of town with gorgeous stained-glass windows, a bell tower, and pristinely manicured gardens. Mourners in black crammed the lawn, giving Aria an eerie sense of déjà vu. The last time she'd been there was for Ali's funeral a year and a half ago. And now, on this sunny Tuesday morning, she was there to mark another death: Gayle's.

Emily and Spencer, who'd ridden with her, stared at the church silently as they pulled into the parking lot. They'd all come as a favor to Hanna—her dad was forcing her to go because Gayle had meant so much to his campaign, and she was too creeped out to go alone.

Hanna's Prius rolled up next to them. Hanna cut the engine, got out, and greeted the others. Then she looked around with a shiver, her gaze narrowing in on the weeping willow tree next to the front path. "*That* doesn't bring back good memories," she said in a foreboding voice.

Aria knew exactly what she meant. It was under that willow that they'd received a threatening note from the very first A. *I'm still here, bitches, and I know everything.*

Now they were in the same position. New A was still here. New A knew everything. And none of them knew where or when A would strike next.

The Abbey's nave was even more crowded than the lawn, the air humid and stuffy with bodies and the noise level deafening. Hanna's father stood by the doors, talking to a reporter. A bunch of people from the Rosewood Rotary Club chatted near the holy water. Naomi Zeigler and her parents stood quietly in a corner, looking at the program. Aria wondered how Naomi's family knew Gayle.

The priest funneled everyone inside the hall. At the end of the long aisle was a closed mahogany casket covered with huge bouquets of flowers. Mr. Clark stood next to it, his hands folded and his head bowed. He looked like he hadn't slept since the night they'd seen him at the police station—there were purple circles under his eyes, his skin looked flaky and pale, and his hair badly needed combing. Every so often, he'd flinch, as though startled. And as Aria squinted, she swore she saw his lips moving ever so slightly, as if he were talking to himself.

Hanna leaned into Aria. "My dad told me that the police think Gayle's killer is a guy who's been breaking into houses in Gayle's neighborhood. They have him in for questioning. What if they convict him?"

Spencer shrugged. "Better that guy than us."

Emily's eyes popped. "How can you say that? It was awful when they thought we did it, but we can't just let someone else take the heat."

Spencer raised an eyebrow as she slid into the pew. "Who knows? Maybe the person who's breaking into houses *is* A."

"Or maybe the person breaking into houses *did* murder Gayle—maybe it's unrelated to A," Aria suggested. But even as she said it, she looked unconvinced. Everyone else did, too.

Spencer crossed her legs, smoothed out her black skirt, and stared straight ahead. After a pause, Aria slid into the pew next to her, and the other girls followed.

The organ music stopped, and the heavy doors closed with a *clonk*. People shifted in their seats. Aria craned her neck over the heads in front of her. Mr. Clark was stepping to the podium and adjusting the microphone. When he cleared his throat, a screech of feedback rang out through the room, and he winced. Then, there was a horribly long pause. Mr. Clark stared out into the sea of people, his mouth trembling. There were a few polite coughs, then several concerned nudges. All the while, Mr. Clark didn't move.

Aria's stomach jumped. It was terrible seeing this man so wrecked, especially over something *they* might have caused. What if A had killed Gayle only because of them? That meant they'd ruined his life not once, with Tabitha, but twice. And Aria was even more to blame—it had been her hands that had pushed Tabitha off that roof. She stared at them now, horrified at what she'd done all over again. Her fingers started to tremble.

Finally, Mr. Clark cleared his throat. "I never thought I'd have to do this twice in one year," he said, his voice cracking. He clutched a handkerchief tightly in his fist. "It's heartbreaking enough when your daughter is taken from you, but when you lose your wife, too, your world starts to crumble." He sniffled and wiped his nose. "Many of you knew Gayle as an incredibly giving philanthropist. But I knew other parts of her, too. Sides of her so special and unique . . ."

He went on to tell how Gayle rescued every dog she saw, took pity on a poor family they met while on a vacation in Curaçao and paid for them to build a new house, and volunteered at soup kitchens every Thanksgiving. Each of the anecdotes was rambling and often nonsensical, but they made Gayle seem utterly un-A-like. A had so expertly convinced them otherwise.

Mr. Clark continued with his eulogy, every so often pausing to stare off into space or to wipe away a barrage of tears. When Aria heard the words "murder," she perked up, suddenly alert.

"As much as I don't want to give my wife's murderer any attention on her day, I have to say something about it," Mr. Clark went on in a grave voice. "Whoever you are, for whatever reason you did this, I will find you. Just like I'm going to find the person who killed my daughter."

The crowd erupted into whispers. Aria blinked hard, the words taking a few seconds to sink in. She looked at her friends. What *did he just say?* she mouthed. Her head started to spin. *This can't be happening.*

Mr. Clark made a waving motion for everyone to calm down. "This is going to come out, so I might as well tell everyone here. I had an autopsy done on Tabitha's remains. Her cause of death wasn't alcohol-related. She was murdered."

Everyone started to talk even louder. The back of Aria's throat tightened so much that she could hardly breathe. Her friends were staring back at her, just as stunned.

A loud *buzz* sounded from Aria's phone. A half-second later, Emily's phone lit up, as did Hanna's and Spencer's. Aria looked at the others in puzzlement, then glanced down at her phone. Her throat closed and her stomach suddenly felt on fire. *One new text message,* the screen said.

Aria opened it. Her vision momentarily went white.

That's right, bitches—Daddy's on to you. How long do you think it'll take the police to realize you were at both crime scenes? —A

"Oh my God," Spencer whispered. She whipped her head up and looked around. "Guys, is A . . ."

". . . *here?*" Hanna finished.

Aria stared out at the church full of people from school, from town, from her past. A high-pitched giggle spiraled through the air and at that very moment, a figure slipped out the back door, slamming it shut.

WHAT HAPPENS NEXT . . .

Don't you love a story that ends with a bang? And those aren't the only fireworks I have in store for the liars. They're gearing up for a week in the Caribbean with students from all over Pennsylvania— and me! I'll be manning the periscope, watching Spencer, Aria, Emily, and Hanna get up to no good.

Let's start with Spencer. She had such *high* hopes for getting into Princeton's most exclusive club. But after the brownie bacchanalia, it looks like the only Eating Club she'll be joining is the food line on the eco-cruise ship. Fingers crossed she doesn't go *overboard* . . .

Aria's ready to leave the Kahn-dram in her rearview mirror and cozy up with Noel on the rear deck. But while Aria may look better in a bikini than Mr. Kahn does, at least he wears his heart on his sleeve. Noel forgave her this time, but when he finds out that Aria's still keeping secrets, will he want to keep *her*?

As for poor little Emily, now that the cat—or rather, *baby*—is out of the bag, all hell will break loose at Casa Fields. Will the cruise be the perfect getaway from all the baby-mama drama? Or will returning to the scene of the Tabitha crime cause Emily to drown in her sorrows?

And Hanna might have looked like a beached whale in her pole-dancing class, but she did get Mike back. Now if only the rest of the school would forget her stint as Rosewood's latest—and, *ahem*, lamest—stalker. But some things will never be forgotten—or forgiven. Like, say, the horrible thing she did last summer. The girl can hit and run, but she can't hide. Especially in open water.

The liars better enjoy the smooth sailing while they can. I hear there are sharks in the Caribbean Sea, and they can always smell blood . . .

Anchors aweigh!

—A

ACKNOWLEDGMENTS

As usual, I want to thank Lanie Davis, Sara Shandler, Josh Bank, and Les Morgenstein at Alloy for all their efforts on this book. It was a tough one to write—there were lots of distractions—and I'm so happy I can count on you guys. Thanks also to Farrin Jacobs and Kari Sutherland at Harper for your keen insight—and for knowing these characters so well. My best to Aiah Wieder for all of your help, as well as Kristin Marang for the website and online promotions—I love connecting with the fans!

To my family and friends—you know who you are. To Kristian, who is lovable beyond words and such a growing, crazy nut. I also want to thank the booksellers who have been such champions of the Pretty Little Liars series from the very beginning, specifically Shelly at Harleysville Books in Harleysville, Pennsylvania, and Kenny at Books and Greetings in Northvale, New Jersey. I've met a lot of other amazing booksellers along the way, too, as well as fantastic librarians, teachers, and—of course—readers! Without any of you guys, the success of this series wouldn't be possible. I am so grateful to all of you.

Also, this book is dedicated to Caron Crooke, who is lovely and wonderful. We love having you as part of our family!

PRETTY GIRLS DON'T PLAY
BY THE RULES...

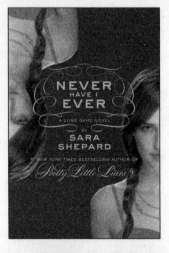
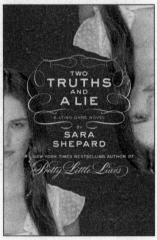
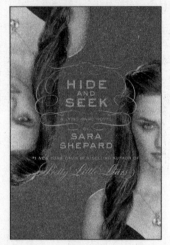

THEY MAKE THEM.

DON'T MISS THE LYING GAME,
A KILLER SERIES FROM SARA SHEPARD

WELCOME TO THE NEW AMERICA

Don't miss a single page of the forbidden love and extraordinary adventure in the Eve Trilogy.

Visit TheEveTrilogy.com to follow Eve's journey.

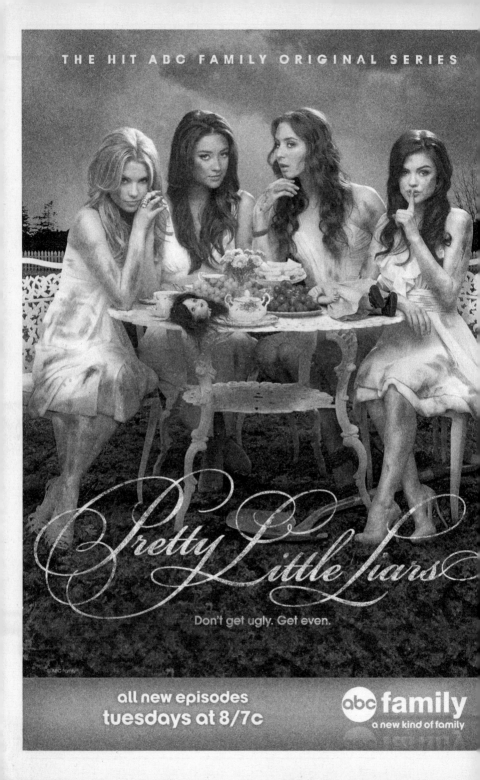